SON OF A DUKE

JESSIE CLEVER

SOMEDAY LADY PUBLISHING, LLC.

SON OF A DUKE

Published by Someday Lady Publishing, LLC

Copyright © 2013, 2016 by Jessica McQuaid

ISBN-13: 978-0-9984192-0-6

Cover Design by The Killion Group

For Indy

CHAPTER 1

*A*s she watched everyone enjoying the ball, she stood there and made a list in her head of all the other things she would rather be doing.

ITEM 1: Polish the staircase spindles. All 106 of them.

Item 2: Scrub chamberpots.

Item 3: Take Lady Gregenden's opinionated Pomeranian, Mr. Fitzherbert, for a walk.

WELL, the last one was not all that bad, but it was true she would much rather be doing that than standing there watching some of the most elite members of society pretend they were having a lovely evening when in fact most of them spent every night doing about the same thing, and she did not know how one kept one night straight from the next.

. . .

ITEM 4: Beat out the hall rugs during a wind storm.
Item 5: Help Cook dice onions.

TONIGHT WAS TURNING out to be another success, which she was sure surprised Hawkins to the tips of his well-polished shoes. But she was not one to be disappointed in the expectations of a rather dour butler. When, in fact, she could not really blame him for his expectations. Hawkins had been at this game much longer than she, and time tended to weigh on people in her chosen profession. But she was also certain Hawkins would congratulate her at the end of the night when this was all over, and she was just as certain when next it came time for her to plan another gala, he would be the Doubting Thomas once more.

ITEM 6: Massage Lady Gregenden's feet.
Item 7: Scrub chamberpots.

OH, wait. The last item was already on the list. But she felt it really belonged there twice, because she would rather do the chamberpots twice over before standing where she was at that moment. Women in brightly colored gowns swirled across the dance floors, held painfully erect in the arms of unwilling gentlemen who all succumbed to the rules of society because of unique ulterior motives.

Lord Niles Turning sought after wife number four, whom he knew would finally give him a son to inherit. Lady Fielding was happy to listen to the dowager Duchess of Cornington drone on and on about her crocuses if only to secure an invitation to the next most fashionable night of the season while Lord Fielding purveyed the year's crop of debutantes, wondering how many he could debauch in a single season.

It was all very tiring for her, and she knew then that she was getting old. Not old. She was turning into Hawkins, and that was a sight worse than just getting old. She would have to rethink her assessment of him and his dour outlook. Perhaps, he was simply just right.

But she sincerely hoped he was not. She hoped, too, that she could continue to keep the corners of her mouth just slightly upturned, thinking about all of the good things that she still had in this life even if she were stuck in the middle of an excessively stuffy ballroom filled with people who had a bit more luck than she had had in life. That sentiment was not fair either. She had been more fortunate than most. She had a respectable position that promised to provide for her security for years to come. The other staff members respected her as housekeeper and Hawkins, well, he at least maintained a kind of civility with her. If they were not exactly friends, she could at least think of them as allies.

But family was not something she could think herself lucky in. Her parents had died young, leaving her with Aunt Martha. Aunt Martha had already had seven children, and another had just been a burden oft forgotten. Not that she had minded much. Aunt Martha was harder on her than the rest, and she had learned quickly how to polish silver, scrub floors, and cook. It would not be until she was an impressionable seventeen, arriving in the big city of London for the first time, that she knew those skills would be useful. They would secure her first post as a chamber maid at Gregenden House. And she would never speak to Aunt Martha or the seven children she was supposed to have called cousins again.

But a kind of family had inadvertently fallen into her lap. A family she had not asked for, but that she now could not have lived without, no matter the consequences. She felt the flinch that always came when she thought on it, but it had dulled with time, molding into something soft and indistinct that no longer left the tang of bitterness in her mouth. And even though it had happened, a part of her could still wish it happened in another kind of way.

And now she stood in a richly appointed ballroom filled with beautifully dressed people. And suddenly, she felt it easier to keep the corners of her mouth upturned. Hawkins could keep his doubting ways. She had still come a long way from where she had been.

She would even remove one of the items involving chamberpots for her list.

"Miss Quinton," came a voice behind her, and she turned a precise quarter turn.

It was Sophia, a young maid they had acquired from another estate that had a less hospitable reputation than that of Gregenden House.

"Yes?" she asked.

Sophia bent her head, the candlelight of the ballroom glinting off hair so blonde it was almost white. The young woman's fine features looked fresh and relaxed in the heat of the ballroom, and Eleanora thought of a time when she had been that young and new to this world. But now it just all felt too familiar.

"Mr. Hawkins wished me to tell you the buffet is set, but he is not sure we have enough footmen for the evening. He is quite concerned, Miss Quinton."

Now her smile came easily. It was not a happy smile, but rather one dripping with appeasement.

"Sophia, you can assure Mr. Hawkins that I have calculated everything precisely, and the evening shall not fail. He need not worry."

Sophia smiled an equally sarcastic smile back at her. "I told him that, Miss Quinton, but it seems he will not listen to me. I assured him no one would get the better of Miss Eleanora Quinton, but he did not take that to reason either."

She nodded. "Very well, I shall speak with him myself."

Sophia looked quickly behind her, turning back to Nora with a look of worry. "But you cannot, miss. Mr. Hawkins is below stairs. You cannot leave the ballroom. What will happen?"

She smiled with affection now for the young woman, remembering when she had been such a novice.

"Fear not, Sophia. The ballroom shall still be here when I return."

Sophia nodded, the worry sliding from her face. "If Miss Quinton says it is so, then it is."

The maid nodded once and slipped into the crowd.

Eleanora turned back to the ballroom, taking in the couples still dancing, the women still gossiping, and the debutantes still preening.

ITEM 8: Assuring Hawkins that nothing would go wrong.

SHE TURNED her back on the dancing couples and moved into the crowd.

SHE WATCHED the infallible Eleanora Quinton from her place beside the refreshment table. Everything was going according to plan until that young maid had come out of the crowd and whatever she had said to Miss Quinton had caused the housekeeper to leave her post. She was certain she could do her part of watching the vigilant housekeeper as long as she remained in the ballroom, but if she left to go below stairs, it was anyone's guess as to what trouble the young woman could cause.

The events of the night had been meticulously planned. The man to complete the necessary, if rather heinous task, had been carefully selected. His movements in and about London were carefully orchestrated so as not to arouse suspicion. Even the supporting players, including herself, had been chosen with care to support tonight's attempt at assassination.

For that really was what this was all about. The more elite gentlemen of the War Office could label it whatever they liked, but in the end, a man was to be killed for treason. It was all really quite simple.

But too much effort had gone into the affair for a mere housekeeper to foil the plot. Even one as robust as Miss Quinton.

She looked across the room, and her eyes easily found his. He stood at his post by the exit to the card room, lazily sipping on champagne. A smile played at her lips as she took in the sight of him in his crisp evening attire of black jacket and snowy white cravat. Even after all these years, she could still find herself drooling over him. But now was not the time for such things. Perhaps later she could enjoy some mindless drooling.

But now she waited for some kind of signal from him. He only watched her, his eyes dark and unreadable in the soft light of the chandeliers. But she knew he had seen the housekeeper move. She knew that he knew said housekeeper would be far more trouble outside of the ballroom than in it. Because if anyone were to notice a person who was not to be there, it would be the infallible Eleanora Quinton.

Jane Black, the Duchess of Lofton, had spent the last few weeks in town getting close to the housekeeper, as was her task, so she could ascertain just how much trouble the woman would be if a murder were to occur in the house of which she was in charge. And she had finally drawn the conclusion that the housekeeper could be very much trouble indeed. If the woman had known, she should have been quite proud that not one but three agents had been assigned the task of watching her.

Not even Guy Fawkes had been watched this closely.

But now he gave her a signal. He reached up and touched his hair ever so briefly. She did not hesitate.

The Duchess of Lofton moved from her place and stepped directly into Eleanora Quinton's path. "Miss Quinton."

She saw the skin tighten around the housekeeper's eyes, if that was even physically possible. The maid was thin, too thin. Her cheeks dipped ever so slightly in her face, and her neck stretched delicately from the collar of her dress. Her eyes appeared larger than they were in her too thin face, and her elbows pointed out like the knobby branches of a tree in her starched black uniform. But the housekeeper's lips never twitched as she looked up to face the woman who had stepped into her path.

"Yes, Your Grace?" she pronounced with a polite dip in recognition.

"Your presentation tonight is quite lovely as always. Lady Gregenden must be quite brilliant to think up such themes for these galas."

Not a muscle moved on Miss Quinton's face as she calmly replied, "Yes, indeed. Brilliant is exactly the word I would have chosen as well."

Lady Lofton knew that to be as accurate a fact as the one in which she herself appeared to be the Queen of England. Lady Gregenden was a dreadfully dull woman of equally dull fortitude when it came to things such as entertaining. The woman only got where she did on the arm of her husband. But Miss Quinton was not one to face any sign of degradation. Even if it was coming from a duchess.

"I see then."

For weeks now, she had been working to gain closer entry into this young woman's world, and the duchess liked to think she had been successful. She tested her theory as she swirled the champagne in her glass, catching it with the light so that it reflected directly at Miss Quinton's eyes.

"Why are you doing that?" Miss Quinton asked, her voice never fluctuating from its low monotone cadence.

"To see if you flinch."

"Oh bother, you still have not given up on that?" Her voice changed then, slightly softer and mischievous. Something flashed in her eyes, and the duchess knew for a brief moment that she had relieved the housekeeper of some boredom, even if it was but a moment.

Then a great bloke of a gentleman smashed into her backside and sent the housekeeper careening directly at the duchess. Caught off guard by the unexpected movement, Lady Lofton had not been prepared for the housekeeper to come falling toward her, and so she could do nothing to stop them both from falling directly into the Earl of Stryden.

The earl caught them both quite neatly, tipping the duchess back up gently with a quick grab but holding onto Miss Quinton's shoulders a slight touch longer than may have been appropriate. The duchess doubted anyone else noticed the entire affair, but concern for the rest of the evening's plans at the forefront of her mind, she did a quick check of those around them. They all looked ready to impale themselves with the nearest frond from one of the ghastly potted ferns that littered the room. She returned her attention to the little scene playing out before her.

This was not at all a part of the plan, but neither had it been a part of the plan for Miss Quinton to leave her post. If she were quick enough to improvise, surely Stryden was as well.

"Are you all right, Miss Quinton?" the Earl of Stryden asked the woman.

"Quite, thank you." She was straightening the ties of her apron when the earl stepped behind her and very simply spun around the bloke who had knocked into her.

The startled man looked absolutely bewildered at the dark look on the earl's face. Of course, the stupid man had to look up about a foot to see the look, which made it all the more intimidating.

"I believe you owe the lady an apology," Stryden said, ever so softly and deadly.

And it reminded her that if anyone could sound deadly, it most certainly was the Earl of Stryden with his chiseled features, nearly black hair, and piercing green eyes. A much younger version of a man the duchess was happy to wake up next to every morning, and she could not help but smile.

The bloke stammered, "My apologies, Your Grace." He bowed slightly toward Lady Lofton, shaking too much to bend any more than he did.

"Not that lady," the earl growled.

The man looked around him, his gaze moving swiftly past Miss Quinton as if she were not there.

Lady Lofton cleared her throat a little and batted her eyelashes at Miss Quinton just to give the man a hint. He was up against Stryden, and well, he was definitely dim-witted, which meant he had a very large disadvantage. The duchess had to help a little. She was not that impolite.

Miss Quinton, however, remained quiet as ever, looking straight ahead with her lips curving at the tips, jaw square, and chin up.

The man stammered some more, "I do beg your pardon, my lord, but I do not see any other lady around whom I might have bumped."

Sweat was starting to pool along the ridge of his collar, streaming down to his intricately knotted cravat. He was tugging nervously on the lapels of his jacket, leaving the fabric, an awful coral color, all wrinkled and stained with the cold sweat from his beefy palms.

"Miss Quinton nearly fell to the ground from your clumsiness. I would not call that a bump." Stryden stepped between the man and Miss Quinton before the bloke could form even a stammer. "See that it does not happen again."

The duchess sipped her champagne in silent salute. Stryden had the man simpering without even a threat of fatal violence to the man's bloated body. Well done, indeed.

Stryden turned his back on the man and bent to look at Miss Quinton.

"I am terribly sorry about that, miss," he said. "Some members of the *ton* were simply born to their status and did not earn their titles. Are you sure you are all right?"

She gave a quick nod. "Yes, my lord, quite all right. I do thank you for your trouble."

"It was no trouble." He bowed to the duchess. "Jane, I hope you are all right as well?"

"Fine, thanks, lad." The duchess saw his lips tighten at that. Oh, how she did love to call him lad still.

He smiled slightly before replying. "I assume you are having a lovely time tonight?"

"Oh yes, quite lovely. Except for that fat—"

"Oh yes, I am sure there's something fat around that

displeases you, Jane. But let's not share it with the world, shall we?"

The duchess hid her smile as she sipped her champagne. It was so fun to annoy the boy. "I was not planning on telling the world, just you, Alec." She cocked her head and pursed her lips.

He laughed right in the duchess's face. He was the only one who ever did. Even her husband, the Duke of Lofton, would not laugh in her face. Oh, she was sure there were many times when her dear husband would want to laugh in her face, but he never did. Jane Black, the Duchess of Lofton, had a reputation that quelled laughter where it formed.

"Miss Quinton, the décor is quite lovely this evening. You have outdone yourself yet again." Alec smiled that smile that had made a thousand women swoon, often right into his bed. But Miss Quinton did not flinch...again. The chit was getting annoying herself.

"Thank you, my lord. I am pleased you are enjoying your evening."

"Oh, I never said I was enjoying my evening. Just your décor."

Miss Quinton actually wet her lips. It was a habit Jane had observed. The housekeeper did it when she was hiding a smile. The Earl of Stryden had made her smile? The duchess determined that she could probably safely die now, because she had most likely seen it all.

"Perhaps you will find more pleasure in the gaming rooms, my lord." Miss Quinton pointed discreetly in the direction of the parlors that had been set up with tables of whist or some other such barbarous game.

Duchess Lofton gazed casually in the direction that Miss Quinton pointed and felt a slight start when she saw the Duke of Lofton had left his post by the card room door. She quickly turned back to the conversation when she heard Stryden's voice again.

"Perhaps. Unfortunately, I must do my civic duty and mingle in the society into which I was born."

He winked at her.

Oh, dear. Jane should have warned him. A wink might give Miss Quinton heart pains. But Jane was certain she would not swoon. She was not the type, really.

And then Miss Quinton smiled, and the duchess herself felt chest pains. Given her delicate age of eight and fifty, she did begin to worry a bit. But they soon passed when a screeching voice—well, *screeching* really did not do it justice. She thought of the sound that comes from running one's knife in the wrong direction against one's plate. Yes, that was exactly the sound that was produced when this creature opened her mouth.

"Stryden! You silly, silly man. I have been looking everywhere for you," Lady Dendrigeshire squawked, jostling her enormous girth through the crowd to the poor Earl of Stryden.

Stryden turned his shoulder so only Miss Quinton could see his face. And what he did then the duchess did not know, but it made Miss Quinton *blush*. The damn chit blushed! Jane snapped open her fan and started swinging it violently through the air. It was not cooling her any, but she suddenly felt the need to release some recent onslaught of energy.

"May I have this dance, Your Grace?"

The sound of his voice sent a familiar shiver down her spine, and the duchess turned toward her husband.

Richard had not always been her husband, and seeing his smiling face in front of hers always brought a sharp pain of reality to her, a pain that made her infinitely happy that she could now be his wife.

"Well, I suppose it is a part of my lot for being wed to you, is it not?" she replied, and Richard smiled even more.

She moved her eyes in Miss Quinton's direction, indicating that she still had a part to play, but Lofton was already putting his arms about her and leading her toward the other dancing couples.

When they were safely out of ear shot, he spoke. "Well done, Your Grace. He's in."

His voice was low and brushed across her ear like velvet. She shivered again.

"That quickly?"

"Of course. The War Office did not choose just anyone for this job."

"No, I suppose they did not," she said and allowed him to twirl her across the floor.

ELEANORA STOOD for a moment by the refreshment table as she gathered her thoughts about her once more. It was not every day that she inadvertently mingled with duchesses and earls in quite such proximity in the middle of a ball. And thank goodness it was not for she would never be able to keep such a close eye on the happenings about her if her attention were always so judiciously averted. Especially by the Earl of Stryden. She knew he was married, even though she had never seen his wife, but she also knew that did not matter when it came to his seductive powers. And for the first time that she could remember, Eleanora suddenly wondered what it would be like to be seduced by a man. A real man. A gentleman.

She physically shook her head in the middle of the crowded ballroom as if to shake the thought from her head. The heat was clearly getting to her, and she would have to seek fresher air or risk collapsing on the spot. She moved quickly then, sliding around the refreshment table and escaping through a door at the back of the ballroom. Her sturdy shoes made no sound as she quickly moved below stairs, expertly dodging the footmen as they carried the trays of champagne above stairs.

It was a maze of hallways and staircases on this level of the house, and Eleanora moved quickly through them. She knew Hawkins was likely to be in the kitchen if he were not above stairs where his energy could be put to good use. Eleanora would speak to him about that tomorrow, but tonight it would do her no good to argue with the man.

She dodged a rather green footman who still carried his tray with two hands and rounded a corner to turn expertly out of the way of a rushing kitchen maid exclaiming something that sounded like the hen is on fire. Eleanora did not spend a moment's worry on whether or not that was exactly what the maid had said for she trusted Cook to have everything under control. Finally, Eleanora spun into the kitchen and stopped.

Hawkins hovered in the doorway on the other side of the room where another staircase lead up directly into the dining room where an elegant banquet table had been laid with the night's supper assortments. There were to be plates of cold roast beef and ham, a radiant display of cheeses and rolls, and decadent savory pastries and sweetmeats for the guests to enjoy. And Hawkins should have taken his place amongst the footmen in the room to ensure that the meal neatly progressed. He should not have been below stairs worrying a hole in the floor with his concerned pacing.

Eleanora approached him carefully. "Mr. Hawkins, I do believe you have expressed concern over the number of footmen with us this evening."

She kept her hands behind her back, tucked under the

bow of her apron. She felt the scratch of starch even through the fabric of her gloves. She wondered for a moment what it would feel like to wear clothing of a more luxurious fabric like the gowns she had seen on the dancing women upstairs. The thought was preposterous, and she quickly banished it to take care of the matter at hand.

Mr. Hawkins paused in his pacing, turning his sagging face toward her. Every time he cast her a look of dismay, she thought of the long face of a Basset hound and felt the corners of her mouth pull upward, which never helped the situation involving Hawkins.

"There are only eleven footmen, Miss Quinton. Surely, we need an even dozen."

Eleanora nodded in sympathy. "Yes, Mr. Hawkins, I can see where an even number would feel more solid and provide a sense of security, but Gregenden House is fortunate enough to say the best footmen that can be found in all of London are here tonight, and they are serving the guests above stairs now even as we speak. But do you know what would make it a solid dozen servants above stairs ensuring the meal is as much of a success as the ball itself?"

She watched Hawkins peel himself out of his misery as if it were a physical thing that clung to him like a wet cloak on a dreary day. It gave her such a start to watch it unfold, and she knew that she had him.

"You, Mr. Hawkins," she continued, "You would make a solid dozen servants and a perfect completion to the evening's meal."

Hawkins straightened, a noticeable change coming across his features.

"That would be a dozen, indeed, Miss," he said, scanning the room above her head.

What he was looking for, she had not a single idea, but it did not matter as long as he moved his body upstairs.

15

She turned quickly, snatching a tray from a footman's outstretched arms. She shooed the young man away, pushing the tray into Hawkins' ready arms. He looked down at the tray as if it had magically appeared.

"You are our twelfth and most gifted footman, Mr. Hawkins. Now, go up those stairs and make this a memorable occasion."

Her talks with Hawkins were starting to sound like the drivel found in ladies' novels, and she worried her mind would turn to philosophical mush. But Hawkins only stared at her in no apparent sense of recognition before turning and moving up the stairs before her. She waited until he had reached the top and disappeared through the door leading into the dining room before she turned around.

Cook watched her from the other side of the large table that took up much of the center of the kitchen. The table was strewn with bits of mauled vegetables and scattered pieces of dough.

The older woman's red cheeks rounded in a smile.

"You get better at that every day, love," she said and moved away to retrieve bread from the ovens.

Eleanora relished the moment of resolving another issue but put aside her feelings to return to the matter at hand. Guests who required attention and a lord and lady to serve. But what would it feel like to have no one to please? No one to serve? Would it be as refreshing and exhilarating as Eleanora imagined?

She quickly looked over her shoulder, down the hall that led off the kitchens to a door at the very end of the corridor, hidden in the dark recess, and just as quickly pushed the ridiculous thought away.

Returning to the ballroom, she found it just as she had left it. Not that she had any doubt that anything would be amiss. Hawkins was in his place, and supper could be served.

The grandfather clock in the hall chimed midnight. One, two, three strokes of the bell so far. The guests should start milling into the other room where the banquet table was set up. A few had straggled in, but most were still here in the ballroom wanting to gossip a little more while their mouths were free of the ridiculously expensive food set out for them in the opposite room.

Eleanora looked to the footman across the floor guarding the doors to the buffet. He shook his head once to the left. Less than ten people had moved then. Well. She would have to make an announcement to get the rest moving, or they would never get them out of the house by dawn.

She stepped away from the pillar she had been pushed against as she had come back into the crowd and began to make her way to the orchestra in the far corner. It was a crush as always, and various bodies stuffed into outrageously huge garments impeded her way. She had said *Pardon me* more times now than she cared to count and suddenly did not feel like saying it any more. She just started pushing as the rest were pushing back against her. It really was the only way to move some people.

The grandfather clock had struck four more times now. Seven down, five to go. She had almost reached the orchestra. The crowd was starting to lessen over here. It being so close to the orchestra was probably the reason. One cannot gossip with loud music pounding in one's ears. She passed the Earl of Stryden, and he winked at her again. Blasted man. Why did he keep doing that? She nodded politely back at him and thought once again of his reputation of seductive powers.

Seduced by a man as wickedly handsome as the earl?

She wondered again ever so briefly before her mind snapped away from the thought.

She reached the platform where the orchestra had been

17

set up and turned to face the noisy crowd of the *ton's* most important peers. She cleared her throat as the clock in the hall tolled its twelfth stroke. She opened her mouth to get the crowd's attention.

Then a gunshot cracked through the air, and a body fell from the balcony above to the ballroom floor.

Eleanora closed her mouth, realizing she really should give Hawkins more credit for all his worrying.

CHAPTER 2

*P*andemonium.

This was what pandemonium must look like.

Ladies started dropping faster than rain, swooning into the nearest gentleman's arms, only said gentleman was not prepared for a lady to suddenly appear in his arms and was subsequently knocked into a potted fern, sending the lady, the fern, and himself tumbling to the ground in the most undignified and colorful heap Eleanora had ever seen.

The ladies that did not instantly collapse at the sight of the very dead body in the middle of the dance floor felt the immediate need to scream with all the air they could push from their lungs. Upon finishing their screeching, they ran for the nearest exit, which was usually on the other side of one of those humps of fabric, dirt, arms, legs, and potted fern. The ladies never made it over the heaps and simply added themselves to it. Some of the more stout gentlemen who had managed to catch the ladies that collapsed on them were standing in a state of complete stupidity, having not a single, bloody clue what to do with an unconscious woman in their arms. And in most cases, the gentleman did not even

19

know the lady, and her being unconscious did not help matters at all.

Eleanora stood on the orchestra platform with her hands neatly tucked under the bow of her apron and watched everyone resort to sheer panic. The members of the orchestra behind her had already escaped out the terrace doors, leaving them open to the cold, night wind that amazingly refreshed Eleanora as she waited for everyone to calm down enough for something useful to be done.

Ladies were coming to now, staring around with wide eyes, not remembering exactly how they had managed to get into such an awkward position. And then, of course, they saw the body again and either swooned...again...or ran. And until Eleanora saw it, she did not believe a woman could run that fast in a ball gown. But Lady Dendrigeshire proved her not only wrong in the fact that a woman is very capable of running in a ball gown, but also that Lady Dendrigeshire could move all of her girth in such a timely fashion. It really was quite astonishing. Other ladies began following her and soon the doors to the outside hall were clogged with women, scrambling to get through the opening. The men hung back, gesturing with their arms and opening and closing their mouths but really doing nothing at all.

And then a single lady turned around to see who was standing on the back of her gown when she noticed the open terrace doors. The woman stopped and stared for a full minute before the significance of the open doors hit her. And then she moved. Her skirt ripped under whatever foot was holding it down as she threw herself at the open doors.

And thus into Eleanora.

The woman had moved too fast for Eleanora to have a chance. But suddenly someone was grabbing her out of the way as the entire herd of hysterical women stampeded the terrace doors. Whoever had grabbed her pulled her off the platform and over his shoulder, carrying her to the side of the melee to set her down by an overturned fern. She watched as the entire ballroom emptied in less than a breath. The entire room, moments before filled with so much noise she had not been able to hear her own heartbeat, was perfectly quiet and deadly still.

"Well, it was a good party, up until about the point where that poor bloke got shot."

Eleanora turned around to stare at the Earl of Stryden. His cravat was crooked and his jacket wrinkled, his dark hair falling over his forehead. Seductive powers, indeed.

"Thank you," Eleanora said. "I might have been killed by the stampede."

"You are welcome, Miss Quinton." He ran his fingers through his hair as if to push back the lock across his forehead. It immediately returned, but he did not seem to notice.

Eleanora turned back to the wreckage in the ballroom. Footmen and maids were starting to come out of their places of hiding, popping out from behind pillars and refreshment tables. And there was Hawkins, emerging from the dining room, a tray of champagne in his hands, his face drawn, eyes wide. And Eleanora knew that no amount of talking would get him to see the good side of the events of the evening.

She heard Lord Gregenden before she saw him. He was at the far end of the room, being sick into someone's hat. Lady Gregenden was lying on the floor at his feet, completely still and staring at the ceiling as if it were the most fascinating thing in the room. Eleanora had been in the Gregenden's employ for nearly twelve years, and something this catastrophic had never occurred under her watch. Would they sack her for this? Surely, they would not. It was not as if she had orchestrated this chaos, nor could she be held responsible for it happening. She thought of the small room below stairs, and a hand went unconsciously to her stomach.

She could not lose her post. People depended on her, and she must make this right. However one made a murder right.

She let out a sigh and jumped when the earl put his hand on her shoulder. She turned slowly to look at him.

"I'll go get the authorities."

Eleanora nodded once before stopping herself. "I am sure that is not necessary, my lord. Hawkins will be pleased to handle that matter."

Stryden looked over his shoulder, and Eleanora followed his gaze to the distraught butler who still stood with the tray of champagne Eleanora had thrust in his arms only moments before. He stood unmoving in the doorway as footmen gathered about him. The footmen not moving because their leader was not moving.

And Eleanora acquiesced. "Perhaps, it would be good of you to see to the matter, my lord."

The earl turned around and left before she said anything else, which left her with one ballroom and one dead body to clean up. Looking back at Hawkins, she amended her thoughts with the unfortunate characteristic of having to do all of that on her own.

"Was this part of your plans for the evening, Miss Quinton?"

Eleanora turned to her side to see the Duchess of Lofton standing amidst fronds, champagne glasses, and the remains of a lady's broken fan and another's glove. A rather pretty lilac glove, Eleanora thought.

"No, Your Grace, it was not." Eleanora bent down and picked up the lilac glove, running it over the palm of her hand. The silky fabric moved sleekly over the coarse fabric of her practical service gloves. Eleanora had never owned something made of silk.

"I had thought not. But it would have been rather adventurous of you had you indeed planned the whole thing." The duchess surveyed the mess.

Eleanora pulled her gaze away from the glove. "Adventurous? I would think the whole thing appalling."

Jane looked back at her. "Oh no, my dear. I've been to too many of these things now, and this is the most exciting thing that's ever happened at one of them. Truly adventurous, really."

Eleanora stared at her. But really, she would expect that of the Duchess of Lofton. It had only been a few weeks since Eleanora had had the pleasure of making the acquaintance of the Duchess of Lofton at a tea held at Gregenden House, but the older woman had taken a kind of liking to Eleanora for which she could not find a reason. It was odd the relationship that had grown up between them, but Eleanora thought that this must have been what it would have been like to have a mother. The thought was as ridiculous as Eleanora imagined, but imagine it she did.

"Do you not have somewhere else to be, Your Grace?" Eleanora smiled slightly at the older woman as she looked about for the Duke of Lofton who was mysteriously absent.

Eleanora had heard that theirs was a different kind of relationship, but having no experience with relationships at all, she had to take the word of the gossips for it, which she could admit was not that reliable.

The Duchess of Lofton tilted her head. "The old bugger can wait. I want to see what happens."

Eleanora slipped the lilac glove into the pocket of her apron. "Very well, then. If you're going to hang around you can help clean up." She bent over and righted one of the potted ferns.

The duchess smiled. "Only you would put a member of the peerage to work, Miss Quinton."

"I find some members of the peerage are there only out of luck, not that they have earned it."

The duchess raised her eyebrows. "Am I one of those there out of luck then, Eleanora?"

Eleanora smirked again. "Loads of luck, Your Grace."

HE DIDN'T BOTHER GRABBING his coat or hat as he walked out into the crisp dark night. He did not have far to walk. The drive in front of him was full of the mob that the ballroom had been full of just moments before. Ladies were scrambling to get into carriages as men pushed from behind, shoving the wads of fabric through the carriage doors that were much too small. Especially for Lady Drendrigeshire's fat arse. Alec observed for a moment that her behind looked quite like the signal flag of a ship as it attempted to make its way through the tight carriage door, and he pondered whether the signal flag would be depicting distress.

He turned right at the end of the walk from the front door and headed down along the side of the drive, ignoring the ladies who shouted at him for assistance and the men who plodded into him while trying to shove the women into the carriages. It really was just a great mess.

Stryden met the street and crossed quickly between two passing carriages to the other side. Walking toward the corner, he ducked down an alleyway before he reached the intersecting street. His shoes clicked, the sound ricocheting off the brick walls that enclosed the back gardens of the townhouses along the alley. The light from the street did not penetrate the darkness very far. But the hack was pulled only so far in, facing the street in case the occupant had a need to leave quickly. Stryden walked up to it, pulled open the door, and climbed in.

"Nice shot." He rubbed his hands together from the cold.

"Thank you." His brother's teeth flashed white in the darkness as he smiled. "Thank you for the distraction. Is she really all that Jane says she is?"

"That and more, I'm afraid. I thought I was in over my head." Stryden relaxed against the cushions, keeping one eye focused out the window for movement.

He had been rather surprised by how ardently Eleanora Quinton had surveyed the room. It was as if she herself had served in the military and knew exactly what it took to correctly manage a battalion of soldiers. Or in this case, housemaids, footmen, and an unpredictable bunch of peers. But quite impressed he still had been.

When he had taken on this assignment from the War Office, he had thought it would be simple enough. A typical assassination of a treasonous lord. He had not taken the time to realize all of the possible scenarios where things would become truly difficult. An assassination meant to look like payment for untold debts and rights wronged and all of that glory nonsense that winners spouted about the morning after the duel in which they had survived and some other poor chap had not. Alec did not know who really had the energy for such drivel. What happened to being a gentleman and all that that stood for?

"You? In over your head with a woman? I doubt that," Nathan said, and Alec looked at him through the darkness.

It still startled him to see a face so like his own, and he felt again the rush of affection for his older brother. Although Nathan had been born first, it was Alec who had carried the title as Nathan had been born on the wrong side of the sheets. It saddened Alec to know that a title Nathan so richly deserved was one he would never have. But their father had not neglected Nathan, just as the Duke of Lofton had not neglected any person under his care in his entire life. He had taken Nathan as a son when the baby's mother had died in childbirth, and Nathan had never wanted for anything. And Alec had had a big brother to look up to.

"Do not doubt, dear brother," he said now. "She's an eagle. I thought I was going to have to ravish her right there on the dance floor to get her to stop eyeing everyone and everything." He straightened his coat. "I have never seen anyone more observant in my entire life. Including you."

Nathan sat up. "Including me?"

"Yes, you." Stryden watched the lines of his brother's face in the darkness. "No." His brother did not move. "No, you are not going to meet her."

"Why not?" Nathan sat forward so a shaft of moon fell across his blue eyes, revealing features so like Stryden's that he paused again in consideration.

This was his brother. The one he fought next to on the battlefields in France and returning to England, they had been partnered by the War Office to fight in a more intellectual game, one of espionage and stealth, played out in drawing rooms and clubs instead of battlefields. And now the bloody bastard was going to ruin everything he had worked so hard to accomplish that night because he wanted to meet a woman?

"I flirted outrageously with her in order to get you in there without her seeing you. And now you just want to waltz in and meet the chit?"

"Oh, come now, Alec, I would not call her a chit. You just said she was an eagle. Most gracious and noble bird that is." He reached for the door. "I believe I shall have a look."

Alec grabbed his brother's hand in midair. "Think about what you're doing. Your life may never be the same."

Nathan sat back. "Yes, maybe it will get better."

"I think it will get a lot worse."

"She's that incredible?"

26

"She reminded me of Hurst."

Nathan leaned farther back in the seat. "Hurst?"

"Yes. Holds her hands behind her back in just the same manner."

"Oh my." Nathan sat all the way back against the cushioned seat, remembering their commanding officer from their days in the field.

"And what about the mission, Nathan?" Alec tried a different tactic. "This was supposed to have looked like a revenge killing."

Nathan seemed to ponder this. "Do you think anyone will believe that?"

Alec shrugged. "I do not know. I have never seen a revenge killing before. It is not like they happen regularly at balls."

Nathan gave a sound as if to agree but spoke no further.

The two sat for a moment staring out the window. They heard the horses shift their feet in the cold, sending their reins jingling in the stillness.

"They should be coming soon. I should head back." Alec opened the door and climbed down. He turned to shut the door, but Nathan was climbing out behind him.

"No." Alec tried to physically push Nathan back into the hack.

Nathan swatted his little brother out of the way. "I think my life could use an adjustment."

* * *

STANDING in the doorway to the ballroom, he knew, quite quickly in fact, that this was more than just an adjustment, and his life really may never be the same again. She was beautiful. Well, not beautiful in any normal manner. In fact, she looked like she could put him in his place faster than make him buckle at the knees with want. Both options sounded vastly appealing, though.

She stood in the middle of an absolute mess. There was what looked like the remains of some kind of shrubbery strewn across the floor. Why shrubbery would be in a ball-room, he had not a clue. But a herd of society's finest had done their best to maim the poor plants. Maids and footmen were gathering the fronds in piles growing almost too large to hold. Others were carefully picking up shards of glass, broken champagne flutes, and plates. More were crawling over the platform in the rear where he had entered earlier that evening. The ballroom had looked quite lovely then.

Miss Quinton was currently folding yards of a sheer, blue fabric, carefully placing it on a table away from the dirt and spilled liquor. Her white hat and apron were as starched and perfect as if nothing out of the ordinary had transpired that evening. The corners of her mouth were slightly turned up. Why? He did not know, but for some odd reason, he really wished to find out.

He felt Alec staring at him as he stared at Miss Quinton.

"Hurst, indeed."

"Do not do it, Nathan. You still have time to flee. She has not seen you yet."

Nathan glared at him. "I'm not going to run with my tail between my legs from a mere woman."

"Who is this, my lord?"

The sharp tone made Nathan swing his head around. He stared openly, knowing his mouth was hanging down to his chest and not caring in the least.

Alec opened his mouth to speak, but Nathan moved first, grabbing her hand and bringing it to his lips. "Mr. Black, of Bow Street, Miss Quinton."

He lowered her hand, letting her fingers slide slowly through his own before fully letting go of her.

Alec attempted to hide a laugh under a strained cough.

A little lie was not going to hurt things at the moment. After all, he had just killed a man.

Except Miss Quinton did not flinch.

Nathan straightened fully and smiled his most devilish smile.

She cast her eyes down along the length of him and back up. "Here is the body, Mr. Black." She turned away from him, gesturing to the dead man on the floor about ten feet away.

Nathan frowned. Deeply. Had she just given him the once over and then dismissed him completely?

He threw a scowl at Alec who just shrugged his shoulders and moved to follow Miss Quinton. Nathan also moved and found his path blocked by one of the decimated ferns. He kicked it out of his way and continued on.

"Be careful, Nathan."

He almost jumped out of his skin. He swung his head to the side to see Jane smiling at him. Where the bloody hell had she come from, and why was she still here?

He raised his eyebrows at her, and the crotchety woman stuck out her tongue at him. He went back to making his way across the cluttered ballroom toward the swiftly moving Miss Quinton.

"I apologize for the mess, Mr. Black. My staff is deeply horrified by such a tragedy and is trying hard to move past it. They are cleaning up this mess as promptly as possible, so that they may retire for the evening. And it has been quite a long evening, I'm sure you understand. I have not allowed them to touch the body, however, in case you may find some clue with it."

She stopped three feet from the body and by God, folded her hands behind her back under the starched bow of her apron. He quirked a brow at Alec, who just shrugged again. He dared to look at Jane, who winked at him.

29

"Very astute of you, Miss Quinton." Nathan bent down to look more closely at the body although he knew quite well who it was and what that *who* was. Lord Archer had been passing information to the damned French. It had been a pleasure to shoot the bastard. Nathan reached out and removed the man's handkerchief from his coat pocket to cover his face. He straightened up and turned to speak to Miss Quinton.

"Why did you do that, sir?" She had her lips thinned out, no longer turned up at the corners, her head cocked, looking quite perplexed. He thought he heard Jane laugh behind him.

"I do not want your delicate sensibilities to be offended by the look of death." Nathan smiled gently.

"I assure you, sir, my sensibilities are far stronger than you might think. A dead body is just a dead body. I have seen far worse." She straightened her head and rolled her shoulders back. She became a full two inches taller, or perhaps that was an illusion. But Nathan took a step back anyway.

And that time he definitely heard Jane snort.

"I apologize for making an assumption, Miss Quinton. Please forgive me."

"Of course, sir." She nodded. "What do you plan to do with the body? It is quite upsetting to my staff."

Nathan pulled his gloves off and tucked them into the pockets of his greatcoat, bumping into the pistol still in his pocket. He bent down and rolled Archer over from the bent position he had landed in. It was pretty spectacular that the bloke had plummeted off the balcony after the bullet had smashed into his chest. Nathan really had not expected that to happen.

Alec squatted down beside him and leaned close. "I warned you."

"Yes, please do remind me to heed your warnings in the future," Nathan whispered back.

They both stared at the body without a bloody clue what to do with it. This was Rogers's territory.

And as if on cue, Rogers appeared. "Very sorry, sir. Was detained by a very large, irate butler in the entranceway." Shiny Flip Rogers looked like a weasel that had been smacked in the face with a rug beater. But really the most trustworthy and kind fellow once you got to know him. True, he was a body snatcher. But he only sold the bodies to the really elite schools of medicine, none of those dodgy, experimental quacks.

Alec and Nathan stood, moving apart to allow Rogers and the two men he had brought with him to approach the body. He would take Lord Archer off their hands, and no one would miss him. And the dead lord would be contributing to the advancement of science. How thoughtful of him.

"Irate butler?" Nathan quirked an eyebrow at Miss Quinton. He thought he saw her assess the statement for a moment as if the description did not match an idea she held in her head. But she quickly recovered and moved on.

"Would you not be irate, Mr. Black, if someone went and got himself shot and kept you from your bed?"

Nathan found he had no response.

Miss Quinton's mouth returned to its normal position, corners slightly turned up. She actually looked pleasant then, looking up at him from under the stark white cap on her head. He noticed thin tendrils of hair had fallen out from under the cap around her ears. It was brown. No, red. Maybe both. The thousands of candles around them were setting it on fire, and he wasn't sure what color it really was.

He cleared his throat. "Mr. Rogers," he pointed behind him, "will move quickly and get Lord Archer removed, so that your staff may finish their cleaning and be in bed before long."

"Lord Archer?" Miss Quinton bent her head to look at the body.

"Yes, the, um, dead man." Nathan watched her face, fascinated by the movement in her eyes, wondering what she could possibly be thinking.

"That is not Lord Archer, sir."

Nathan had not thought she had been thinking that.

"Of course, it is Lord Archer." Nathan turned back to the body.

"No, it is not." Miss Quinton stepped forward and actually bent down. "This is his brother, Frederick. Or Mr. Westley, as his brother is the elder and inherited the title of lord while Frederick is a mere mister." She tugged on the man's cravat revealing a scar along one side of his neck. "He got that in a duel over his mistress's honor. Most preposterous thing." Miss Quinton stood back up. "Lord Archer is in Wessex at Lord Heathenbaum's house party."

Nathan, Alec, and Rogers all stared at Miss Quinton. Jane bent over and looked at the scar, letting out a soft *Oops.*

Alec spoke first. "What?"

Nathan thought that a profound statement from his little brother.

Miss Quinton drew in a deep breath and held it a moment. She released it slowly through her nose in a soft sigh. "Franklin, Lord Archer, is in Wessex attending a house party with his mistress while his wife is in Rome recovering from a bad chest cough which involves the personal attention and care of one Monsieur Pierre, last name unknown." She stared directly at Nathan.

Nathan pointed at the body. "That is not Lord Archer," he said.

He felt his throat closing.

"Precisely, sir." She adjusted her apron, which did not

need adjusting, and placed her hands carefully behind her back.

Nathan moved his gaze over to Alec, who in turn looked at Rogers.

Rogers, daft idiot that he was, blurted out, "Even though it's the wrong bloke I still get the body, right?"

Miss Quinton's spine straightened. Her whole body seemed to lengthen, and Nathan knew, had she been a dog, her ears would have stood up. Her gaze sharpened. "Mr. Black?"

Jane stepped up. "I really think you should tell her. If anyone can understand the need for discretion right now, it would be Miss Quinton."

Nathan's mouth was open again without sound coming out. Second time in two minutes. That was not a good sign. He took Miss Quinton's elbow and tried to turn her away from poor Frederick. She did not budge an inch, and he thought his own elbow might have been dislocated from the jarring.

"Tell me what, Mr. Black?"

"It is a rather delicate affair, Miss Quinton—"

"Mr. Black, you are operating under a false impression. I am not a stupid, fragile girl like the rest of the debutantes in this society. I have lived things that you only have night-mares about, so could you please stop assuming that I am going to break at your every word?"

Nathan nodded, not daring to open his mouth.

"Thank you, sir. Now what is going on here?"

Nathan actually turned to look at Alec, but somehow, Miss Quinton ended up in front of his face. "Do not try to avoid me, Mr. Black. I would like an explanation."

"Very well, madam, but only in some place more private." He grabbed her elbow and swung her around, not caring in the least anymore for her delicate sensibilities. She ended up smacking into his side, but he just scowled at her. Her cap had fallen back on her head, and she looked up, her eyes huge.

Nathan forgot what he had been doing.

There was fear in her eyes.

Stark, naked, and piercing fear.

He immediately let go of her, thinking his touch had brought on the sudden terror in her. She backed up, two whole steps, her eyes never leaving his face, always wide and watching as if waiting for him to strike. Her hands were bunched in the front of her apron, making the fabric crease with jagged wrinkles he was sure she absolutely would have hated had her mind been functioning. But he could see her mind was completely focused on him.

She was scared to death of him.

Nathan pulled his gaze away from her, hoping to stop whatever his touch had begun. Alec and Rogers were both staring at the suddenly silent Miss Quinton. Jane was staring at her hands. Nathan stepped in front of the men to block their view. Leaning close, he whispered, "Take the body. Alec, go to the Office. Tell them what has happened. Find Lofton."

Rogers snapped his fingers at the two men with him and started to gather the body for transport. Alec stepped over the dead man's leg to take Jane's arm to lead her away. Jane would not budge.

"I am only leaving if Miss Quinton says it is all right for me to leave."

Nathan looked back at Miss Quinton. Her hands were now pressed flat against the fabric she had moments before tried to rip to shreds. Her eyes were blank, and her face frozen as it had been before Nathan had touched her. The corners of her lips were no longer turned up.

"It is all right, Your Grace." She never took her gaze off of Nathan.

Nathan flicked a glance at Alec. He had not been aware that Jane had gotten quite this close with Miss Quinton.

Jane turned to let Alec lead her away.

"Um, sir?"

Nathan wanted to rub his hands over his face in exhaustion, but instead he turned to Rogers with an eyebrow raised.

"Are you going to be all right alone with her?" He pointed rudely at Miss Quinton.

Nathan stupidly followed the line of his finger and instantly watched the blood drain from the poor woman's face at his look. He supposed he would have reacted the same way if two strange men were whispering and pointing in his direction.

He quickly shifted back to Rogers, grabbing the offending finger and shoving it against the man. "I will be fine. Rest assured, Rogers, I can handle one woman."

"I would never doubt it, sir. Normally. But this is not just any woman." Rogers leaned in. "She could cut your ballocks off with that tongue. Mark my words." Rogers leaned back and gave him a frightful look.

Nathan cleared his throat and adjusted his jacket, covering the front of his breeches. He hoped the gesture looked casual, or Miss Quinton was going to faint on him.

He wondered then what had happened. She had been confident and sure, even a bit demanding. And then suddenly, she had withdrawn, pulling so far in on herself she had disappeared from his grasp. Leaving her dead. And scared. Absolutely terrified. He thought her eyes would have never shown emotion beyond efficient progression, and the emotion they had shown was not something he wanted to see in them again.

But he also wanted to know what had put it there. What had happened to Miss Quinton that had made her so reflexively nervous? What had her pulling away from him?

He stepped over some fronds, slowly approaching her again. "Is there somewhere we can speak privately, Miss Quinton?"

"His lordship and ladyship will wish to be informed of anything that involves their home. They have retired for the evening, however." It appeared the confidence had come back.

Nathan nodded, acknowledging the validity of her statement. "You can tell them anything you see fit tomorrow when they rise, but I will tell you some things you should not even know and therefore, I cannot let you tell them." He watched Rogers and his men carrying the body out wrapped in canvas. "It is state business."

"State business."

Her tone made him look at her.

"Is that what it is called?"

He nodded.

"Very well, Mr. Black. It appears I require a lesson on the definition of state business."

CHAPTER 3

*M*iss Quinton spun on her heel, and he moved to follow, watching his feet to avoid tripping over any plant parts, champagne glasses, or...was that a shoe? He collided with her before he could answer his own question. His body weighing a great deal more than hers sent them both sprawling. He wrapped his arms around her waist, hoping to roll her on top of him, keeping her from landing directly on the floor and everything that littered it. He landed on an urn and spun backwards over it. Landing quite solidly on his back, he tried to roll to gentle the impact, tucking Miss Quinton quite nicely under him. He came up on his elbows before squishing her. A plant frond had become affixed to her white cap, and more hair had fallen down around her face. It was brown, he decided. No, it was definitely red.

He went to reach for it when he noticed her eyes were shut. Tight.

His hand paused in the air over her cheekbone. Her skin was so white he thought no blood ever flowed through it. It was paint. Her face was painted with that horrible powder women put on their faces to hide age. It smothered her features. If he had not gotten so close, he would never have noticed. But around her eyes, he saw the weary smudges of too many sleepless nights. And by her right ear, there was a long, thin scar that was hidden nicely by the powder. No one would ever notice it just by looking at her. But he saw it all, and the strain around her eyes from holding them shut so tightly.

He was not sure anymore what to do with his hands. He thought if he touched her she might have an attack of the heart and simply die. But the skin around her eyes was strained so tightly he thought it might just snap off. He rested a hand on her shoulder. Surely that was a safe spot. But she did not budge. He looked down at her chest. He needed to see if she was breathing. Which he found she was not. At all. He moved his hand to her cheek. Her eyelids squeezed tighter, sucking her lips in at the same time, removing all hint of color from her face.

"Miss Quinton." He slid his hand along her cheek, down her neck and around, cupping her head. He placed his other hand along the side of her face, rubbing his thumb over her lips.

She trembled. Under his thumb, against the palm of his hand, against his chest, against his legs. It was a full body tremble that vibrated right through all of her clothes and all of his.

He tightened his grip and shook her. Picking her head right up off the floor, he shook her. "Eleanora."

She tossed her head in his grip. Her lips parted, and he heard her mumble, "No."

He leaned his head down, pressing his lips to her ear. "Eleanora. Wake up, Eleanora. It is all right. Nothing is happening to you."

Her eyes snapped open. He felt the flutter of it against his cheek. Pushing back on his elbows, he raised his head to look at her. The frozen look had returned, except her mouth hung slightly open. She darted her tongue out to wet her lower lip.

Nathan thought he might die right there on top of her. But then that would have been rather rude, seeing as how she had already had one dead body on her hands tonight. He did not want to add another one. But he could not help the way his body responded to her.

She blinked rapidly now, coming out of whatever fog had washed over her. Her hands flew up before he saw them coming, striking against his chest, wiggling out from under him. He rolled off of her and stood, reaching down for her hand. She looked at his hand as if it might give her leprosy and stood on her own.

She brushed at her skirts and apron, pulling on the loops of the ridiculous bow at her back. Her cap was still lying on the floor, and he picked it up, feeling her warmth still in it. He was tempted to hold it up to his nose and take a deep breath except she saw it first and snatched it away from him. The jerky movement sent the last remaining hairpin flying out of her hair.

And her entire mane of silky red-brown hair went cascading down her back.

Nathan felt his knees give and summoned the strength to remain standing.

She really was beautiful. He wanted to grab her, wipe that horrid white paint off of her face, and see her for what she really was. But not with that stark fear in her eyes. He wanted her eyes wide with excitement, her face flushed with the passion he put there, he wanted—

He felt himself choke, and he coughed several times before his lungs began functioning properly.

When he felt he could control himself, he looked at her again. Somehow she had twisted the hair into a braid that she coiled and pinned at the nape of her neck. Her hands flew and suddenly the cap was fixed back on her head as if nothing had happened. Setting her hands on her hips, she looked at him. "Are you coming, Mr. Black?"

Small wisps of hair fell down along the sides of her face, and she tucked them behind her ears. He sighed, absolutely exhausted. "Yes, madam. I'm coming."

He walked five steps behind her. He counted. She took five whole steps before he even took one. She took him toward the back of the ballroom and the platform where the orchestra had been set up. Sheer drapes fluttered in the wind by the terrace doors. Miss Quinton picked her way carefully past a chair that had fallen off the platform and scooted around the stage to the terrace doors.

"Miss Quinton?"

"It is faster to go out these doors and around to the study through the parlor doors." She did not look back at him as she spoke.

He felt the wind shift and welcomed the cold that washed over him. The wind shifted again, and his head snapped up. He saw the bush move before the moon glinted off the barrel of the gun. He dove for Miss Quinton, once again wrapping his arms around her and sending them both to the ground.

The gunshot sliced the air above them as they landed behind one of the doors, pulling down a drape as they slid into the corner behind the platform. Nathan struggled to get the damn drape off of them. He freed his arms from it and began to work Miss Quinton free. He grabbed her shoulders and dragged her up the length of him, which he had to admit felt just too good, even if someone was trying to kill them.

Her arms were wrapped around herself, but her eyes were wide open.

"What sort of state business are you involved in, Mr. Black?"

* * *

NATHAN PICKED UP MISS QUINTON, depositing her rather unceremoniously on the floor by a tree in the corner, perfectly sheltered behind the platform. What the hell a tree was doing there, he had not a clue.

He stuck his finger in her face and waited for her to push up her fallen white cap so she would see it. "Stay."

He treated her rather like one would a furry companion of the canine variety, but he would make up for the disrespect. For now, the burning need to keep her safe propelled him forward without a conscious thought as to propriety.

Thankfully he had reloaded his pistol after shooting poor Frederick, and he grabbed it out of his greatcoat pocket. The weight of the gun felt secure in his palm, as he waited for one of the drapes along the doors to flutter again. It shifted, and he darted out on the terrace, mixing his movements with the fabric. Anyone watching from out in the gardens would have seen just one movement, not being able to discern his dash from the flutter of fabric. He pushed his back against the post of the staircase leading down into the dark gardens. The shot had come from the left. He turned his head, thinking again why it was a good thing he did not wear a hat. It would be a serious encumbrance right now.

It was late spring, but the night still held a chill in the air that had Nathan watching his breath to ensure he did not accidentally give himself away. The largest rhododendron bush he had ever seen loomed up on the left of the staircase. Its blooming branches obscured his vision of the remainder of the garden, and he leaned a little outward to see around it. He held the pistol wrapped in his right hand, nestled in his left for balance. He raised it now, stepping out with his left foot. His stance was firm as he surveyed the bush more clearly. A flash of red caught his eye, and his finger started to squeeze the trigger even as his mind was stepping ahead of it.

The red scarf was stuck to one of the flowers. Whoever had shot at them was long gone. He lowered the gun to a smaller angle but did not release his grip on it. He went down the staircase sideways, crossing one foot in front of the other, his eyes traveling the length of the garden to the left and back again. A fog was starting to come up as the night grew colder. The hedges were just gloomy lumps in the dark. He reached the ground and took a wide circle around the bush.

The ground was too firm, which meant no footprints, and he was reminded again of how the evening was not going according to plan. He stuck the pistol back in his pocket, grabbing the red scarf off the bush. He ran it between his fingers. It was silk with small, white rosebuds along the edges. A woman had taken a shot at him? That did not fit with the information he had received about Archer, and if this attempted shooting was related to the matter, he did not see how it fit.

He took another sweep of the ground and started back up the stairs to the terrace. The agents who had relayed the information on Archer's whereabouts were dependable, solid operatives. He could not imagine why the information had been corrupt. He paused at the top of the staircase and looked back through the night and fog. All was still, the wind the only noise in the darkness.

The ballroom was blindingly bright when he returned. He did not bother looking in the corner where he had deposited the demanding Miss Quinton. It was pretty certain she would not have stayed where he left her. Her confidence and surety at commanding the situation would have propelled her to seek him out and ascertain the gravity of the event and what was necessary to rectify it.

He was studying the scarf in his hand now that he had more light when he heard her voice from behind him, so soft he almost missed it. "Mr. Black?"

He spun around. She was still on the floor behind the tree. Her knees were drawn up, her arms wrapped around them. Her chin was up, her eyes clear and piercing. For a moment, he simply stood and stared. She looked so young there in the candlelight, shadows dancing across her fine, too thin features. The vulnerability of her stance struck him, and his breath caught in his chest. His mind flashed on a long ago time when he was a young boy, helpless in his youth, and then it had been a different woman who had been so vulnerable. A different woman he had been unable to help even when her pain was clearly visible in the bruises on her face. A shift in the wind through the terrace doors brought him back abruptly, and he pushed the memory from his mind.

"It is all right, Miss Quinton. They are gone." He shook the scarf at her. "This was all they left behind."

She started to get up from the small place she was squeezed into between the obnoxious tree and the wall. Her feet slid across some fronds on the floor, leaving her slipping back down to the ground. He waited, unsure if he should help her or if his presence and touch would send her into hysterics once more. But when she looked up at him, his breath stuck in his lungs once more at the abject innocence he found in her eyes. He wanted to pick her up, hold her against him, carry her away from all of this and—

And do what?

Support her on the salary of an agent for the War Office? He thought it unlikely. And once again, he felt the helplessness of a child engulf him. A helplessness that raged unbidden in his mind.

"Mr. Black, I seem to be incapable of getting up. Would

43

you please assist me, sir?" A more politely worded request he had never heard before in his life.

"Certainly, madam." She was holding up her hands to him, so he took them very gently in his and pulled. Her feet would not gain purchase on the floor, and she began to slide directly between his legs, first her own legs disappeared between his and then her torso and then he saw her face heading for—

His arms were under and around her, pulling her upright faster than even he thought he was capable of moving. Her face smacked into his chest instead of his more delicate areas, which he considered a good thing. But by the way Miss Quinton immediately tensed at such a close proximity to him, he knew she did not think it a good thing at all. His arms were snuggly around her, her head tucked just under his chin. He could not help but think how perfectly she fit, and how good it felt to hold her with her scent invading his senses. Lemons...and wax. She smelled like cleaning formulas. He wanted to pull her closer, which was most likely impossible, but he very much wanted to try anyway.

Instead, he took a deep breath and a step back. He had not even realized that she had been holding onto him as tightly as he had been holding onto her until her hands slid along his back and around to the front as he stepped away from her. Her eyes were closed or looking at her feet or something, but it was killing him not to see what they were saying. Was she scared, terrified, ready to kill him for touching her?

It seemed an eternity before her lids rose, and her brown eyes flickered in the candlelight. Wariness. He saw wariness in them. And insecurity. But not fear. There was not any fear in them. The air rushed from his lungs, and blood surged to his head making him dizzy. He sat down casually on the edge of the platform to cover his sudden euphoria. She was not scared. A little wary, a little insecure, a little unsure, but not scared of him. Uncertainty was easier to work with than outright fear.

The scarf was still in his hands, so he handed it to her. "Found this. That is all. The ground is too firm for footprints." She took the scarf from him, which left his hands free to scrub over his face. He had been staring at her so hard that he feared his eyes were going to fall out of his head. He pushed his hands into his hair, rubbing his scalp, hoping to clear his brain, which was suddenly cluttered with thoughts of lemons, wax, and red-brown hair.

"Bridget Davies was wearing this. She left about a half hour ago with Daniel Flattery." She held the scarf out to him.

"Bridget Davies?" That name had not appeared anywhere in the intelligence on this mission. He did not even recall a Bridget Davies having been on the invitation list for the evening's affair.

"They have not come back yet. I am hoping they heard the mass exodus and left discreetly through the back. Or tongues will be wagging tomorrow." She sighed, looking to the spot where the body had been. "Well, they will be wagging more."

"What do you mean they have not come back yet?" He knew his mind wasn't so befuddled with lemons and wax that he could not understand English any longer.

"They went for a stroll in the gardens, Mr. Black." She pursed her lips at him as if any idiot would know to what she referred.

"Oh, quite," he finally said and looked back at the floor.

This entire affair had gone drastically wrong, and nothing seemed to be improving matters. He had the wrong man dead, Archer was still out there somewhere, and now someone was shooting at him. And then there was Eleanora Quinton. Nathan should have listened to his brother and never gotten out of that hack.

"Mr. Black, did you hurt yourself?"

He raised his eyebrows. "Not that I recall."

"You are bleeding."

He jumped up as if a dog had taken a bite out of the seat of his pants. "Where?"

She cocked her head, her lips moving into...a smile? His night was already not going very well. He did not need to add an injury to it.

But then Miss Quinton approached him. Slowly at first and then with more assurance, and then one tentative hand reached for the sleeve of his jacket. He felt the barest of touches tug at the fabric of his greatcoat, and the smell of lemons flooded his senses.

"It looks like the bullet was closer than you thought," she said.

He had been staring at the top of her head, and her voice shook something inside of him. He followed the line of her hand to where it perched on his upper arm. He saw where the jacket had torn, and dried blood stained the ripped fabric. It was not the first time he had been shot, but it did not mean he liked it any more.

"It will be fine, Miss Quinton," he said, pulling his arm away from her touch.

She finally looked up at him then, and he saw something move across her features.

"Nora," she said, and the softness of her voice had his body relaxing unwillingly. "You may call me Nora."

He wanted to smile. He wanted grab her and pull her against him. He wanted...her. But he did nothing and simply replied with, "And I am Nathan."

She did not move and neither did he. They both stood, staring at each other amongst the wreckage of the ballroom.

A sudden commotion in the hall had them both turning toward the door. Feet struck the hard floor in rapid staccato as someone dashed along its length. Bursting through the doors, a boy of about ten slid into the mess of the ballroom and stopped, staring at the mutilated ferns, broken glasses and various pieces of apparel. His mouth was hanging open, as his straw straight brown hair fell into his eyes.

He finally saw Nora and Nathan standing down the room and shouted even though he really need not have.

"Did someone really get shot, Mama?"

* * *

NORA DID NOT MOVE.

She did not dare to breathe.

Of all the things she had expected to happen this night, none of the events that had actually transpired were on her list. Not a single one.

If she were to learn anything from tonight, it would be to always listen to Hawkins even if his ramblings bordered on ludicrous.

"Mr. Black—" she began, but he cut her off.

"I'm afraid someone was shot, young man," Nathan said, stepping towards the young boy in the doorway.

Nora had not realized quite how small her son still was. She had been watching him every day for more than nine years, and he always amazed her with his capabilities and sheer presence. She often forgot he was still just a little boy with his too thin features, large dark eyes, and mop of pin straight brown hair that continuously flopped in his eyes. She took a protective step forward, but Nathan was still ahead of her.

"You need not worry on it. This was strictly an affair of the War Office of mother England. You are quite safe, lad."

Nora watched Samuel back up as Nathan approached. She could not remember when it was that Samuel had taken to retreating from men. She worried it was an indirect influence from her, but she could not be sure. Still, watching him recoil from a perfectly fine gentleman made her heart sink as a mother. Was she truly that quick to react to a male's presence? Did Samuel pick up on it that easily?

"What is your name, son?"

Nathan advanced more, and Nora still tried to get in front of him. But then she noticed Nathan's hand. The one closest to her was open, palm wide and fingers splayed as if telling her to stay back. What was he doing? This was her son, and she was not just going to stand back while he cowered with insecurity in the doorway.

"Samuel." Her son was not shouting any more. He was barely pushing out enough air to make noise.

"Samuel. That's a fine name. How old are you?" Nathan continued, and Nora held her breath.

"Nine, sir."

"Nine. That's fantastic. You're almost old enough to be a spy yourself. Ever thought about being a spy, Samuel?"

Nora looked at Nathan. She was not sure what she had expected Nathan to say, but the topic of espionage was not high on her probabilities list. She looked back at Samuel and realized he watched her. He was doing that thing that Nora so often did. He looked over Nathan's shoulder instead of at him, making it appear as though he were looking through Nathan instead. Nora felt her mouth go slack. Never had her mothering skills been so apparent to her.

She smiled. She was not sure what made her do it or even where the energy for it had come. But she did, and she saw Samuel twitch. It was a physical thing, and she held her breath as Samuel answered the question.

"No, sir. If I'm a spy, I won't be here to look after my mother."

Nora's heart dropped again. She knew the bond with

her son was strong and close, but she had not quite realized how much of a parental role her own nine-year-old boy had assumed. He should not have been doing thusly. He should have been playing marbles or jacks or running around causing mischief with other boys his age. He should not have been taking care of his mother, much less worrying over her. Nine-year-old boys were not supposed to worry.

Nora looked about her suddenly, taking in everything around her, and feeling the weight of the house itself and her station in it press down on her.

Samuel should not be here. He should be running through fields and catching frogs and scraping his knees. That's what she had always wanted to do as a child instead of running Aunt Martha's household for her and her seven brats. She looked back at Samuel and saw him watching her, not looking at Nathan in the slightest and she wondered if the two of them had asked a question of her. But then Nathan spoke.

"Samuel." Nathan's voice came out on a soft tone, and Nora wondered if he realized Samuel's trepidation. "What are you thinking of doing if spying is out of the question? Perhaps you would like to be King of England?"

Samuel scowled. "Indeed not, sir. I would not like people to know my name when I passed them on the street. Everyone would be bowing down to me, and it would be a nuisance. The streets would be clogged with bowing people, and no one would get anywhere."

Nora saw Nathan blink and felt a pang not knowing what he thought of her son.

"What would you like to do then?" Nathan asked.

"I want to be a lamplighter." Samuel smiled, huge and proud, tucking his hands into the pockets of his well-worn breeches as if he were a real, grown up man. The last of the unease slid off his shoulders, and Nora imagined it falling to the floor in a dissolving puddle.

Nathan sat on an overturned urn. He crossed his legs and leaned his head on his fist, assuming a serious face. Nora smiled honestly now, watching the scene unfold before her.

"And why a lamplighter, Samuel?"

"The lamps make the streets safer at night. It would be a huge and noble responsibility to be the one to light those lamps."

"Yes, a very important task. Are you sure you're up to it?"

"I'm working very hard on being responsible, sir. My mother helped me plant some flowers in an old cup, so that I could tend them. And if I do not tend them, they will not grow. It's teaching me responsibility."

Nora realized she was still smiling as maids began to filter in from adjoining rooms armed with mops and rags. Footmen carried large buckets to remove the debris, and Nora wondered on the time. Her son should be in bed.

"That is exactly right, Samuel. Now, I think you have taken up enough of Mr. Black's time." Nora started to move briskly toward them and placed her hand on her son's shoulder to draw him away.

Samuel's face turned red. "I am very sorry, sir. I did not mean to be going on about such things."

Nathan stood up and walked over to kneel in front of the boy, ignoring Nora's attempt to pull the lad away. Nora's heart flipped again, and she wondered how much more she could take in one evening. No man had ever knelt down to her son's eye level, but she was not sure if it was because no man had ever bothered or if she had never let anyone get that close to her son.

"I think such things need a lot more discussion. Perhaps, you will have time this week to discuss responsibility further with me. And call me Nathan, not sir. My father is sir, and I am definitely not old enough to be called sir. Understood?" Nathan said.

Nora felt a pang in her stomach. What was it that Nathan promised her son? Surely, he could not be speaking of seeing her son again. And if he were speaking of promises he did not intend to keep, she would not have him around her son.

Samuel looked up to his mother, back at Nathan, and back up to Nora.

Nora spoke. "I do not believe you will have the pleasure of seeing Mr. Black again, Samuel, but it is kind of him to make such an offer."

Nathan stood so abruptly, Nora backed up involuntarily.

"I would have hoped you would allow me to see more of you and your son, Miss Quinton."

Nora watched Nathan's eyes in the lamplight, sparkling blue in the dimness. Something gripped her. She did not know what it was or what it meant, but it felt like she was suddenly safe. Like all the worry and anxiety she carried on her shoulders had simply been removed.

"We are quite busy during the week, si-Nathan. I am not sure we would have a moment."

She was not certain why she was defending herself, pushing back an offer from a gentleman that was nothing less than decent. But there lay a niggle of suspicion still deep within her, and she could not yet let it go and wondered if she ever could.

"Of course," Nathan said, and Nora watched something change in his face.

The moment was gone as quickly as it had come, and Nora instantly regretted whatever she had done to make it disappear.

Nora gently turned Samuel's face up to her. "Will you run to the kitchen and grab the medicine box for me, please?"

"Is it for the man who was shot? I do not think a medicine box will help, Mama."

Her ever practical son was not yet mature enough to feel the undercurrents moving between the adults in the room.

Nora felt her lips turn up just slightly at the tips. "No, it is not for him. Bring it along to the study, and then you should be off to bed. The music room drapes need to be beaten out tomorrow. You will need your rest."

Samuel nodded sharply with a stern, "Yes, ma'am," before taking off like he was on the most important mission in the world. He skidded to a sudden halt at the door to look over his shoulder at Nathan. "It was a pleasure speaking with you as well, Nathan." He disappeared through the ballroom doors.

Nora finally turned to look at Nathan, the shroud of seriousness returning with the unexpected suddenness of a cold wind on a spring day.

"We should move along to the study. It is getting late, and there is still quite a bit we should discuss."

Nora just nodded at him and turned toward the door, not bothering to pick up her skirts as she made her way through the mess.

CHAPTER 4

"*I*s that going to sting?"

"You will never find out if you do not allow me to tend your wound." Nora shoved him into a chair by the fire, feeling he was more trouble than Samuel ever was.

She busied herself with the supplies from the medicine box even though she really need not have. She was suddenly unsure if her nerves were up to touching him, and she would be touching him a great deal to clean his wound. It was only a small slice across his upper arm, but she would still need to rip his shirt to get to it. Or have him remove his shirt. She grabbed the table to keep from falling down. No, he would definitely not be removing his shirt. She refolded the clean cloth she was going to use to bind the cut with for the eighth time and decided she had had enough of her own foolishness.

Nathan sat rather calmly while Nora worked up the courage to actually touch him. It was a remarkable thing to watch her face, watch her eyes glint as one thought passed into another, her lips turned slightly up at the corners again but pressed solidly together in the middle.

He had removed his coat and folded it across the back of the chair into which she had pushed him. He had contemplated removing his shirt as well, so she could better access his arm. Remembering quite clearly her reaction to previous encounters with him, he left his shirt in place and would just let her rip the sleeve as needed.

His arm was starting to throb. It was throbbing enough to distract him from the fascinating expressions of a dithering Eleanora Quinton. He bent his head at an unnatural angle to get a better look at his shoulder, but all he saw was the spattering of blood on the white of his shirt. He looked back at the dithering Miss Quinton.

She was coming toward him, rather resolutely for a change, which made him sit up straighter. A white bandaging cloth and a bottle of a threatening elixir were her weapons of choice. He was thoroughly anxious to see how she would use them.

"I must rip your shirt, Nathan." She put the items down on the table beside him, moving the lantern that sat there back a bit.

There was enough light now for him to clearly see the layer of white on her face, saw where it faded into the high collar of her gown.

"Why do you wear that?"

She looked down at herself. "Because it would be improper for me to go without clothing. Surely even a rogue such as yourself would know that, Mr. Black." She pursed her lips at him.

He sat back slightly, inexplicably displeased that she had decided he was a rogue.

"It just so happens I am not a rogue—"

She laughed.

And he forgot what he had been saying. The sound of her laugh was musical and unexpected. Why it was unexpected, he was not sure, for surely she had occasion to laugh. But there was something about her serious posture that had precluded the thought from his mind. Her mouth was open, her teeth white and straight, her eyes sparkling in the lantern light.

And then she stopped.

And he remembered.

"I am not a rogue, Miss Quinton," he spat out her name as sharply as she had used his. "I simply enjoy the company of a fine woman."

Her eyes remained still on his face, not sparkling, glinting, or flashing. Not even blinking. Her lips were firmly together, corners turned up; her hands rested against her white apron.

"I see." She bent down to grab his shirt.

He sat back. "You see?"

"Yes." She made to grab his shirt again, making him sit almost on the arm of the chair to get away from her.

"You see what?"

"Lots. Now are you going to let me rip off your shirt or not?" He knew the moment she realized how the words she had said sounded. Her eyes went blank, both at the same time and sharp as a lightning strike. And he really did have the gall to smile just then, slowly...dangerously.

And he leaned towards her.

Her hands gripped the sleeve of his shirt and pulled with more force than he had been expecting. It even tugged him forward a bit, making him grab the arm of the chair. The white lawn of the shirt ripped easily under her hands, falling away from the slice in his arm. She grabbed his hand then. The contact sent a shock clear to his stomach and back. She adjusted his arm against the chair, turning his bicep into the light.

Her slender, reddened hand wrapped around him. Well,

obviously it did not wrap entirely around his bicep, but she had enough of a grip on it to cause more throbbing. He tilted forward to relieve some of the pressure. Her hands were callused and rough. When she had first removed her gloves, he had stared at her hands, never before having seen a woman's hands so badly mutilated from scrubbing and working, working to stay alive. It had made him think, and he realized suddenly that he had forgotten she was a housekeeper.

"Some of the blood has already dried on. I will have to wash it before I dress it."

"Wash it?" he asked.

She let go of his arm and walked away from him, across the room and out the door.

Nathan blinked at the open door. The clock above the fire ticked into the silence while he just sat staring at the spot where she had been standing. The woman was completely unpredictable. Nothing in her profile had indicated the slightest hint of a life of unconventional nature, and it had suggested impropriety be completely out of the question. But the infallible Miss Quinton had a son. And a son had meant that somewhere along the way, she had slipped up. But that thought did not fit right in his mind. He doubted Nora ever did anything of a reckless nature. The only other option would be if she had been...

He could not form the word in his mind.

He heard the tapping of her shoes on the floor in the hall several moments before she swished through the door, shutting it softly behind her. She carried a small basin, a blue rag hanging over the side of it. Walking briskly over to him, she set the basin on the table by the bandages and elixir before grabbing his arm again.

Her grasp was so tight a small *Ow* slipped from his lips. She raised an eyebrow at him. He stared at her face. No woman had ever raised an eyebrow at him. He was thinking up a scathing retort when she smacked the wet blue rag against his damaged skin, and instead of a retort, a curse popped from his lips.

She raised both eyebrows and frowned.

"I beg your pardon," he mumbled, gripping the armrest of the chair.

She nodded and bent to wash the dried blood from his arm. He looked at the fire, allowing his mind to drift away from the unpleasant thoughts he had been thinking on just moments before.

"What are you thinking?"

Her words made him jump, and he looked up at her. She had stopped bathing his arm, held the cloth in her hand, and looked at him thoughtfully.

"You looked suddenly serious, Mr. Black. Quite an unusual expression on your face, and I having only just met you. You can understand what an odd occurrence it was."

"I was thinking on your son." He smiled softly, skirting the truth without lying.

"Were you?"

Her lips formed a tighter line if that was possible, making them go almost white with lack of blood. She went back to bathing his wound.

"And just what were you thinking?"

"He loves you very much." She stopped to stare at him again, only this time, he saw the real Eleanora Quinton, not the one with the white face paint putting on a good show for everyone. He saw a strong woman, a mother trying her hardest to make sure her son grew up safely, healthily, and most importantly, happily. He saw a woman he very much admired. "He is lucky to have you."

"I think I am the lucky one." Her voice lost its boldness,

the words flowing delicately from her lips, almost as if she could not be saying the words aloud.

"How are his flowers coming?" Nathan found he liked this Miss Quinton best and tried to keep her around a little longer. "And you do realize he talks like he is eighty instead of nine, do you not?"

"His flowers are coming along wonderfully, and yes, I know he talks like he's eighty." She washed out the rag in the basin. "That is probably my fault." She smiled, or was it a smirk?

"Yes, probably."

They fell into silence then, mostly because Nathan could not think of a damn thing to say. Too many things were crowding in at once, so many questions he wanted to ask her, so many things he wanted to learn. He shifted in the seat, and his back scraped along the shape of his pistol in his greatcoat. And he suddenly remembered why he was here, alone with her, a slice across his shoulder from a bullet that was meant to kill him.

"Miss Quinton—"

Her eyebrows went up. "Oh, we are back to Miss Quinton. This must be the serious portion of the evening." The clock suddenly chimed two above the fireplace. "Or should I say morning?" she amended.

Nathan was not sure he liked all the eyebrow raising. It was normally he who did the raising. "I need to discuss with you some...things."

She finished with the washing and moved to get the bottle of clear stuff from the table. He sat straighter in the chair.

"Sometimes, Mr. Black, I wonder where you learned to speak. You are just so profound at times."

The woman's wit was either going to drive him insane or —well, yes, it would probably just drive him insane.

"My father, I guess, mostly taught me how to speak." Her eyebrow went up. "He is a duke," Nathan finished.

Nora froze. Nathan really had not believed it possible for her to go whiter under all the rice powder, but her skin definitely went down a few notches on the color scale. The blood must have drained from her entire head. He leaned forward just in case he would have to catch her in a faint.

"I beg your pardon...my lord. I had not realized." She ducked her head to work the cork out of the bottle.

"I am not a lord." He closed both of his hands over hers to get her attention. She jerked once, but he thought that was mostly from the sudden contact and not from an attempt to get away from him. He waited until she looked up at him. "I am the result of a burst of excitement, if you understand my meaning. I am no lord and never will be." He released her, but she did not move. He pointed at the bottle. "Do you need help with that?"

She looked down at her hands, looking as though she was not really certain how they had become wrapped around the bottle. "No, thank you." She pulled the cork, making a loud pop cut the air.

* * *

SHE WAS ACTUALLY GOING to have to touch him now. There was nothing else left to be done. A large cleaning rag had been barrier enough, but to apply the medicine, she would need to make contact with his skin again.

Nora felt the bile rise in her throat, her lungs constricting any passage of air.

She focused on a spot above his shoulder where the fabric of his great coat blended through the intricacies of the fabric of the armchair. The firelight glinted on the threads, and she let her eyes lose focus, wallowing in the undefined state of not seeing.

Eleanora Quinton could do this. She had left Aunt Martha's at the young age of seventeen and made a way for herself in London with no reference and no one to help her. She could dab some medicine on the arm of a Bow Street runner. Surely, she could. She had survived far worse.

She watched her hand drift in front of her, wondered as it moved of its own volition. The tips of her middle fingers brushed his skin first. He was warm and strangely soft. She wondered why this astonished her as she did not have anything else on which to base an assumption of how his skin would feel. It was not as if she made a practice of going about touching strange men. Or any men, for that matter. But still, she had expected him to feel...tougher, if that were the correct word.

There was something about his presence that just suggested strength and absoluteness, no room for yielding or tenderness. But when she touched him, she felt something entirely different from the aura she exuded.

He stared intently into the fire; his eyes squinted, focusing on the flames. She wondered what he thought. She was finding Nathan Black to be an odd man, if not particularly in his actions but in his moods. He often swung from one end of the pendulum to the other, keeping her guessing as to what he would say next. He could be charming at the beginning of a sentence and serious at the end. It was disconcerting.

She took the moment to actually look at him, really see what he was made of. She had never studied a man before, picked him apart piece by piece, put the pieces back together to see what they made. Men were never very interesting to her, less so after... Well, after. But this one was suddenly drawing her attention, for what reason she did not know. He was just like all the rest, perhaps a little more charming, a little more...friendly. Perhaps it had been the occasion of their meeting, something in the suspense and tension of murder that made her take notice of him. But she doubted that.

The pull was intrinsic. She could feel that much. There was something in Nathan Black that spoke to her. Her stomach churned, not wanting in the least to find out what it was.

She stepped back, lifting the alcohol soaked rag from his shoulder. Nathan was still staring at the fire, not noticing that she had moved. His dark hair fell across his forehead. The light did not touch the recesses of his eyes, making her wonder what color they were in the firelight.

He was so tall and broad, that she had not dared look at him before. She had looked past him, over his shoulder, making it appear as though she looked through him. But looking at him now, she found he was quite...pleasing in his makeup. His shoulders easily spanned the width of the chair back, and his large hands rested casually on either arm of the chair. His legs were stretched before him, too long for him to sit comfortably without stretching them thusly. His clothes were of fine quality but not quite as fine as that of a gentleman of the realm. But he had said he was the son of a duke. An illegitimate son. The notion opened many questions, but she did not dare to ask a single one of them.

His mouth was relaxed, tiny lines framing it. She had a sudden urge to run her fingertips over his lips, across his jaw, and along his cheekbones, to feel the scrape of his skin along hers. She wanted to touch more of him, see if all of his pieces felt the same as the skin of his arm. She wanted to know what it would feel like for him to touch her.

She stepped back so quickly she smacked into the table she had set the medicine box on. The whole thing shook, sending the lantern light swinging recklessly across the room. Nora grabbed for the lantern first. The last thing she needed tonight was to set the study on fire. The other clean rags fell off the table to the floor; the lid of the medicine box tottered shut with a snap. Steadying the lantern, she turned her head, knowing Nathan had heard the racket.

He had turned his head as well, but otherwise looked exactly the same, completely relaxed and calm.

"Skirts," Nora said. "They tend to get in the way."

"I can only imagine." His voice was soft with the slightest inflection of mockery.

She turned her head back to the lantern and bit her lip. She was slowly losing her mind, assuming she had not lost it already. First, she wanted to run her fingers all over his face and then suddenly when he had teased her, she had wondered what it would feel like to kiss him.

"Are you finished with me?" Nathan said behind her.

Nora bent and retrieved the fallen rags before turning back to him. "Yes, you will be fine."

But she very much doubted she would be equally as fine. This man was doing things to her she had never imagined any man could. And then he stood, and her stomach made a motion inside of her that had never occurred before. He towered over her, and it was not fear that she felt. It was an inexplicable tightening, an uncontrolled spasm deep within her.

"Excellent," he said and stepped toward her.

She would have stepped back, but that would have meant running into the table again. She knew her mouth had fallen open, and she probably had meant to scream, but it stuck in her throat. But no, that did not feel right. She was not afraid of him any longer. She was the very opposite. Something about him pulled at her, wanting him to come closer, wanting him to touch her.

And then he did, and the air rushed from her lungs.

Nathan reached for her. No, he was reaching around her, and the sudden feeling of loss that the near touch sent through her left her reeling. He picked up a clean rag and dipped it in the basin of water. Wringing out the excess water, he looked back at her.

She could see his eyes now, brilliant blue even in the soft light cast from the fire. The moving light played over his features like moonlight across the even surface of a lake. The planes and crevices invited her in, begged her fingers to explore. She did not know what was happening to her, but she did not want it to stop.

And then Nathan spoke.

"My turn," he said and finally touched her.

NATHAN THOUGHT she looked absolutely terrified. But there was the slightest softness around her mouth that made him doubt the validity of his observation. It was not terror. It was unwanted curiosity he saw masking her features.

She wanted to see what he was going to do next, and he was not leaving tonight without seeing what her face really looked like. He wanted the rice powder off of her skin. He wanted to see Eleanora Quinton for what she really looked like. He wanted to see her.

He gripped her shoulder first, and she did not flinch. She did not move at all under his touch. He swiped the wet rag along the line of her jaw, making a streak in the rice powder. He unearthed the curve of her cheek, the line of her nose, the soft angle of her jaw. The scar running from her eyebrow to the corner of her jaw became paler as the powder was wiped clean from it. He pulled the rag across her forehead, his fingertips inadvertently brushing the softness of her hair. Finished, he tipped her face up with a hand under her chin and studied her face in the lantern light.

The scar was more pronounced now, but it was not sinister or revolting. If anything, he simply wondered what had caused it. He traced it with a single fingertip, running his finger down the side of her face. He watched her. He watched the breath slowly slip from her slightly open mouth, saw the rise and fall of her chest. He felt the tightening in his stomach as he drank in the nearness of her.

And she had freckles. He could not have been more delighted. They dusted her nose and sprayed her cheeks, adding just a touch of color to her pale face. There were dark smudges under her eyes, making them look rather sunken, skeleton like, and he let his fingers run across her skin to one of the bruised patches. She blinked when his fingers came close to her eye, but she did not move. His gaze fell to her lips. They had taken on color and dimension without all the powder surrounding them, dimming them beyond recognition. He let his fingers drift down, running along her jaw to cup her chin once more.

And then he stepped back.

Cold air rushed between them, and he ardently wished he had stepped closer instead of back. It had already been a long and trying night, and from what he knew of Nora and what he had discovered of her this night, he knew she had already been through enough. Her emotions must have been straining even if she did not visibly show it on her person. He needed to give her some room, so she could adjust to his being there. Being in her life.

When he had started out that night, he had not thought it would end like this. He had been going out to complete an objective for the War Office. That was all. A rather typical day for him, but a rather typical end it was not. He knew he was not going to forget Eleanora Quinton, and he knew he was not going to let her slip from his life.

He looked at her, with the defiant set of her chin, the dusting of freckles, the parted lips that begged for another touch, and he took another step back.

"Franklin Archer is a man suspected of treason," he heard himself say, moving over to the fire. "I was given the task of eliminating him before he could pass more secrets to the French. It was to look like a revenge killing. That is why it was staged to occur tonight at the ball. I regret the disturbance this has caused you and your staff. The powers that decide these things do not always think on the repercussions of their actions. They only think of the best way to resolve an unfavorable situation."

Nora did not speak. He turned slightly to look at her. She had not moved from her spot by the lantern, and her face had not lost its sheen of curiosity. He needed to finish what he had to say and leave. He was already feeling the strain of keeping his emotions intact. If he was alone with her any longer, he could not be held responsible for what would occur. And something in the back of his mind made him feel disgusted with his own urgings, and he checked himself.

"It is unwise for you to share this information with anyone, and I advise you to think of another story to tell the lord and lady of the house. Knowledge of this information could prove deadly if discovered. Do you understand, Miss Quinton?"

He had been watching her, and at the last of his words, he watched the delicious spell that had swept over her break away and dissolve into the air. He wished it back almost instantly, but he knew it was for the best.

"I understand, Mr. Black."

Her voice was neither that of the demanding Miss Quinton he had met in the ball just hours before nor that of the mother who directed her son so carefully. He suspected this was the Eleanora Quinton that stayed hidden in the depths of the infallible housekeeper in an ardent need to feel safe.

Nathan was suddenly very tired and let his gaze drop down to the fire in the hearth.

"Thank you, Nathan," she said then, and he looked quickly back up. "Thank you," she continued. "For explaining the situation."

He nodded and reached for his great coat. It was past time for him to leave.

"I only regret that I cannot tell you more," he said, but then he paused. "Nora, I am uncertain as to what will happen next with this situation. There may be an issue with you knowing about Franklin Archer. I will not know until I speak with my colleagues."

Nora only nodded, and the simple response made him want to take her into his arms, close her within his grasp, and keep her safe from anything the world wanted to do to her. But he did not have the luxury of being in such a position to protect anyone. He never really had.

"I will be in touch as soon as I learn of what is to be done next, but I want you to understand that I do not know when that will be or what it will entail. I apologize now for this could cause an upset in your life."

Nathan recalled the many innocent people who had gotten in the way of War Office business and were suddenly transported to obscure places like the colony of Rhode Island or whatever such thing it called itself now. He wanted Nora to be able to grasp the gravity of the situation without frightening her.

She nodded again, and he moved toward the door. He had almost made it to the hallway when a question made him stop.

"Nora, do you have any family?"

Her face revealed nothing as she replied, "It is just Samuel and I."

He had suspected as much, and he wondered both why he had asked the question and why the answer had made him sad.

He nodded. "Thank you for your corporation, Miss Quinton. I bid you good night."

He turned once more to the door, but this time continued through it before the enticing image of Miss Eleanora Quinton could get the best of him.

CHAPTER 5

*N*athan turned left at the end of the drive heading toward the park. The air was crisp, making the part of his face exposed above the collar of his coat sting with each step. His footfalls were silent on the pavement, the fabric of his greatcoat eerily swooshing in the stillness. In the distance, a carriage passed on a cross street, the horses' hooves striking the road in a syncopated rhythm.

He reached the cross street and turned left, heading up along the park. It would have been quicker to cut through the park, but even he was not brave enough to go through the park at night. Even with a gun. Who knew what could be lurking in there. Rapists, robbers, or worse, snakes.

The houses lining the streets were dark except for a small glowing window here and there in one of the upper floors. Members of society readying for bed after long evenings spent at balls, musicales, and soirees. Wives brushing out their hair; husbands checking the children one more time. He stopped and stared up at one such window. The shadow of a woman passed across it, and the window went dark. He wondered suddenly where it was Nora and Samuel slept in Gregenden House. Was it a nice room? Was it drafty? Did they have an adequate bed to sleep in?

He pulled his collar up higher and continued down the street.

His father's house stuck out amongst the others, and it struck Nathan that it looked oddly welcoming, even at this early hour of the morning. There was light in the study, pouring out into the small space between the house and the one next to it. Alec had probably relayed what had happened to his father, and hopefully, they were getting started on what to do about the situation of mistaken identity. It was not every day that Nathan shot the wrong person. One slip could not be held against him, especially when the men in question looked so very similar to one another.

He climbed the steps and opened the door without knocking. Most likely the servants were all in bed, and he did not want to wake them by knocking. He remembered what Nora had said about the butler, what was his name? Hawkins. It would be very inconsiderate of him to wake the servants at this hour when he was certain he could open the door himself.

He stepped into the hall, closing the door softly. The light flickered as wind shifted from the open door. He put the lock in place and stepped over to pick up the lit candle Jane had probably left for him. He cupped his hand to protect the light and made his way down the hall.

Third door on the left was slightly ajar, and he heard the low tones of his father's voice. Nathan stopped to just listen to it. He could not make out the words, but he did not have to. His father's voice had always soothed him. As a small child, whenever he could not sleep or a nightmare had awoken him, he would find his father and make him read to him. Nathan could never remember any of the stories. It was just the sound of his father's voice that he had wanted to hear.

He walked up to the door and pushed it open, blowing out the candle as he stepped into the study. Jane sat on the sofa in front of the fire, a glass of sherry in one hand. Richard Black, the Duke of Lofton, stood leaning on the mantel, the fire behind him, casting his face in shadow. Alec sprawled in one of the wing chairs, legs spread, head hanging down to his chest, staring into the fire as if it were the most interesting thing in the world. An empty glass hung from his fingers.

Richard turned as Nathan entered and stepped away from the fire. His face became visible, and Nathan did not like the expression on it. He prepared himself for the worst.

Richard gestured with his glass before asking, "She did not emasculate you, did she?"

"Very nearly, yes. I just escaped in time." Nathan matched his father's serious tone.

"Want a drink?"

"A very big one."

Richard nodded and headed over to the whiskey decanter. Nathan went to the other winged chair and collapsed into it, not bothering to remove his coat. His pistol thumped against his thigh as he settled in. A glass of straight whiskey appeared in his hand, and he downed it in one gulp. The glass disappeared again, only to be returned a short moment later filled again. This time he only took a sip.

His father settled onto the sofa, slipping his fingers through Jane's out of habit. Nathan smiled. Jane and his father were one constant in his life. He remembered thousands of times that they had sat together on the same sofa, holding hands as if that was the normal way of things. Nathan wondered why they had not wed sooner in their lives, but Jane's past was not a topic easily broached, and Nathan left it at that.

Nathan turned his attention to Alec, who had not so much as blinked. His position in the chair looked less than comfortable, but he doubted Alec thought so, or cared for that matter. Nathan crossed one leg over the other and waited for his father to tell him what to do. Even at two and thirty, he could always depend on his father to tell him what to do.

Nathan wondered if Nora had anyone to depend on even though she had said she had no family. But perhaps there was a friend, a confidant, someone she could go to for help. Samuel's small face rose up in his mind, and he thought it not likely that she did. Instead, she had others depending on her. He wondered if she would let him change that, and he wondered if he would have the means to do so.

"Poor Frederick," Richard finally said.

"Poor, old Frederick." Jane sipped her sherry. "But really the world will not miss him. Bastard."

Richard nodded his agreement.

Alec mumbled something from his seat. Nathan did not catch it, but Jane responded, so it must have been English.

"He liked little boys, Alec. Everyone is better off without him."

"What do we do now?" Nathan asked the room in general, changing the subject.

"The Office is attempting to create a cover. Nothing too flashy. A debt unpaid. Revenge exacted. So on and so on. Same line just a different tilt to it to cover Frederick and not Franklin." Alec raised his glass to take a drink, realized it was empty, and just scowled at it.

Nathan nodded. "What about Archer?"

Richard shifted. "The Office does not want to do anything

for the time being. Both brothers being shot so close together will look more than fishy. We will keep intercepting the correspondence. See where it leads us. In time, we will form another strike."

"And meanwhile, what do I do about Miss Quinton?"

Richard raised an eyebrow, looking uncannily like the face Nathan saw in the mirror every time he went to shave. "Does Miss Quinton need to be...done?"

Jane elbowed him in the ribs.

"Someone shot at us from the gardens shortly after Alec left."

Finally, Alec sat up and looked halfway human. "Someone?"

"Whoever it was was gone by the time I made it to the gardens to check." Nathan sipped from his glass, hoping they would let that pass.

Alec, of course, would certainly not let something like that pass. "In the time it takes for a bullet to leave a firearm and almost strike you, the assailant was able to escape because you were..."

He let the sentence hang, but Nathan could imagine all of the things he was finding to finish the sentence with. And Nathan probably would not approve of any of them.

"I was sticking Miss Quinton behind a tree. Or maybe a fern. It was something to protect her from any more fire." Nathan waited, staring into his whiskey.

His feelings surrounding Miss Quinton were still quite a logjam in his chest, and he did not have the energy to sort them out just then.

Richard finally made a noise in his throat and said, "Protect the lady first. Good job, son."

Nathan looked at Alec. But Alec was only staring wide-eyed at the fire. Probably thinking of more possible things that Nathan had been doing in between the moment the bullet zipped past him and the moment he had made it out to the gardens. Nathan scowled at him, even though his brother was not looking in his direction. The scowl at least made Nathan feel better.

"The ground was too firm to leave footprints, and otherwise, there was nothing left behind."

"And Nora? Is she all right?" Jane asked in a concerned tone.

Nathan thought a moment, the image of Nora on the edge of curiosity, begging to be kissed as he left springing up in his mind. "She will live," he decided to say.

Jane pursed her lips but let it go.

"Her son is more than fine though." He took a drink and realized that everyone was staring at him as if he had suddenly grown horns.

"Her son?" Jane's voice was no longer filled with concern.

"Yes, Samuel."

"Miss Quinton has a son?" Alec's eyes were squinting now. Nathan wondered how his brother ever managed to win at cards. His emotions ran wild across his face.

"Yes, Miss Quinton has a nine-year-old son."

Jane's mouth was opening and closing, but no sound was emerging. That was not good. Jane knew everything about Miss Quinton. It had been her assignment. If she did not know about Samuel, then it was because Nora did not want Jane to know. Nora probably did not want anyone to know, and now he had gone and told three different people at one time.

He felt like a cad.

But if Nora loved her son, why did she not tell anyone about him?

"That explains some things," Jane said.

Richard only nodded, and Alec kept squinting like the sun was in his eyes.

Nathan felt like an idiot.

His father, thank the good Lord, changed the subject. "So we have someone shooting at you and Miss Quinton and the wrong man dead. Overall, I think it has been a rather horrible night." He turned his head. "Jane, what do you think?"

"Horrible, indeed."

"Well, I think I would disagree." Alec leaned back, a wise expression splattered on his face. "I think this night has seen immense progress. We—"

"Alec." Richard frowned at his youngest boy as if he knew he was going to say something he probably should not. And Alec shut his mouth, just as Richard had probably expected at the tone of his voice. It was amazing how children never really stopped being absolutely petrified at the sound of the parental voice. God knows Nathan was still scared of it. Richard looked back at Nathan.

"How do you plan to proceed with the Gregendens? They did have someone murdered at their ball."

Nathan settled deeper in his chair. "I spoke with Miss Quinton and imparted the gravity of the situation. I advised her to think of a line to tell the lord and lady and that I would return once I knew more."

Richard frowned harder. "Jane told me that she knew."

Nathan nodded, staring absently into the fire. Nora knew quite a lot.

"I also advised her that I would find out what will happen to her now that she is privy to state secrets."

Richard nodded, his expression glum. "I guess that is all we can do for this evening then." Richard rose, bringing Jane up with him. He took her glass and his over to the table in the corner and set them down next to the decanter. Alec began to pull himself out of the chair as well, searching around for wherever he had thrown his jacket. And his cravat. And his collar.

Nathan got up as well, pacing over to his father and setting down his glass next to the others. Richard put a hand on Nathan's shoulder, drawing his attention. Once again, Nathan was struck by how much they looked alike. Nearing nine and fifty, Richard had only a splash of gray throughout his dark hair, deep lines around his eyes and mouth from years of smiles, and soft brown eyes that still speared him.

"Get some rest," was all that Richard said, before turning to take Jane's hand to leave the room. Jane smiled at him and disappeared through the door behind Richard.

Alec had finally unearthed his collar and cravat but had yet to find his jacket. He probably had flung it over the staircase railing as he had come in.

Nathan stuck his head out into the hall and sure enough, saw it hanging crookedly over the banister.

"It is out there, brother." Nathan pointed out the door.

"Oh." Alec smiled goofily. "Are you coming home with me or are you staying here?"

On a War Office salary, Nathan could not afford to keep a place in town and mostly just stayed at either his father's or his brother's home. It was better than renting a room the size of a cupboard in some dive in Whitechapel.

Nathan heard his father and Jane moving around upstairs. "I am coming with you."

"Great." Alec smiled brilliantly.

"Why do you always find it so much fun when I come to stay with you?"

"Because you are my brother." Alec walked past him into the hall to find his jacket.

Nathan remembered Nora's answer to his question about family and guiltily followed his brother from the house.

* * *

Nora's head hit the pillow just as the clock chimed three. She had two hours to sleep before getting up to start the fires in the kitchen. And as exhausted as her body was, she cherished that two hours like nothing else.

But after five minutes with her eyes shut, Nora knew she was not going to fall asleep any time soon. She kept thinking about Nathan. About the way he had talked with Samuel, about the way he had stared at her so completely dumbfounded after she had pointed out that he had shot the wrong man, about the way his face looked when he was concentrating on the fire in the study, about the shifting color of his eyes.

About how his callused fingers had felt rasping across the soft skin of her face.

She rolled over, scanning the darkness opposite her until the outline of Samuel, sleeping soundly on the cot in the corner, came into focus. His chest rose and fell with the deep steady breaths of contented sleep. She watched him, wishing she were sleeping a contented sleep as well that did not involve images of Mr. Nathan Black.

She rolled over again to stare at the boring white wall of their small room. The fire was banked for the night and barely flickered against the wall. Nora concentrated on what tasks she needed to complete the next day, trying to bore herself to sleep. It was not working. The one task she kept thinking of was how she was to tell Lord and Lady Gregenden what had happened. It was all Hawkins could do to get them to retire for the evening without speaking with the presumed Bow Street runner who had come to the house to fetch the dead body. It was then Nora suddenly realized she was no longer sure if Nathan truly was a Bow Street runner. What had he said about the War Office and state secrets? Was he not a Bow Street runner at all but really a...spy?

This line of thinking was not going to get her to sleep any sooner than thinking of a story to tell her master and mistress.

She rolled again, this time to stare at the ceiling. The ceiling was just the bottom of the floor above her, the wooden beams and criss-crossing of floorboards. When she realized she had started counting the floorboards, she sat up and rubbed her hands across her face. This was never going to do.

Pulling the covers back, she swung her feet to the icy floor and stood, letting her nightdress fall down to the floor. The whole thing sat like a tent on her, letting air seep up the bottom and cool her skin. Her braid of hair hung across her shoulder, and she pushed it back before scooping up the top blanket on her bed and moving over to the small fireplace. It was more of a stove than a fireplace, but it suited her needs for having something to stare at while she brooded.

She stopped by Samuel's cot, just to look at him as he slept before settling into the worn armchair in front of the coals, pulling the blanket about her like a cocoon.

Every night she discovered new places on her body that could in fact be worn out to the point of painful aching. Tonight it was the spaces between her toes. She tucked her bare feet under her and spread the blanket over her and the chair, creating a bastion of comfort. She watched the coals fade and brighten, changing as air shifted across them. But even as soothing as that was, sleep was avoiding her. Or maybe she was avoiding it. She could never really tell anymore.

Samuel made a noise in his sleep, a soft mewl as he dreamed. Nora looked over to him and smiled softly. At least someone was sleeping well these days.

And as if to remind her, an image of Nathan rose up in her mind.

What was she to do with him?

Perhaps nothing, the sensible part of her mind scolded her. After all, Nathan had said he was not sure when he would return or what he would have to say on the matter then. His words had often been cryptic, but she was sure she had grasped at least the notion of what he was attempting to communicate to her. She now knew something that she should not, and her life was going to change as the War Office saw fit.

She looked over at Samuel again.

Perhaps they could leave. Leave at dawn. Just run away from it all. But then where would she go and without a reference? How would she secure employment? How would she care for Samuel? It was not as if she had family to help her, and she was not returning to Aunt Martha. She was honestly not even certain if Aunt Martha was still alive to help anyway.

She could do none of the things she wished would come easily. She had her son to care for, and she needed her good name and a solid reference to keep him safe, warm, and fed. She could not just leave in the morning and think all would be well.

Sleep would not be coming to her that night.

NATHAN PUNCHED his pillow for the tenth time, this time adding whispered curses as if they would somehow make the pillow more comfortable. After laying his head back down, he discovered swearing at pillows did not in fact make them more comfortable. He groaned, swooped the pillow from under him, and stuck it on his face, to groan even louder into it.

He had been lying there for more than an hour. It was not like him to not sleep. He was a champion sleeper. He always had been. He just had to lie down and roll over and bang, he was asleep. So why could he not do that tonight? He knew why. It had red brown hair and freckles. That was why he could not sleep.

And what was he to do about the red brown hair and freckles?

Nothing.

That was the answer that was keeping him from sleeping. There was nothing he could do. He remembered a time long ago, as a little boy, when he had been witness to a tragedy another woman he loved had faced, and then he had been helpless, too. He wrestled with the sheets, wanting to wrestle with the unfairness in life instead.

But he sat up and threw the pillow into the corner. It was childish, but it made him feel better. He got up and walked over to the window, drawing back the curtains to look out on the sleeping city. The houses were built up in this area, blocking his view. He saw the edges of the park in the distance, a few of the larger homes off to the west, and the tip of St. Paul's on the horizon. It was all cast in a silver cloak of moonlight, encasing it, preserving it until the sun returned. Nathan swung the curtain back in place, not caring in the least how magical it all looked.

He just wanted sleep. But he had a feeling he was not going to find it tonight. He reached for his dressing robe, not wanting to be discovered wandering around his brother's home stark naked by some young maid, who would either faint or jump him. He preferred neither tonight.

Out in the hall, things remained in darkness, the light of the moon not penetrating far from the window at the end of the hall. Nathan did not need the light, however, and moved quickly to the stairs and down, in search of some strong drink.

Not only did he find the strong drink, but he found his brother drinking it.

"Cannot sleep tonight?" Nathan asked Alec's reclined body on the sofa by the fireplace in what might have been a library if Alec had ever bothered to read the books that were in it. As it was now, it was just a storage room in which the books could collect dust.

Alec mumbled something from underneath the arm he had thrown over his eyes.

Nathan poured himself a drink from the liquor cabinet and sat down on the floor, leaning back against the sofa. He waited for Alec to summon the energy to speak more clearly and surveyed the room in the meantime. Alec had tossed his coat on the chair behind the mahogany desk that he never used. His collar was on the floor by the liquor cabinet. And his cravat had somehow become draped on the hilt of the crossed swords above the fireplace. Nathan took another swallow of drink, not wanting to contemplate how the article of clothing had gotten up there.

It took him a whole two minutes, but Alec finally spoke intelligible words. "Sarah is coming."

Nathan choked on his drink. "Sarah?"

Alec might have replied in the affirmative, but he was back to mumbling, and Nathan could not be sure. Nathan felt a sudden surge of delight that he was not the only person plagued that night with thoughts of womanly woe.

Sarah involved a whole lot of explaining most of the time. Technically, Sarah was Alec's wife and thus, the Countess of Stryden. But in reality, Sarah could not stand to be in the same room as Alec for more than three seconds. (Nathan had counted once.) And she was only married to Alec because the

War Office had made them get married. Sarah was an orphan, the result of a prostitute and a man with some extra money. She had been taken in by St. Mary's in The City and pounded with the Bible, day and night. She later had been rescued by an old woman with a lot of money she did not feel like leaving to anyone in her family. She adopted Sarah and conveniently died three days later, leaving Sarah with a fortune at the age of fourteen. Of course, Sarah, being only fourteen, did not exactly have control of the money, but neither did anyone else. The money was left in trust until Sarah completed her education. And what an education it was. It rivaled the education of some of the men of the upper echelons in England. And that was how Sarah came to work for the Office. She was smart and rich. The two important aspects of being a good spy.

The only problem was Sarah's unmarried state. A single woman could not go to the same places as a married woman, especially not alone. That was where Alec had conveniently entered the scene. He would marry Sarah (in name only or it would be over Sarah's dead body) in order to allow her more freedom to carry out Office business. But a marriage meant every once in a while, they actually had to appear to be married or the whole thing would be seen as the ruse it was.

And this was probably one of those times they were meant to appear actually married. Which would then account for Alec's less than chipper disposition and the empty glass on the floor, just beneath his dangling fingertips.

"When is she due to arrive?"

Alec moved his arm to look at the clock above the fireplace. "Seven hours, four minutes, and five seconds." He slid the arm back over his eyes.

"Ah." Nathan took another drink. "Want to talk about it?"

Alec moved his arm again to scowl at the back of him. "No, I do not want to talk about it."

The thing Alec did not want to talk about was the fact that he was completely and totally in love with his 'in-name-only' wife. He had been since the day they were married four years ago. Four years was a long time to be in love with someone who absolutely hated you. Nathan felt very fortunate that he was not in Alec's shoes. He only wished he had better shoes to be in himself at the moment. Ones that did not remind him what a useful man he was.

"Have you spoken to her recently?"

"No, just a letter, letting me know when she was coming." Alec swung his arm off his face to rest on the back of the couch. "How quick does arsenic work?"

"Not quick enough. Let me know when you want the deed done, and I will just shoot you in the back of the head."

"Oh, thank you, brother."

"You are welcome." Nathan swirled the liquor in his glass. "As long as you will do the same for me."

Alec studied Nathan's profile. "She is the reason you cannot sleep?"

"Yes." Nathan set the still full glass down on the rug to rub his face with his hands. "I cannot seem to rid her image from my mind."

"I hate to be crass, but I did tell you so. When will you see her again?"

Nathan looked up to the clock as Alec had done before, but unlike with Alec, it held no answers for him. "I do not know. I think that may be a part of the problem"

"Ah." Alec looked back at the ceiling. "Have you thought about what you are going to discuss the next you see her?"

"How to get her dress off."

"Good topic. Do you think she will agree?"

Nathan felt his mood dampening. "No."

"Thought not."

The two were silent for a while, listening to the fire and the tick of the clock.

Alec finally broke the silence. "Why do you think God created woman?"

"To give all men an idea of what Hell would be like, so they would lead better lives in order to avoid going there."

"Oh, yes, that does sound right."

CHAPTER 6

$\mathcal{N}$ora pinched her cheeks again, harder this time and winced.

"Ow!" she hissed.

Why on Earth women submitted themselves to such torture regularly, she had no idea. Instead of her cheeks turning delicately pink as desired, her whole face had gone red from the exertion. Her decision to forgo the rice powder this morning was starting to look unwise, even if Mr. Black had expressed a dislike of the stuff. She stuck her tongue out at her reflection. Now she certainly looked attractive.

It was not as if there was any certainty that she would be seeing Mr. Black that morning. It had been four whole days since last she had seen him. Four whole days of wondering and waiting and watching. The anticipation was enough to do more than keep her awake at night. She had been eating even less than usual, and Cook had begun to notice. She struggled to keep her demeanor as pleasant as usual, but even that was becoming a strain. Her head ached, a consistent dull pounding just at her temples. It was as if the anxiety teased her with a constant reminder but refrained from taking any shape she could rail against.

And now she stood in front of a mirror pinching her cheeks like a green debutante. The maids were cleaning the drawing rooms today. All four of them, and Nora had to be there to supervise. She especially needed to monitor the young maids who had just joined the staff a mere three weeks before. They had reminded Nora of herself, young and unknowing, and bumping about in society without any real direction. They required her attention like none of the other staff did, and yet, she was trying to make herself...

What exactly?

More attractive?

And if so, for whom and for what?

Four days was a very long time not to hear from someone even if he had said explicitly to her that he did not know when he would return or what information he would carry with him. When she sat awake at night, her gaze often strayed from the warm glow of the coals to her sleeping son, and she wondered again what was to become of them.

What was a little murder really, she thought to herself. Surely she and her son meant nothing to the great behemoth that was the War Office. Nora and Samuel were sure to go unnoticed. It was at least possible, she continued to tell herself, at least for the sake of Samuel.

"Mama?"

Nora jumped, sending her hip into the table below the hall mirror she had been scrupulously studying her reflection in. Goodness, her son was much too quiet for a child his age.

"Yes, Samuel?" she asked, rubbing carefully at her hip so as not to disrupt her starched apron.

"Mr. Black has arrived. He is waiting in the servants' hall," Samuel said.

He had a streak of dirt above his left eyebrow, and his hands had turned brown from beating out all the drapery that could be found on the second floor. But Nora suddenly did not notice how unkempt her son appeared.

"I beg your pardon?" she asked and realized she need not be so formal with her son. Perhaps this was why he now spoke as he did.

"Mr. Black, Mama. He is here. In the servants' hall."

Nora did not have a response. After four days of waiting, she would have thought something would stir in her mind, but there was simply nothing.

"Mama? Are you all right?" Samuel asked then.

No, she was not all right, but she was not about to discuss why she was not all right with her nine-year-old son.

"Please tell Mr. Black I will be down shortly." Her voice did not sound right, and she looked toward the mirror again. Perhaps she had pinned her cap on too tightly this morning. Her sudden change in condition had nothing to do with Mr. Black or the news he carried with him.

Samuel had not moved when she looked away from her reflection.

"What is it, Samuel?"

"I have never seen you look at yourself in a mirror before, Mama."

"Of course, you have. I have looked at myself in a mirror before this." Her hands were wrinkling her apron now. She felt the starchy fabric crinkle under her fingertips, but her son's quizzical gaze prevented her from relinquishing her grasp on the garment.

"Not for this long."

"Perhaps we should go greet Mr. Black together." She took Samuel's shoulder to steer him toward the stairs.

"But I have already greeted him."

86

Nora almost missed the first step. She grabbed the banister at the last moment and looked at her son. "You did?"

"Yes."

Samuel did not elaborate but began to move down the steps, forcing Nora to follow because she was still hanging onto his shoulder.

Samuel did not greet visitors to the house. He often stayed in the room where he was working and did not seek out interaction with visitors or even staff for that matter.

"Where did you see Mr. Black?"

Samuel rounded the banister at the bottom step and moved into the hallway that led to the back of the house.

"He was in the servants' hall when I was coming from the kitchen. I had to fetch a glass of water, Mama. The dusty drapes made me thirsty."

Her son stopped then and peered down at his shoes as if guilty of something.

She raised his face to hers with a finger under his chin. "That is quite all right, Samuel. And you saw Mr. Black?'

He nodded then, his expression melting into one of happiness she only saw on his features when they read together at night.

"He asked me how my flowers were doing."

"He did, did he?" Nora asked, putting her hands on her hips and smiling down at her son.

"I told him the violets have poked through the dirt."

Nora felt her mouth curve into a smile. "What did he say to that?" she asked.

"He asked me what other flowers were growing. And I told him all the different kinds but—" He stopped so abruptly Nora looked behind her to see if someone had appeared in the hall to interrupt them.

When she looked and found no one there, she prompted

Samuel to continue. "But?" she said, nudging his shoulder a little.

"I was not sure if I was speaking out of turn. Lady Gregenden is always saying children are to be seen and not heard. Was it all right that I spoke to Mr. Black, Mama?"

Nora's heart twisted in her chest at the sight of the suddenly crestfallen face that peered up at her. She bent down, getting her face next to his.

"Samuel, I am going to tell you something that I probably should have told you long ago, but it is something that you cannot share with anyone nor let anyone know that you know of it."

Samuel nodded to show he was listening.

"Remember when I told you to listen to adults? That they know better than you because they have been around longer?"

Samuel nodded again.

Nora swiped her hands in the air between them as if erasing an invisible sentence that hung there. "Well, that is all rubbish, Samuel. There are some adults who are just plain nitwits, and you should not listen to them at all."

Samuel took a step back from her, a look of astonishment on his face. "But Mama, you said—"

Nora cut him off with a quick shake at his shoulders. "Do not listen to what I said then, Samuel. I was clearly wrong."

His face told her he still did not believe her.

"You can trust me, Samuel," she said then, as if stating something so clear and basic would get his approval.

But Samuel only nodded at her, his eyes wide with incomprehension.

"Mama?" he asked, his voice small in the great front hall.

"Yes?" Nora prompted, her hands still on his arms, her knees bent, not feeling how her muscles protested the awkward stance.

"Is it all right if I ask you to tell me which adults to listen to and which not to? I think I may find this subject very confusing in the future."

Nora smiled. "Of course, you may. Now we have kept Mr. Black waiting long enough," she said, not vocalizing that she believed keeping a person waiting for four days was long enough as well.

* * *

NATHAN BLACK SAT at the long table that took up the majority of the servants' hall. He heard the bustle of the kitchen maids moving about in the kitchen beyond the room, and he watched the scullery maids with their buckets of rags scurry up the staircases and down. He had come to the back door of the house, thinking it unwise to approach the front and raise the notice of the lord and lady of the estate. He had heard tales of Lord Arthur Gregenden from Jane and had no wish to meet the man. If he stayed below stairs, he was unlikely ever to have to confront him. And as for Lady Gregenden, well, he was not discussing state business with a woman whose greatest triumph was picking out which gown to wear every morning.

He heard small footsteps on the stairs and looked up, watching Samuel's thin legs come into view. He stood, his heart picking up speed, as the unmistakable starched white apron of Miss Eleanora Quinton appeared in view. It had been four days since last he had seen her, and only last night had he been able to sleep even for a few hours. For yesterday, he had learned of what was to become of Miss Eleanora Quinton and her young son, and his mind found some semblance of peace.

When they reached the bottom step, Samuel bowed to his mother.

"Here you are, Mama," he said and then straightened to look at Nathan. "It was nice to see you again, sir." He bowed again and turned back to the stairs.

Nathan spoke up quickly. "Leaving us so quickly?"

The young boy paused on the stairs, a look of confusion plastered across his features.

"There is work to be done, Nathan," he said, the pitch of his voice so soft, Nathan thought he leaned forward to hear it.

"Quite right," he said. "You cannot be a lamplighter if you do not exercise restraint in one's work ethic."

Samuel's face melted into a grin, and he nodded, continuing his way up the stairs.

Only then did Nathan allow himself to look at Nora, and the breath stopped in his chest.

She was beautiful. Of course, she was beautiful, but a tiny part of his brain that focused on survival had convinced him that perhaps she was not as beautiful as he had believed. But that tiny part was not only wrong, it was entirely mistaken. For Nora was not the beautiful he had remembered, but a kind of beauty that had him stepping forward, bringing his hands up as if to grasp hers, but she stepped back, and a wall of cold washed over him.

"Not here," she whispered then, and the cold seeped away as quickly as it had come. "It is good of you to come, Mr. Black," she pronounced then, more loudly than was necessary for him to hear, and he knew it was not his ears with which she was concerned. "I will speak with you in my office."

She turned then and moved down the hall that led past the kitchens and around the two sets of staircases that disappeared into the bowels of the house. He followed until she disappeared through a door on the left, and he entered quietly behind her, being careful to keep a necessary distance between them. It was a small room, smaller than he had imagined in the dark hours of the night when he had decided to torture himself by thinking only of her. But then he had imagined a small, cozy room with worn but lush carpets and a comfortable chair and beds for her and Samuel. But the small room she had led him to was none of those things.

The first portion of the room appeared to be an antechamber of sorts with a desk that was repaired with a piece of wood that looked suspiciously like the banister from a staircase. There was no chair for the stool, but instead a wooden crate pushed under its recesses. The top was neatly organized with stacks of parchment, pens, and ink. A lamp sat at one corner. Nora stood in the space between the desk and the wall on one side, her hands primly folded in front of her. But just over her shoulder through a door, he saw what looked to be two cots. They were not significant enough to be called beds, and the chair by the fire looked neither lush nor comfortable. And it all was filtered through the watery light of a small window set in the wall, panes mottled with age. He averted his gazed back to Nora, not wishing to see anything else.

"Well, Mr. Black, I hope your arm is better this morning. No ill after effects from that night's incident?"

"Well, Miss Quinton." He paused to see if she would notice the use of her name. She did not so much as blink. "I am well. Thank you."

"Would you care for tea?"

He shook his head, "I would not put you to the trouble."

"It is no trouble," she said, and before he could stop her, she stepped around him and ducked her head into the hall. He heard mumbling and a response of more mumbling from a voice he did not recognize. A moment passed, and Nora straightened with a tea tray suddenly in her arms.

"That was quite efficient of you," Nathan said, stepping

back to allow her to place the tray on the desk in the room. She gestured toward a wooden crate that had been set against the wall on the far side of the desk. Nathan thought it likely he would crush the decrepit thing if he were to set himself upon it, but Nora was attempting to make him feel comfortable as a guest, and so he sat, hoping the whole time that the crate did not collapse.

Nora picked up the flowery pot on the tray and poured the tea into a cup that would take Nathan a half year's salary to buy.

"It is not really a matter of efficiency, Nathan. The kitchens are just on the other side of that wall, and we keep tea trays set up for the lady of the house. She is always calling for one."

Nathan nodded. "Quite remarkable of you, Nora. I understand from Jane that you are an accomplished housekeeper. I can see that it is true."

He saw the almost imperceptible wobble of the tea pot as she regarded him, and he waited for her to reply in some scathing way, but she did not. She changed the subject instead.

"Samuel tells me he has already greeted you. That is most unusual for him. He does not take to strangers." She looked up as she offered him the cup. Nathan found her looking straight at him, not at a spot above his shoulder like she had done the night of their first meeting, and he took comfort in the change.

"But you are here on business. So let us proceed." She motioned as if to physically summon the words he was about to say. But he took a moment instead to look at her in the filtered light from the window and watch the way her eyes moved with such precision. It was then he noticed she was not wearing the rice powder.

"You are safe from the clutches of the War Office for now,

Miss Quinton," he blurted out, wresting his eyes from her enticing features and taking a drink from his tea cup.

"That is it?" she asked, and he knew that the statement was quite lackluster after the emotional buildup of four days of waiting. But that was how the War Office worked. A long wait for a not very long response.

Nathan set the tea cup on the desk in front of him. "I am afraid so. Government bureaucratic machines are never really well-oiled as you can imagine," he said.

Nora shook her head. "I cannot say that I do know that, Nathan."

He looked at her then and let his gaze linger. "No, I guess you do not."

And then silence fell on them, but he knew exactly what she was thinking because it was what he was thinking. This may be the last time they saw each other. The thought made him wince internally, and he wished there was something he could say to prolong the moment, make the conversation last for hours, days even, however long it took to convince her...

Of what?

What were his feelings towards Eleanora Quinton?

He was afraid they involved more than just a passing acquaintance, and anything more than that was beyond his power. The notion left him deflated. But he was saved once again by Samuel's impeccable timing.

"Mama!"

Samuel burst through the doors and stopped, the epitome of calmness, just as he had done the night of the ball "Sorry, Mama, but it is Lady Gregenden. She's—" He halted and looked at Nathan.

Nora looked at Nathan and nodded. "It is all right, Samuel. What is the problem with Lady Gregenden?"

"She is up."

"She is up?" Nathan swung his head back and forth between the pair like the pendulum on a clock.

"Yes, she is up," Samuel confirmed.

"It is only ten o'clock." Nora set her cup down abruptly, sloshing tea into the saucer.

"And she is asking for you, Mama."

Nora looked away from her son but not quite back at Nathan.

"Samuel, will you please stay here with Mr. Black until I can take care of Lady Gregenden?"

A smile instantly lit Samuel's face. "Of course, Mama."

Samuel stepped up to Nathan, grabbed his hand, and pulled him from the antechamber to the little room beyond so quickly he missed the look of disbelief on Nora's face. He heard her slip from the other room and even heard the door click before Samuel stopped pulling on his arm.

"Both of you sleep in here? At the same time?" Nathan could probably touch both walls if he stretched out his arms while standing in the middle of the room.

"Yes, is it not wonderful?" Samuel sat on what was probably his cot in the corner, surveying the domain. "We even have our own fireplace. Not everyone gets their own fire."

Nathan now saw the entirety of the ratty chair in front of what Samuel called a fireplace, but was really nothing more than a stove on which to brew coffee, and suddenly recalled the dark circles under Nora's eyes. How many nights had she spent in that chair staring at the flames in the stove? How many more nights would she spend there? He wished he had the power to make it none.

"Do you have such a nice room, Mr. Black?" Samuel asked.

Nathan thought of his room in his brother's house with its fine draperies and heavy, dark furniture and his other room in his father's house with the intricate carpets and plush chairs. "No, Samuel, I do not believe I do."

Samuel smiled softly and tilted his head in contemplation. What he was contemplating Nathan could not imagine.

"Samuel." Nathan moved to sit on the bed opposite the cot when an image rose of Nora in a virginal white nightgown, her hair loose and scattered over the pillow, her face flush with sleep, her mouth—

Nathan settled into the ancient chair, put his elbows on his knees, leaned closer to the boy, and demanded his mind behave.

"Do you like it here? Do you like working for the Gregendens?"

He watched the boy's mouth begin to form an answer, but then the dark eyes so much like Nora's changed as if Samuel realized his answer was not correct. "I do not know anything else," he finally said.

Nathan wanted to take the boy's hand, grab Nora, and walk out the front door without ever letting them come back. But he could not do that. He could not take care of them. He wanted Samuel to catch fireflies in a glass jar, hide frogs in his bed to scare the maids, and climb to the top of trees just to see the sun set. He wanted Nora to be able to sit in a better chair in front of a bigger fire before she went to bed and slept in his arms.

But he could not promise any of that.

And who was he to say the life he wanted to give them was better than what they were living now? People lived as Samuel and Nora did for years and died happy and fulfilled. But he knew a different life, lived a different life, but it may not have been that way if his father had not taken him in when his mother had died. His birth mother had been a maid like Nora, and if his father had not come for him, Nathan would have lived a life much like Samuel's was now. He could

95

not imagine being without his brother or his father. He could not imagine not having Jane in his life when he was a rebellious teenager. But what Samuel had said was true. Samuel did not know anything else.

So instead of continuing with a conversation that was sure to make him frustrated, Nathan reached into his pocket for the deck of cards he kept there.

"Now, have you ever played poker, Samuel?"

It was nearly thirty minutes later when Nathan realized that although Samuel may have been a novice at cards, he was also a quick learner.

"A full house beats a pair?" Samuel asked.

"Of course, it does." Nathan gathered the cards strewn over the surface of Samuel's cot.

His knees screamed at having been bent for so long as Nathan precariously perched on one end of the cot. But Samuel's happily enraptured face was enough to keep Nathan from moving for hours. Maybe even days.

"I won again?" Samuel asked.

Nathan watched his hands deftly shuffle the cards so Samuel would not see his smile. "Yes, you won again."

He felt only a minor prick of annoyance that Samuel had indeed won again with no help from him.

"Have you ever gotten a royal flush, Nathan?"

"A royal flush?"

At the shrill sound of Nora's voice, Nathan dropped the deck of cards, scattering them over the cot. Samuel's ears immediately turned a delirious shade of pink.

"Mr. Black, are you teaching my son poker?"

Nora stood just inside the door of the small room with her hands on her hips, her jaw clenched, her lips not in the least turned up.

"Um—" Nathan began, but Samuel was already standing up.

"It was my fault, Mama." He tilted his head back to look his mother in the eye. "I should not have exhibited nor manifested so much enthusiasm for the game. I apologize, Mama."

Nora opened her mouth, but Nathan jumped up before she could speak, sending aces, eights, and some fours to the floor.

"It was my fault, actually, Miss Quinton. I forgot my place." Nathan looked her in the eye also, hoping Samuel knew some secret trick of defense that he did not.

Nora's mouth suddenly softened, and she squatted, her hands on her knees to bring her face closer to Samuel's face.

"Did you win?" she asked her son.

Samuel took a step back as if his mother's question had stung him. "Yes, Mama."

She smiled. Now it was Nathan who took a step back.

"Good," she said and straightened. "Mr. Black and I must finish our conversation, Samuel. Why don't you run out to the stable and ask Michael if he needs your help with the horses today?"

"Yes, Mama." Samuel repeated, apparently the only phrase stuck in his brain.

When he did not move, Nora softly smiled again. "Samuel?"

Samuel blinked and shook his head. "Right, Mama. I am sorry, Mama."

He disappeared out the door.

* * *

NOT ONCE IN nine years had Nora ever caught her son doing anything that so much as whispered impropriety. The fact that the first time she did, Samuel was in the company of one Mr. Nathan Black did not strike Nora at all as odd. She sort of fancied the notion.

"Did he really win?" she asked, knowing she was smiling more brilliantly than she had in years.

Nathan did not respond. At least not with words. Instead he took a step forward, bent his head, and laid his lips gently on hers. Nora kept her eyes open and did not move. Nathan's lips were soft, barely even a presence gliding across her lips. His eyes were closed, and his long, black lashes fanned his cheeks. His broad shoulders blocked out the rest of the room. Except for his lips, he did not touch her.

And then he was gone.

Nora still did not move even as Nathan stepped back.

"Yes, he really did win," Nathan said.

Nora had never been kissed before, at least not kissed willingly, and she did not know what one said after such an occasion. So she stood there in her room with the man who had done the kissing, hoping he would notice her awkwardness and respond accordingly.

"Perhaps we should finish our conversation." Nathan gestured toward the chair while he sat on Samuel's cot.

Nora was pretty sure that that was not what someone said after sharing a kiss, but in the circumstances, it was appropriate. So she sat.

And plunged through the awkwardness she still felt with practicality.

"If you please, Nathan, is it common practice to shoot spies?" Nora asked.

Nathan seemed unsurprised by her question as he answered readily.

"Unfortunately, in this case, yes. Archer is in too deep for us to pull him out and give him a fair trial. Removing Archer would be like declaring to Napoleon that we had found him out and then his resources would scatter. We would lose track of them, and a network would set up and start the whole process again. Only this time we would not be able to watch them. Elimination is the only option."

Nora leaned in. "Are you usually the one to do the eliminating?"

Nathan grinned sheepishly. "Uh, no. I try to avoid situations in which there is violence. I prefer to barter in information."

She saw the way his eyes went downward while he was speaking, and she was compelled to ask, "Why?"

He looked back up at her then and frowned. There was a degree of hesitancy about his expression, and Nora wondered if he were about to lie to her.

"I would tell you the entire truth, but it is not mine to tell. The point of the matter being that I do not like hurting people. No matter in what form."

Nora paused before asking her next question, taking a moment to realize that Nathan had not hidden the truth from her but had graciously side stepped the issue on behalf of…another person?

"Then why are you in this position?"

Nathan smiled glumly. "It is expected of the son of a duke, legitimate or not, to enter the military. It just so happens that in our family, entering the military is a brief cover for joining the War Office in more clandestine opportunities."

"And the other night was a clandestine opportunity?"

Nathan shrugged. "No one on that balcony that night knew who I was. I offered them champagne even as I disappeared."

Nora narrowed her eyes. "How did you get a tray of champagne?"

Nathan narrowed his eyes as well. "Alec and Jane."

"Alec and Jane? You mean the Earl of Stryden? What does he have to do with champagne?"

"He made you blush."

Nora sat up and gasped, startling herself because she had never gasped in astonishment before this. "I knew there was something not quite right about all the attention he was giving me."

Nathan shrugged again. "I hear it was difficult. You really put him to the test."

Nora laughed softly, and Nathan enjoyed the sound of it in the small room.

"So now what do we do?" Nora asked.

She would, of course, voice the very question he had been unwilling to even think, for thinking it led him one step closer to never seeing her again.

Nathan leaned back. "We do nothing. Your role in this act is over, Miss Quinton, and the War Office extends its gratitude. As for the lord and lady of the house, I recommend a lengthy fabrication in which a lot is said and nothing is told. I hear you are quite good at that sort of thing."

"Jane talks entirely too much," Nora said, standing.

"Yes, she does, and we love her for it." Nathan stood.

"It was a pleasure making your acquaintance, Mr. Black." Nora stood as well, extending a hand.

She did not wear her white gloves, and the red patches of dry skin on her hand had him pausing before reaching for it, afraid he would hurt her. He looked up only to notice she was not looking at him, but that she was looking beyond him at a spot over his shoulder, in the direction of the only window in the room.

"Nathan, I think someone is watching us."

CHAPTER 7

*N*athan cupped the side of Nora's face before instinct turned her head. He stepped closer and bent his head, so that whoever was watching saw an intimate embrace and not a stealthily held conversation. He slid his arm around Nora's waist, both enjoying the sensation and fearing she may collapse on him. Instead, he was delightfully surprised to find her leaning in, putting her hands on his chest.

"I want you to look around me without turning your head. Tell me what the person looks like," Nathan whispered against her ear.

He felt Nora's lashes flutter against his cheek as her eyes changed direction.

"He is...small. I can see one of his hands, and it looks almost delicate. His face is hidden by a big cap. It is flopping in his face. There is red hair coming out from under it. His coat is shabby. Stained. That is all I can see." She turned her head, unknowingly nestling it in the side of his neck. "You are in the way."

Nathan forced his grinding teeth apart. "All right. Nora, I

am going to change our positions a bit. I do not want you to be frightened. I just want to get a view of the window. I am not going to hurt you."

"I know," was all that she said.

Her breath stole across the underside of his chin, and his mind worked not to curl his hand tighter into the fabric at her back to pull her closer. And then she snuggled into him, both bracing herself for what he was going to do and sending a tingle that went straight to his toenails and back to the tips of his ears.

He swung her around, sat in the chair, and pulled her onto his lap. He put a hand at the back of her neck and pulled her head down, so his lips met her ear.

"Are you all right, Nora?"

"Yes." Her voice was small but steady. She was much too light in his lap, and he wondered if an inability to sleep came with an inability to eat.

He pivoted his head, bringing his lips to the point where her jaw met her neck. He ignored the sweet smell of her hair and lingering scent of lemons, and he ignored the urge to open his mouth, just a little, to steal a taste. Almost. He belatedly remembered to open his eyes and look toward the window without looking like he was looking. The knot of Nora's hair blocked the bottom corner of the window, preventing him from seeing whoever was spying on them. The knot would have to go.

He speared his fingers upward, sending pins flying. The white cap slid off the top of her head and disappeared somewhere in the direction of the floor. Nora jerked as Nathan froze.

He cradled the back of her head and whispered in her ear, "It is all right. Your hair was in the way."

His other hand stroked her back as her muscles eventually unwound. He flicked his glance toward the window.

The spy was indeed wearing a floppy hat that hid his face. One hand gripped the window ledge, probably holding the man up. It was delicate, almost fine, and the hair escaping the hat looked almost wispy. He looked like a she.

Nathan buried his face in Nora's hair momentarily, and then forgot that he was doing it only as cover because the smell of it had sucked him in. Soap. It smelled like soap, and he had never smelled anything more intoxicating in his life.

Nora made a soft whimpering sound, and Nathan's heart stopped. He did not dare move or speak for fear that he would continue to hurt her. And then Nathan decided he was going to kill whoever had hurt her before.

But the figure at the window moved. He looked over his shoulder as if calling to someone and dropped from the ledge, disappearing from sight.

Had Nathan been a gentleman, he would have released Nora immediately and separated her from him. Had Nathan been a good spy, he would have bolted from the room to follow the man who had been spying on them. But because Nathan was decidedly not a gentleman and currently did not feel like being a good spy, he did none of those things. He kept his arms around Nora and his face in her hair. She had relaxed again, sagging more now against his arm.

Nathan ran his hand along the back of her neck, brought it forward to the soft skin under her chin, and let it drop. He eased her up to see her face. Her eyes were open, and he knew that she was seeing him. Her hair was around her shoulders making her face look thinner than it was. He picked up a few strands and drew them behind her shoulder.

"Are you all right?"

She nodded, still staring.

"He is gone," he said slowly, drawing out the moment unnecessarily. "We can stand up now."

She did not move so neither did he. They watched each

other. The silence began to ring in his ears. He wondered if he should move, maybe help her to stand up, but then he wondered if he really wanted her to stand up. If they stood up, she would think it was goodbye, and for all circumstances, it probably was. But he did not feel like saying goodbye, so he sat instead.

And then Nora leaned forward.

His heart moved, abruptly and none too steadily, into the region of his spleen, and she kept coming at him. She closed her eyes and pressed her lips against his. The angle was awkward and shy. Their noses bumped and kept him from getting closer. She did not deepen the touch, but then he doubted she even knew how. So he closed his eyes, brought his hands up to her face and augmented the angle, bringing her in closer. Her lips parted at the movement, and the blood drained from his head.

He sank.

* * *

HOLY GOD, she was kissing him.

It was only the second time in her life that she had taken any of the courage that she had and put it into some sort of action. The first time had landed her in London with nothing but a suitcase and a will to find employment. She had been a young girl, completely unknowing in what she was about to embark on, and yet, the moment she had stepped off the coach in London, she had felt nary a fear. She was concerned, and she was aware. She knew what she was doing would take confidence and determination. Those were two things she had had in spades when she was seventeen. But life had worn on her since then. Her confidence ran strong but only in select areas. Her determination was much the same. It tended to only push her when it came to her position and her son.

She would be a good housekeeper, so she could provide for Samuel. And she would be a good mother, so Samuel could have a life she had never had the opportunity to even dream about.

And now when her courage had propelled her into another unknown, it was not confidence and determination she felt. It was naked fear. She realized most of the fear came from an unworthy sense of history repeating itself. She had seen men treating women with respect in regards to relations. Lord Gregenden exhibited it to the oblivious Lady Gregenden nearly every day. Even Hawkins doted on Cook with a flair he committed to nothing else, and they were not even wed. It was like something out of a Fielding novel.

But flashes of her past licked at the back of her memory, and she pushed at it, willing the fear to ebb. She would grasp what was in her reach now, and she would see where her courage would take her.

And besides, she liked it.

At least she thought she liked it, liked kissing Nathan Black.

She was concentrating so hard on not doing something ridiculous that she was not really sure what she was feeling. She knew she did not want him to stop, so that must mean that she liked what he was doing. But she kept her hands on his shoulders and her head at the angle he wanted it and didn't move. She was good at not moving. Right now seemed like a time to do something at which she had some skill.

But maybe he wanted her to move.

She had in the past accidentally, and not accidentally, come upon people engaged in torrid embraces and most of the times, the woman had been moving. The woman also had been making weird noises that Nora knew she would never know how to make nor would she probably want to make such noises. But what if Nathan wanted her to make those noises? What if Nathan wanted her to move in some way? What if she was doing everything wrong?

And then she did freeze. And then she realized she froze. And then it was too late to unfreeze without Nathan noticing. And then Nathan was easing her back. The connection of their lips severed, making her shudder at the loss.

She licked her lips and said the only thing that was going through her mind, "Please do not stop."

She did not want to open her eyes, but Nathan did not say anything. She needed to see him. She needed to see what he was thinking or feeling. She needed to see if he smirked at her and her awkwardness. She let her eyelids flutter open, her chest rigid with her held breath.

His eyes were open and clear, and he watched her with a gentleness she had never seen in the eyes of another before then. His face was relaxed, his expression contemplative. His hands had loosened their grip on her, and she realized she was holding herself in his lap, leaning into him with a carefree assurance she did not feel but apparently knew without conscious effort.

"Have you ever been kissed before, Nora?"

She had not expected him to speak, and as she had just begged him to keep kissing her as if she were some tart that had been cast from the enclave of Almack's, she found the question an odd one. She thought on the answer for but a second and mentally stopped her thoughts from proceeding. There had been an instance when she had been kissed, but it had not been of her choosing. She must have made some kind of move or gesture, because Nathan's hands suddenly tightened.

"I beg your pardon," he said quickly then, and she watched the corners of his mouth turn down and his eyes crinkle in concern.

She did not like seeing him thusly, and she blurted out the

only thing she could think of to remove such an expression from his handsome face.

"It is not your fault, Nathan," she said, an answer so obscure even she could not think of what she was removing him from blame.

She rushed on as if a profusion of words would clear up the issue. "Something...happened once, and I...well, it was not..." She sounded like an idiot. "Nathan, it's—"

"I know," he said, cutting off her words.

Nora had been studying the knotting of his cravat, trying to find words that would convey what she needed to without having to say anything at all on the subject, but she looked up then and met his dark blue gaze. She felt herself pitch forward as if pulled into the comfort she saw there, but she had not moved a single muscle. Her breath slowed in her lungs, and her hands curled into the fabric of Nathan's coat. She wanted to ask him what he meant, but she did not need to. She knew what he meant even without asking, and she would not disrespect him by evading the truth in his words. She nodded then, just slightly, as if to encapsulate everything that was reeling through her mind.

But it was all too much, and she suddenly could not, no, she would not keep it all in her head any longer. She wanted it banished. She wanted something good to rid it from the recesses of her consciousness.

"Will you kiss me again, Nathan?" she said and was rewarded with a soft chuckle that vibrated against her stomach where their bodies came together as Nora continued to perch on his lap. His laugh was not malicious, or she would have already been on her feet, moving toward the door with every intent to throw him out. But his laugh had no such intent. If anything, it contained only self-mockery, but for what, she did not know.

"I do not believe it was I who started the last kiss, Miss Quinton, but I would be happy to start the next one."

She blushed, the heat surging across her cheeks and down her neck, but she did not squirm or try to move away, because he was right. She had started the last kiss.

"Yes, I believe that would do," she said, and he laughed again even as he leaned toward her.

She tilted her head this time in anticipation of their lips meeting. This time her mind emptied of anything other than the feel of his lips against hers, and she realized—

She did in fact like Nathan Black's kiss.

His lips were warm and soft, his mouth moving against hers with such demand she felt her entire body go slack in response. His hands held her tightly even as she thought she would surely melt in a puddle at his feet. She moved her own hands, sliding along the muscled contours of his shoulders to the nape of his neck, her fingers twining with the strands of hair that curled over his collar. She thought she heard him moan, but he deepened the kiss, and she forgot anything at all. His tongue traced a searing line around the edges of her lips, and she whimpered, wanting more, wanting everything from him. She splayed her hands along his shoulders and pulled him forward, hoping to convey what she was feeling without knowing how to do so. But he groaned again, and his mouth sank into hers, and she reveled in the feel of the power she had over him.

Power.

She held the power here. He moved with her every command. A simple tug on his shoulders, and he came to her, unleashing his desire exactly as she wished. If she straightened away from him, she knew he would stop. She did not want to try it for fear that the magic of the kiss would be broken, but somewhere in her, the knowledge of the thing drove her forward. She sat up straighter, coming up above him, so that she took control of the kiss. And she returned his demand with a will of her own. She felt him lean back in the chair, felt his hands release and slide to her hips, fisting in the folds of her skirt, no longer holding onto her but waiting as if bracing for what was to come. The power she felt in that moment raced through her, sending her confidence soaring to a place it had never been. Emboldened, she parted her lips, opening herself to him—

And then someone knocked on the door.

Nora fell off his lap.

Literally.

She hit the floor with such a thump Nathan was sure it would send that irate butler, Hawkins, running to the rescue. He wanted to rip out his fingernails to distract himself from the ball of frustration burning in his gut. Looking at the door, he sent silent curses at whoever stood beyond it. Something had happened in the last few seconds of the kiss. Nathan had felt it, had felt how Nora had changed, felt the determination sweep over her. The fear had gone, swept away by whatever feeling of triumph Nora had suddenly embraced. He knew something...beautiful, something...powerful was about to happen when they had been interrupted. If only they had had but two seconds more, Nathan was sure he could have brought Nora to a place she had never been before.

Nora fumbled with her skirts, attempting modesty after the kiss they had just shared seemed ridiculous. But Nathan knew Nora did not feel that way. So he helped her. As much as it made that ball of frustration burn hotter, he helped her. They stood together, bumping against each other, before steadying.

The knock came again.

Nora looked at the door now, her eyes narrowed and her lips strained. Nathan could only imagine her own curses she was sending at the intruder. Then she flicked her hair behind her shoulder, strode over to the door, and ripped it open.

With one hand on her hip, one turning white on the door knob she had just ripped open, she demanded, "What?"

A man that smelled so foul that tears formed in Nathan's eyes from the stench stood in the hallway. The man smashed a hat in his fists and swayed from foot to foot in uncertainty. A line of blood oozed from a crack in his lip.

"Beggin' yer pardon, ma'am. But they've taken 'im," the man said.

"What, Michael?" Nora's hand had relaxed on the door, her other starting the slide down her hip.

"Yer boy, miss. They've taken him."

NATHAN'S HANDS were on her shoulders. She must have moved, but she had not moved. The room had moved. The passion of just moments before was a long departed memory, and her skin flushed cold and clammy. Surely, she had heard Michael wrong.

Samuel.

Someone had taken Samuel?

Her son?

"What do you mean they have taken him?" She heard her voice ask in a faraway place.

Michael smothered his hat with a fist. "Three of 'em. Big blokes. And a wee, little, nasty one. It was no fair fight, ma'am. Me and 'Enry, we tried, ma'am. But they 'ad a pistol, ye see, aimin' right at the lad. We didn't dare put up a fuss."

Nora felt Nathan's body behind her, clear along the full length of her, keeping her upright. If he had done that only a few minutes ago, fear would have swamped her, but now she pushed back into him as if he were the only safe place in her world right then.

"Which way did they go?" Nathan asked.

"Dunna, sir. They pitched me and 'Enry into the stall and took off. The wee nasty one spit on us before running, though. Cheeky bastard. If I'da 'ad my feet under me—"

"I am sure," Nathan cut him off. "Are you hurt?"

Michael shook his head. "Eh, no, sir. Nothing but me pride's been bruised."

Nora had not thought to ask such a question even though the signs of a brawl were evident in the split lip on Michael's face. Her mind was simply a blank page with a single word written across it.

Samuel.

Samuel was...gone?

And then Nathan turned her around. Nora looked up automatically, tilting her head all the way back as their close proximity called for.

"I am going to go out back with Michael and take a look around. See if I can find anything. I want you to pack whatever belongings you and Samuel own. I am taking you away from here. Do you understand?"

Nora shook her head. She did not understand. Leave? She was to leave?

She shook her head again. "I cannot, Nathan. I'll lose my employ."

"It is not safe for you here," he said.

Nora took a step back, nearly colliding with the door. No, she could not leave. This place was her home, the only place that gave her refuge, and now her son was gone. Kidnapped. She could not leave. This was the only place that was safe. Nathan was wrong.

"Nathan, I cannot leave. This is our—"

The word *home* did not come out. Nathan approached her, his hands returning to her shoulders.

"Nora, something has happened. I do not know what, but someone is after you. I had thought it was me because of what happened at the ball the other night, but now that they have taken your son, I have my doubts. You are vulnerable here. Please let me take you to a place where I can protect you."

Nora had not been listening until something suddenly flashed across Nathan's face as he spoke those last words.

Protect you.

There was something there. A long ago pain that Nathan never let surface for she had not seen it until that moment. And unlike the power any words could have over her, the stark, scalding pain she saw in his eyes just then had her mind focusing sharply.

Nathan was right. She could not stay there. They had taken Samuel from the stables of the house. They knew where she was. They would know where Samuel was when they got him back. When Nathan got him back.

She had packed her bags at seventeen and left the only home she had never known without a backward glance. She would do that again if only to keep her son safe. She reached up, completely ignoring the fact that Michael still stood in the doorway watching them, and let her fingers slide along the plane of Nathan's cheek. The skin was rough with beard, but the feeling soothed her. He was solid and strong.

"Please find my son, Nathan," she said, her voice barely above a whisper.

Nathan let go of her shoulders and walked out the door, leaving Michael to scurry after him.

Nora stood a whole minute, just standing, letting thoughts, feelings, emotions seep in, finally penetrating her numb body.

Someone had taken Samuel. Nora's mind flashed to the little man at the window who had stood watching them. He was obviously looking for something, and when he had not found it, he had taken Samuel.

But what was he looking for?

And why take Samuel?

If it was something that Nora had, why not take Nora? Would she not be the one to help them find whatever it was they sought? She was nothing but a housekeeper. What was it she had that these people wanted? A mere week ago her greatest concern was Hawkins' unfounded worries, and now her son was missing.

And Nathan.

Her hand went to her lips unknowingly, the memory of their kisses flashing through her mind like a sparking flame. Her body heated just from the memory of it, and she longed to have Nathan back. Back here in this room, in her arms, making her forget everything but what she felt between them. That moment when she had realized she was in control of what happened between them had supported her, propelled her forward when her weak courage would have given up, given in, and let her past swamp her with a fear that would keep her from ever having more in her life. More happiness, more joy, more laughter, just more.

She turned a circle, looking at everything between the two small rooms. The two beds, the scattered deck of cards, the tiny stove, the ratty chair, and the scarred armoire that held her two other uniforms, an old dress for her days off, and Samuel's few trousers and shirts. The desk that she had spent long nights at, writing carefully so as not to upset its precarious stability. Her hairbrush and pins lay beside the cracked basin on the washstand. A small, dull mirror hung above it. And then Nora was back to the beds. That was it. That had been her entire life for over ten years.

But that was not all that had been in the room when the little man had spied on them from the window.

Nathan had been in the room then, and he must have been what the little man sought. Surely, Nathan could be wrong. Surely, Nathan could have been the intended target. And what he had seen was Nathan and her. They had been in an intimate embrace, which would then have led the man to believe that he could get to Nathan through Samuel. That must be it. But that would mean the man would have to assume that Nora meant so much to Nathan that kidnapping Samuel would get Nathan's attention. She was sure she did not mean that much. But that was not the point. The little man at the window knew nothing beyond what he saw. And what he saw was a couple in a situation that looked very much like they cared for one another.

Did they care for one another?

Nora recalled the look on Nathan's face as he had said he wanted to be able to protect her. Such a look did not come from a person who did not care, but what was it that had made him look so afraid? Nathan had never been anything but strong and resolute when he had been with her. What had made him so suddenly unsure?

She laid her hand against her forehead. She did not have the energy to worry about such things. Her mind kept reeling back to Samuel, leaving her exhausted when she had much to do before she could leave.

Her son had been kidnapped. By big blokes with guns. She should be filled with panic, brimming over with the stuff so that it made her shoes sticky. But she was not feeling panic. She was not feeling much of anything.

Someone else was taking care of her now.

And that someone else had very explicitly told her to pack.

So she did.

CHAPTER 8

*N*athan remained objective as he followed Michael to the stables. If he let the turbulence boiling inside him get out of control, he would be of no use to anyone. And Nora needed him right now. He could not let his emotions, past or present, sweep him up until he could no longer think on the current situation. If Samuel truly had been taken, their time was limited. They needed to do everything in their power to get him back quickly and safely.

Nathan's hands itched with the memory of the softness of Nora's hair, her long slender back, what it felt like to grab ahold of her and pull her toward him. It had felt so natural, so real, so perfect. He did not know loving a person could come so easily. For love was what he was afraid he was beginning to feel. In a few stolen moments and one short week, he knew he was dangerously close to falling for Nora Quinton. That alone was a prospect he did not want to think on in general, let alone now. He could not care for Nora as his wife on a War Office salary, and she deserved no less respect than that of an honest woman.

But the feel of her body against his radiated through him

like nothing ever had, and he feared he would never be rid of that memory. It would plague him for the many long, dark nights his life held ahead of him. And for now, he needed to find Samuel.

The boy was smart and pragmatic. He knew more about life than Nathan had at his age, certainly, and probably more than he cared to admit now. But he was still a child, and he would think on emotion more often than not. Nathan had to get to him before something made Samuel react unknowingly, causing his captors to respond in kind.

Nathan surveyed the ground that spanned the distance between the back of the house and the stables, but the solid ground showed no signs of anything that had transpired mere moments before. The lack of rain was not helpful. Not a drop for near on three days.

While Michael continued toward the stables, Nathan turned abruptly, looking back at the house to find the window that looked into Nora's chambers. It was one of only three on the lower level, and Nathan made his way over to it. He was careful not to look inside. He had left Nora abruptly just minutes before, and although he was certain she had the strength to get through this, he was not so certain he did. The memory of another woman and her sorrow flashed in his mind, and he took a sharp breath. There were certain things that made a woman cry that Nathan could not understand, did not want to understand. For once upon a very long time ago, he had been unable to help another woman's sorrow, and the memory still pained him.

But even more than the ghost of pain, the idea that he would not be able to help Nora now, help erase the sorrow that hung on her like a heavy cloak, that uncertainty gnawed at his stomach, churning his surety like a violent storm on the sea. He could not let her down.

He scanned the ground around the window, letting his

eyes scan up to the wooden sill and around the frame of the window, but there was nothing. No footprints and no discarded clothing or fibers stuck in the cracked wood of the sill. He turned away from the window in disgust, having no more idea of the size of the men, or woman, they were dealing with. He did not know if they were wearing fine leather Hessians or worn work boots, something that would have helped place the person in a social class that could then be dissected for clues. But Nathan had nothing.

He walked back to the stables and the cobbled alley that ran between the houses on this block. It was all stone for as far as he could see once he stepped past the small gardens at the back of the house.

"Did they have a carriage, Michael?" Nathan asked, approaching the man as he shuffled his feet just inside the stable.

Michael sniffed into a handkerchief as he huddled not quite in and not quite out of the stables. "Na, sir. Not 'ere they didna. 'Haps down the way farther."

Michael pointed over his shoulder in the direction of the street. Nathan followed the line of the other man's finger and watched the traffic of the street pass across the space between the rows of houses.

Nathan nodded even as he was moving. His boots sent echoes down the length of the alley to come ringing back at him. He watched the ground, saw the places where the cobbles heaved or where they had sunk in. A cat wandered across his path and disappeared completely into a pile of rubbish. He skirted a stack of carts beside the stable of the neighboring house. The carts smelled rather suspicious, and Nathan wrinkled his nose at them even as he kept moving.

Nathan kicked something with his boot and looked down.

It was a four of clubs playing card.

He picked it up and stared at it a moment, turning the card over in his hand several times. And then he ran.

He made it to the cross street quicker than he thought he would. Traffic suddenly moved directly in front of him, and it surprised him enough to make him stop. He looked around. Fine carriages and the occasional hack. Nathan crunched the four of clubs in his hand and turned back around.

He almost knocked over the street urchin who had approached him.

"Beggin' yer pardon, sir, I 'ave a message for ye." The boy held out an empty hand.

"How much will this message cost?" Nathan gave the boy a look.

The boy glared right back. "What 'ave ye got in yer pockets, sir?"

Nathan grabbed the only money he had out of his pocket. It was only a pence, but he did not have to tell the boy that. He made it look like more and held out a closed fist. The boy reached, but Nathan drew the fist back.

"Message?"

The boy watched the fist. "The message is stay out o' this. It ain't of yer concern."

"That it?"

The boy nodded. "Aye, that's it."

The boy lunged for Nathan's fist, prying it open. The pence fell to the ground. The boy dove for it and stood up.

"This is it?" the boy squeaked incredulously.

Nathan shrugged. "You said what I had in my pockets."

He turned and walked back to Gregenden House, the four of clubs held tightly in his hand.

* * *

Nora had been packed for three minutes.

She had heard the seconds count off in her head. She was at three minutes and thirty-one seconds when Nathan finally came back through the door. She shot out of the chair she had been pretending to sit in, carpetbag beside her like a soldier's rifle.

Nathan stopped and raised his eyebrows at her.

"You packed," he said.

"You told me to pack."

Nathan nodded, looking none too convinced. "You put your hair back." He pointed in the general direction of her head.

She patted the white hat gently to see if it was in place. "Yes, I did." She stopped patting when her hand began to tremble. "Did you find anything?" she asked, although she was not sure she wanted the answer. "Did you find Samuel?"

She could not decipher the expression on Nathan's face just then. It looked like something, and if not regret, then resignation. It was as if Nathan was preparing himself for something he did not entirely wish to do. For a brief second, Nora felt a pang of uneasiness. It was not as if Nathan was here by choice. He was a professional. He had been sent to complete a job, and then something had happened to escalate the situation, and he—

Oh God, she had kissed him.

Nathan would likely have been gone before Samuel had been taken if she had not lingered with him there in her chambers. He would have been out of this situation entirely if it were not for her and her unpredictable emotions. She felt herself shrink inward, and she must have made a motion, because Nathan suddenly stepped in front of her, his hands going to her shoulders. The warmth of his touch burned through her gown, and she welcomed the pressure on her shoulders. She watched him, her breath frozen in her chest.

"I did not find him, Nora. They were long gone by the time I got out to the stables. However, I believe Samuel left us a clue."

He released one of her shoulders to dig something out of his pocket. She waited expectantly before he held up a wrinkled playing card.

"The four of clubs?" she asked when she could see the card.

Nathan nodded, returning the card to his pocket. "Four of clubs," he confirmed, moving his now free hand back to her shoulder. He squeezed gently. "I just do not know what it means."

"Why do you think he dropped that card?"

He watched her, but she could tell he was thinking deeply, not entirely seeing that she stood before him.

"I do not know, but why exactly did he drop that card and not another one? Was it truly a clue or was the card simply lost in the scuffle? But then why did he not drop all of the cards?" Nathan shook his head. "I didn't even see him take this card, let alone any others. So I simply do not know."

From this angle, the watery light from the window made his eyes appear almost the color of midnight, and she felt her body sway toward him. Without realizing it, his arms slipped lower, coming about her waist as he drew her in. She felt his chin against the top of her head as her body came to rest against his. The comfort and protection she felt in his embrace was enough to drive tears to her eyes. She held her breath again lest she suddenly start crying.

Was this what it felt like to have someone protect her? To care for her? Or dare she say, to love her?

Her hands moved tentatively to his back, but her fingers would not curl into the fabric there. Her loose grip was all she could manage just then.

"I also received a message," Nathan said. "From a very greedy street urchin."

"A street urchin?" she asked, her voice slightly muffled in the front of his coat.

"Yes. Apparently, I am to stay out of this. It is none of my concern, which just confirms my suspicions from earlier."

He eased her back a bit, and she looked up at his face. "Is there something you are not telling me, Eleanora Quinton?"

His tone was joking, and she was struck that he could be so teasing in a moment like this, but then she felt her heart lift just a bit, and she knew he did it on purpose. Her lips curved the slightest bit, and she saw the responding softness creep into his expression. He was doing this on purpose, and she welcomed the distraction.

"There is nothing that I am aware of that I am keeping from you. I will not rule out the possibility of me knowing or having something of value that I am not aware of. I do see and hear a lot of things in my position, Nathan Black. I can never know if any of them are of value to another."

Nathan frowned deeply. "That is a good point you make, my lady," he said, his tone playfully serious, but then his expression blanked, and he looked at her more closely. "That is a good point you make," he said again, but this time his tone was wondering.

"You do not believe that I saw or heard something that I am unaware of?" she asked. "That sounds like something from one of those novels, Nathan. Completely fantastical. Those kinds of things do not happen in real life."

"Perhaps not," he said, easing her away from him completely. "But it would probably be best for us not to forget it."

Nathan reached for her carpetbag. Nora instinctively picked it up first and moved it away.

"I have got it," she said.

Nathan raised an eyebrow at her, and Nora felt a flush climbing up her face.

"I beg your pardon, Nathan. I have never had anyone offer to carry my bag before this," she said.

She held out the bag. Nathan took it in one hand and held out his other to her. He was not wearing gloves. The two occasions in which she had interacted with him, Nathan had not been wearing gloves. Nor had he worn a hat. Nora stuck her hand in his before she thought any more.

"Would you like to go out the front or the back, my lady?" Nathan drew her hand through the crook of his elbow.

"I have never been out the front door," Nora said, and in those words, the weight of what she was about to do descended on her.

She looked about the room again, at the small beds and the chair she had spent countless nights in. She was leaving. She was leaving all of this, and she had not told a soul. She was simply going to disappear. She pulled her hand from Nathan's grasp.

"I cannot do this," she whispered, but Nathan was already reaching for her.

"Nora, you must come with me. You are in danger, and I cannot protect you here."

The urgency in his voice had her gaze snapping to his. There was something that plagued Nathan Black. Something that he had not told her, but then there were things she had not told him. Not entirely at least.

"Nathan, I cannot leave my post. How will I find work when we get Samuel back? How will I care for him? I cannot—"

"My father will take care of it," he said, cutting her off and taking her hand once more.

He did not pull at her though. He simply held her hand in his.

"Your father?" she asked, and she suddenly remembered that night when he had told her his father was a duke. "The duke?" she added unnecessarily.

Nathan nodded. "He will find a post for you. I assure you. Everything will go back to what it was before as soon as this is all over."

The words brought comfort, but with it came a sting of regret that she could not understand.

"Would the duke have work for me?" she asked instead of thinking about her sudden feelings of regret. "I know dukes can have advantageous positions in society but—"

"My father is the Duke of Lofton," Nathan said, and Nora stepped back so quickly her hand came loose from his.

She knew her mouth was open, but in that moment, she could do nothing about it. "Your father?"

Nathan nodded, his now empty hand hanging in the air between them.

"Then Jane is...and the Earl of Stryden?" She no longer formed complete questions, but Nathan still nodded.

Without another thought forming in her head, she stuck her hand back into his. "This is a lot bigger than me, is it not? This...situation?"

Nathan nodded again, and she nodded back.

"We had best be going then," she said.

Nathan turned right when they reached the hallway, and Nora walked him to the front door.

* * *

ALEC FIGURED that standing on the front stoop would appear overly anxious. Waiting in the library would be suspicious since he was only ever in there to drink, and noon was too early to imbibe even for him. He had never been in the parlor, and the dining room would obviously look odd.

So that was why he was waiting at the top of the stairs. He could just see out the second floor window down to the street below. He would wait for her carriage to pull up, see her alight, and then start casually down the stairs. If he were in motion the first time she saw him, it would appear that he was a busy, important man.

And not like he had spent the entire morning wondering where to be standing when she arrived, what he should be wearing, or even if he should have his valet try to keep his hair off his forehead.

If he were moving, she would assume that he was actually doing something important.

Which he was.

He was trying to make his wife love him.

When the carriage rolled up out front, he nearly fell down the first stair. Patience. Patience. He had to wait for her to alight. The tiger pulled open the carriage door and first her shoe appeared, a nice, fine, black, traveling shoe. Then pale blue skirt. Then her face, looking up at the house. And then he really did fall down the first stair. He grabbed the banister at the last moment to keep him upright. The fall had dislodged his cravat, and he fumbled with it, trying to get it back into place.

So that was what he was doing when the front door open, and his wife came home.

"Problems dressing yourself, my lord? I thought that that was what your valet was for." Sarah's voice was properly impersonal and slightly biting.

Alec's skin tingled, and his heart beat a little faster.

She was beautiful. Even more beautiful than the last time he had seen her. Her golden hair was swept up under a hat full of feathers or some such. Her skin was pale and glowing. Her hazel eyes were sharp and cunning. Her mouth, her glorious mouth with its slight overbite. Her little nose that pointed up.

And her bosom.

Alec forced his eyes back up to her face.

He tried to think of something witty, something funny, something intelligent to say, something that would have her so impressed, she would fall at his feet in utter adoration.

So he said, "Hello, Sarah."

Her lips parted into a smile, lines forming around her upper lip from the overbite. "Hello, Alec."

Her voice dripped cynicism, and Alec was suddenly deeply depressed.

Why had he thought things would be different this time? Why had he thought she would see him differently? Why had he thought she would care this time?

And then his brother came flying through the door and crashed into her.

Alec fell more than walked down the rest of the stairs. Sarah collided with him, sending them both into the wall. He cushioned her against him, knocking her hat to the floor. Her head came up, almost knocking him in the chin. Her eyes were huge, and what looked like uncertainty swam in them. Then she looked at his mouth. Her eyes swooped down for one short, stolen look. Which made him look at her mouth. It was only an inch from his. If he just leaned forward a little bit, he could take that delicious upper lip—

"I beg your pardon, Sarah. I did not know you were right inside the door," Nathan said from the doorway.

Alec set his wife away from him and bent to retrieve her hat, letting the blood flow back into his head.

"It is quite all right, Nathan," Sarah said cheerily enough to make Alec grind his teeth. "How are you?"

"Fine, thank you, but we seem to have a problem."

It was that moment that Alec's bumbling butler came careening down the hall from the back of the kitchen.

"Is everything all right, my lord?" Reynolds gasped, his rotund belly heaving with the exertion of sprinting down the hallway.

"Quite all right, Reynolds. You may return to your business."

But Reynolds did not move.

"Lady Stryden," he said, bowing in Sarah's direction. "It is wonderful to see you again. Might we be enjoying your company for a suitable length of time?"

Alec was not sure if a more politely worded yet outrageously bold question had ever been asked.

Sarah merely smirked. "That remains to be seen, Reynolds. But I have had a long journey, and I would require some refreshment. It appears we will be having guests as well." She gestured to Nathan standing with his hand still on the doorknob. "Perhaps a cart in the drawing room?"

"Of course, my lady." Reynolds bowed again and waddled back in the direction from whence he had come.

Sarah looked at Alec then, but he did not have energy to speak to her. Reynolds had asked a very important question. How long did she intend to stay?

Alec turned back to his brother. "Problem?"

Sarah also turned her attention to Nathan, and he noticed how still she grew as if her body could absorb bad news more easily if she did not move.

"Someone has kidnapped Nora's son, and I cannot find Father."

Sarah looked around at Alec. "Who is Nora?"

"Miss Quinton," Alec answered, distractedly. "Father was not at the house?"

"He was not at the house or his club. I was hoping you might know where he is."

"I do not have a clue," Alec replied.

"Jane was to meet me here this afternoon," Sarah said, and Alec looked at her.

"You are inviting guests to a house which you yourself fail to occupy on a regular basis?"

"Do not start, Alec Black. Of all the people—"

"Excuse me."

Alec's head shot around to the authoritative voice that spoke somewhere in the location of Nathan's shoulder. Eleanora Quinton stood just inside the doorway, her house-keeper's uniform obscured by a worn cloak, her hands held together firmly in front of her.

"I do not mean to interrupt, but as it is my son who has gotten himself kidnapped, I would appreciate some agility in the anticipated events of getting my son back. Is that reasonable to assume?"

Alec looked at Sarah who stared at Miss Quinton before looking at Nathan.

"Kidnapped? Are you sure?" Alec asked Nathan, but it was Miss Quinton who replied with a question of her own.

"Do you think us incapable of deciphering a kidnapping when it occurs, my lord?"

He had only had the pleasure of spending one evening in Miss Quinton's company, but her sharp retort should have been expected by him. He would do well to keep her bold manners in mind the next time he thought to ask a ridiculous question.

"What are the circumstances?" This was from his wife, who appeared unfairly fetching with that curious mixture of intrigue and concern on her face.

"Have you been briefed on the result of the attempted Archer assassination?" Nathan said.

Sarah shook her head. "Attempted? Was it not successful

then?" She looked at Alec for an answer, and her gaze was so intense he forgot she had asked a question.

"Yes, it was not successful," Nathan answered for him. "And I fear we may have brought Miss Quinton into a dangerous situation with our mistake."

"Miss Quinton?" Sarah said then.

Alec stepped forward. "Sarah, this is Miss Eleanora Quinton, the housekeeper at Gregenden House. Miss Quinton, this is Sarah Black, the Countess of Stryden."

He never ceased to enjoy calling Sarah his countess. He just wished someday that he would mean it.

Sarah bowed her head in Miss Quinton's direction. "Pleasure to meet you, Miss Quinton. I just wish it were under different circumstances."

"Likewise, my lady," Miss Quinton bowed in return.

"Did you set a time with Jane for your rendezvous?" Alec asked.

Sarah shook her head. "No, just sometime about noon. She has a meeting at the college this afternoon. Some lecture on phrenology."

Alec raised an eyebrow, but it was Nathan who spoke. "Phrenology?"

Sarah shrugged. "I have no idea what it is, but Jane seemed quite interested. Let us move to the drawing room to discuss this better. Unless you would like to remain standing in the foyer with the cold draft coming through the front door." She raised her own eyebrow in question.

Nathan nodded and took Miss Quinton by the arm, guiding her in the direction of the first floor drawing room.

Alec moved to escort Sarah, but she pulled her arm out of his way and marched off to the drawing room, moving so quickly she passed Miss Quinton and Nathan. Alec followed more slowly.

Nathan looked like he was trying hard not to laugh as Alec caught up to him.

"The thing I did with the door. Brilliant, was it not?"

Alec did not feel so close to laughing. He frowned instead. "Yes. Bloody brilliant."

CHAPTER 9

*N*ora tried not to touch anything. Such finery could be easily spoiled, and she was still wearing her uniform, the uniform she had been wearing to beat out the drapes. She gripped her hands tightly in front of her and prayed to any god she could think of not to ruin anything. She had chosen to stand not quite in and not quite near the first sitting arrangement she had come to as she walked in the door. The fabrics of the furniture were glistening with wealth. Nora could almost see the pounds that it had taken to purchase such finery. The drapes at the windows facing the street were equally as fine in hues of cream and peach, and it suddenly struck Nora that a man could not have chosen such decor. Her gaze traveled the length of the room to where the Countess of Stryden stood, ripping her gloves from her fingers one by one, muffled curses coming from under her breath.

Literally, the woman swore.

Nora knew such language was unbecoming of a lady, but she had sensed a rather strained relationship between the countess and the earl. Having been in the employ of a large household staff for ten years, such tension was visible to her, but such tension also went without comment. It wasn't Nora's place to judge the ones that would provide for her and Samuel.

A sharp pain coursed through her at the thought of her son. Where was he now? Was he safe? Was he warm, fed, anything? Nora thought of Nathan following her into the drawing room with the Earl of Stryden at his side, and an unnameable calm swept over her. Nathan promised her he would find Samuel. And she would hold him to that promise.

Nora was struck once more by the remarkable resemblance between the Earl of Stryden and Nathan. If she had not known they were half-brothers, she would soon have been asking questions upon seeing the pair in such close proximity. They had the same chins and cheekbones and straight dark hair that sometimes fell into their faces. But the color of their eyes was markedly different. Nathan's so blue and the Earl of Stryden's a striking green. For the first time, Nora thought of Nathan's mother, wondered whom she might have been. This made her instantly think of the sadness she sometimes saw on Nathan's face, the fleeting awareness that something was not quite in his grasp, and she wondered if that momentary insecurity had something to do with his mother. But then she had recalled him saying something about his mother dying at his birth, about his father taking him in. Did he regret not having known his mother? Surely such a loss at an age when memory was so temporary could not still plague him in such an apparent way?

So what was it that made him restless and unsure?

"So what is the situation as it stands, Nathan?" Lady Stryden asked abruptly.

Nathan gestured to the sofa in the seating arrangement where Nora hovered as if she were to sit, but Nora hesitated.

She saw the look of confusion on Nathan's face, but still she did not move. She looked at Lady Stryden.

"Oh, do sit down, please," she said then, making the same gesture toward the seating arrangement.

Nora thought about hesitating again, but a lady had requested that she sit. So she did, pulling in her muddled skirts as best she could in the hopes of not soiling the upholstery of the chair she had chosen.

"You have heard of the miscalculation of the recent assassination attempt?" Nathan asked, taking a seat opposite Nora on the sofa.

Lady Stryden paused as she took her own seat. "Miscalculation?"

Nathan nodded. "It appears we have assassinated the wrong man," he said plainly, and Nora wondered how they could speak of the death of a man without emotion.

"Oh dear," Lady Stryden said in a tone that left Nora wondering whether or not the countess was being facetious. "What are the next steps then?"

"The War Office wants to lie low for a bit. Let everyone settle back in. We do not want to act hastily and ruin all of the hard work that has been accomplished thus far." This was from Lord Stryden who joined them rather belatedly.

Nora noticed for the first time how his cravat was slightly askew and his collar was just a touch wrinkled. She wanted to call for his valet but soon realized it was not her place.

"I see," Lady Stryden said, "And then someone was kidnapped?"

"Yes," Nathan responded, but just at that moment, a maid entered with the tea cart.

Without thinking, Nora stood and accepted the tea cart from the maid. The young girl looked up, startled, and Nora realized what she was doing. Her hands were already on the tea cart, and it stood between them, the object of their missed propriety. But Nora had been serving for ten years, and right then, it was all that she knew was still right with this world.

"May I?" she asked the young maid.

The maid looked over Nora's shoulder, presumably at the lord and lady of the house.

"Nora, you mustn't do that," this was from Nathan, but she ignored him.

"Right now, I must," she said and started to put pressure on the cart to take it from the maid.

"It is all right, Lily," Nora heard Lady Stryden say, and then the cart came free into Nora's hands.

With a task to accomplish, Nora set about serving the tea. She listened to Nathan explain the order of events at the Gregenden ball, poor Frederick being shot instead of his brother, Franklin, and the subsequent attempted shooting of Nathan himself. But when the topic circled around to the kidnapping of her son, Nora's focus narrowed. She set out the tea cups and saucers filled precisely with the steaming tea and with a precision the most astute of maids could never hope to muster, she laid out the cream and sugar. While the necessity of the task did not bring her peace, it brought order. And that was enough.

"Why would someone kidnap the son of a housekeeper?" This was from Lady Stryden. "I do beg your pardon, Nora— I may call you Nora?"

Nora had been nothing but Miss Quinton or Mama for ten years, but if a countess wished to call her Nora, Nora she would be.

"Yes, my lady," she said precisely, coming to stand by the tea cart, hands folded in front of her.

"If I am to call you Nora, you are to call me Sarah. And do sit down. You are making me nervous with all of your energy. We shall find your son. It is only a matter of time. You mustn't worry so."

The countess finished this long sentence and immediately turned to the earl. "I would assume Nora will be needing a place to stay. Is there a room available here at the house?" she asked.

Nora was in the process of sitting when she heard this question asked. Surely, she could not ask for residence in the home of an earl. But where else had she to go?

"I was thinking of finding a place for her at Father's," Nathan chimed in.

"A place for who?"

Nora's head, along with everyone else's, swiveled in the direction of the door as Jane came through it, peeling a ridiculously plumed hat from her head. Nora stood immediately. The countess may have asked her to sit, but when a duchess entered the room, one stood without question. The motion must have caught Jane's attention for the woman looked at her, a flash of concern moving across her features.

"What's happened?" she asked quickly, stopping in the middle of securing a pin in her hair.

Nathan stood as well.

"Samuel has been kidnapped," he said, and even though she had heard that word many times now, it still stung.

"Good Lord," Jane said and came over to Nora. When the duchess embraced her, Nora froze. Her gaze traveled over Jane's shoulder to Nathan's face, and she watched him watching her, a look of concern on his features unlike anything Nora had known before. And then Jane released her, taking only Nora's hands in her own. Nora looked down at the fine gloves Jane wore and wanted to pull her own hands back, but such a gesture would be simply rude. Nora looked at Nathan again, completely unsure as to how to function in this place where she found herself.

"Of course, you shall be staying with us," Jane said. "I'll send a note to the house immediately to have rooms made up. We should also send for Richard. He is meeting with his solicitor, but that can wait." Jane turned directly to Nathan. "Are you still assuming that shot was meant for you and not Nora?"

Nathan shrugged. "I am not sure what to think any longer."

Jane nodded, squeezed Nora's hands once more and let go.

"Let us have tea and discuss this. Surely we are more intelligent than traitors and Frenchmen. We can figure this out over a cup of tea."

The duchess moved to the tea cart, but Nora reacted instinctively, moving to fill a cup for Jane.

"Goodness, Nora, do you ever stop serving?"

"I beg your pardon?" Nora asked, handing Jane the cup.

Jane simply shook her head. "Never mind. And sit down. You mustn't be on your feet at a moment like this."

At a moment like that, Nora was getting weary of everyone telling her to sit down.

"Actually, perhaps not." This came from the countess.

Nora stopped in mid-seat as the countess stood. Jane choked on her tea.

"Whatever for?" the duchess asked when she could breathe again.

"We cannot have Nora dressed like that."

The countess pointed at Nora's worn cloak and the visible service gown underneath. For a moment, she wanted to sink entirely through the chair and the floor beneath it, but then the countess spoke.

"Whoever is doing this will be looking for a maid. Therefore, we cannot be seen with a maid. I can surely remedy that."

Never in her life had Nora felt her station more than at that moment and neither had she ever felt like it did not matter in the least. A countess was paying attention to her as if she were a real person and not just a servant.

Stryden asked, "What do you have in mind?"

The countess tilted her head. "What do you think, Jane? Between the two of us I am sure we can find something that will fit her."

Nora instantly looked down at herself. Fit her? Did they expect her to produce a new gown?

"I have no other gowns," she said quickly. "Well, at least not the kind that would convince people I was not a housekeeper."

"Oh, but I do," the countess said with a smirk and moved toward the door of the drawing room.

"Jane, will you be so kind as to assist me?"

Jane set down her cup. "My darling Sarah, when have you ever had to ask for my assistance when it involves perusing a countess's collection of gowns?"

Jane took Nora's arm. "Come, Nora. The tea will have to wait." The duchess turned to the men in the room. "Boys, see that a note is sent for your father. We will be busy for the foreseeable future."

And with that, Nora let herself be led from the room.

NATHAN REMAINED STANDING LONG after Sarah and Jane had swept Nora from the room.

"At what moment exactly did we lose control of that conversation?" Alec asked.

Nathan shook his head. "I am not certain we ever did have control of that conversation."

Alec mumbled something and sat. Nathan felt his legs

move but did not really understand that he was moving to sit until he was once again next to Alec. His mind was spinning, moving from one thought to the next before the first one had a chance to complete itself in his brain. He thought of the look on Nora's face when she had learned of Samuel. He thought of the way she had stood resolute when he had returned to remove her from Gregenden House. He thought of the quiet that had descended over her when they had climbed into the hack that had brought them here, to Stryden Place.

What was she thinking right then? What was she feeling? Did she really trust him to find her son?

What if he did not trust himself? What if he failed? Failed Nora? Failed Samuel? Failed all of them?

"I can see why she would keep you up at night," Alec said then, and Nathan's mind spun to a catastrophic halt at the sudden voice.

Nathan nodded, not sure he could articulate the words that were burning in his mind.

"She trusts you, you know?" Alec continued.

There was a glimmer of panic that he would continue on the subject that was most pressing in Nathan's mind, but Alec suddenly fell quiet again.

The pair listened to the ticking of a clock somewhere in the drawing room. The sound of traffic filtered in from outside, the rattle of carriages and the clipped staccato of hooves.

"I shall have Reynolds send a lad to fetch Father," Alec said then, rising from the sofa.

Nathan still did not move as Alec went to the corner of the room and pulled the braided cord to summon the butler.

Reynolds arrived briskly and, just as briskly, accepted direction from Alec before retiring from the room. Nathan did not so much as blink as he sat on the sofa staring into the empty grate of the fireplace before him. Alec eventually returned as the sofa dipped with the new weight.

"So how about Webbly?" Alec finally asked.

The question startled Nathan so deeply, he forgot with whom he was speaking. "Who the hell is Webbly?" Nathan asked.

"Duke of Worcester. Accidentally stabbed himself in a duel with John Langford."

"What was the duel over?"

"Langford insulted Webbly's mother."

"Who is Webbly's mother?" Nathan asked.

"She's now the Countess of Dendrigeshire."

"Dendrigeshire?" Nathan grimaced. "What did Langford say?"

"He said she was a big-boned woman."

Nathan turned his head to Alec. "How is that cause for a duel?"

"Langford thought Webbly was his mother."

"Oh, I see."

The silence took over once more, surrounding them like an impenetrable enemy.

"I am sorry, brother, that is all I have at the moment," Alec said then.

Nathan nodded. "It is all right. Father will be here soon, and he will speak enough for all of us."

The sound of the traffic outside once more flooded the room. Nathan listened to the sound of his brother's breathing as if the cadence would bring calm to his troubled thoughts. His mind kept racing, and Nathan looked about the room, at the forgotten tea, the heavily adorned windows, the intricate carvings in the wood around the fireplace.

"How is your lady wife?" Nathan suddenly asked, and Alec groaned in response.

"That is the subject of which you wish to speak? In this, your hour of most need?"

Nathan shifted on the sofa, so he could better see Alec. "It is not my hour of need. We will find Samuel. I am just having trouble focusing. That is all."

Nathan stood and walked to the end of the room where a heavy cabinet stood in the corner. He picked up one of the thick glasses that sat on top of the liquor tray that rested there. He motioned to Alec.

"At only midday?" Alec said.

Nathan only shrugged. "I will keep asking after your wife."

Alec waved a hand at him. "Yes, all right then."

Nathan poured each of them a glass before returning to Alec. This time he took the chair that Nora had occupied so briefly. "So things with the lady wife are going well?"

Alec answered after taking a sip from his drink. "The things with the lady wife are going nowhere at all."

Nathan swirled his drink, having yet to take a sip. "You mean to tell me that you had not swept her off her feet by the time I came through the door?"

Alec gave him a look that clearly questioned his intelligence. "It is quite more complicated than that."

Nathan reached over and set a hand on Alec's knee. It was a gesture he had made a thousand times when they were boys. Nathan may have been the older brother, but Alec was usually the one who did the comforting. There was something about Alec's casual confidence that led him naturally to support his sometimes cautious older brother. But there were the few times when Nathan made the gesture as he did now.

"What is it that has her so angry with you?" Nathan asked, and Alec finally looked at him.

There was emptiness in his eyes. Blank slates that

yearned for answers. Nathan recognized the look he had seen on his own face far too many times when he had looked in the mirror.

"Perhaps Father will know what to do. He did eventually convince Jane to marry him, and we all doubted that would happen. You know, after..."

He let the sentence trail off, knowing Alec would understand to what he referred. And he saw the understanding cloud his brother's gaze.

"Perhaps," was all he said.

NORA WATCHED as a line of maids hauled buckets of steaming water one by one through the narrow door of the sitting room. She only thought how fortunate it was that they did not have to carry the buckets all the way into the dressing room across the chamber. She doubted some of the smaller maids would have made it so far with such a heavy load. Nora had tried to help only once, and upon receiving a slap on her hand - literally, the Duchess of Lofton slapped her - Nora refrained from trying to help.

It was a quite difficult task for as Lady Stryden, or Sarah rather, led her deeper into the bowels of what she was learning was called Stryden Place, she began to feel more and more out of sorts. She longed for a chambermaid to instruct or Hawkins to placate or Samuel to smile at her and make her forget everything that surrounded her. If only Samuel were there, she would not have left Gregenden House and the only life she ever knew. She would not now be wondering what was happening to her son and worse, how she was to care for him when Nathan brought him back to her.

As everything welled up inside her, Nora would have

settled for a mere rag and something to dust if only to distract her dangerously tilting mind.

But with each step they climbed up to the family's main living quarters, Nora found herself being pulled further into the conversation between Jane and Sarah. Sarah ordered a bath from a maid descending the second floor staircase while Jane requested a tray of sandwiches. Surely, Nora could not be expected to try on gowns without refreshment. A footman was sent to fetch the countess's lady's maid to freshen the gowns that Sarah kept at Stryden Place. And when they finally stopped climbing, Nora thought they most certainly were higher than the dome of St. Paul's. At least, she was winded enough to feel like it were true.

And now there she was, watching maid after maid haul water to a steaming bath big enough for an entire ballet troupe. And Nora was truly expected to bathe in it alone? A sudden image of Nathan flashed in her mind, and she physically choked, bringing the attention of Jane.

"There, there, Nora," Jane said, coming to her and patting her delicately on the back, "The boys will figure this all out, and Samuel will be back to you in no time. I assure you, darling."

Nora had never been touched so much in her entire life, let alone touched out of comfort. If she had been choking before, she had stopped breathing now. She almost could not stand everyone being so nice to her. If one more person so much as expressed their sorrow, she was sure she would dissolve into the floor where she stood.

But that would soil the fine carpet beneath her shoes. The Floral Room, as Sarah had called it, was opulent if it were anything. Nora stood as still as Hawkins in a musicale in the very center of the room, keeping her worn cloak and soiled uniform from touching so much as a table. She gazed at the delicate furniture with its intricately carved lattices and polished handles. The drapes were divine and of such quality that Nora pondered how the maids cleaned them without damaging the fine cloth. The covers of the bed were lush in deep purple tones with pockets of pure white. She longed to lie down, bury herself in its luxuriousness and forget that her son was missing, that she no longer had a home or employ, that she was falling in love with a spy.

"We will give you some privacy," Jane said then, scuttling past her. "But only for a brief time. There is much to be done, and Richard will likely be here soon."

Sarah approached her with a stack of fluffy towels. It took Nora an entire moment to realize the decadent towels were for her. She accepted them haltingly.

"Do not listen to the woman. Enjoy yourself," the countess said with a wink.

And Nora was sure she did dissolve into the floor.

When the door closed behind the pair, Nora still did not move. It was too surreal. It was too unfamiliar. It was too...unlikely. But just as Nathan had told her to pack, these women had told her to bathe.

She quickly set down the towels on the nearest chair and began stripping her clothes off. First the cloak, then her apron, then her gown. She was careful to fold the exposed sides of her uniform inward to keep the dirt and dust from spreading into the room. She tucked the bundle of clothes away and gingerly approached the steaming tub.

Soaps of varying colors and sizes and smells were laid out on a tray by the tub. Various vials of oils were also displayed by the tray, and Nora wondered what they were used for. She picked up one of the vials and studied the liquid inside of it as it moved back and forth against the glass. Was this how the women of the *ton* smelled so delightful? Nora wondered what Nathan would think of her if she came back smelling like a bouquet of peonies? What would *she* think if she smelled thusly?

Nora set the vial back down and approached the tub directly, carefully placing one foot and then the other into the resplendent bath water. Her muscles flexed at the sudden heat before spooling away in relief, unwinding her very core until she was fully relaxed in the water.

And then she let her mind drift. But the warmth of the water or silkiness of the bath oil or the aroma of the soaps, or perhaps a combination of them all, invaded her senses, and her mind was nothing but a blankness that left her in a cocoon of simple peace. She stayed there for as long as she dared. She stayed there until the skin of her fingers began to pucker from the water, and she feared the water would grow too cold before she had truly completed bathing. She stirred, reluctantly, pulling her head up from where it rested against the rim of the tub.

Reaching her hand over the edge of the tub, she randomly selected a bar of soap from the small table and drew it to her nose. It smelled like something floral, but having never had an occasion to bath in such finery, Nora could not give the scent a name. She dipped the bar into the water and began to scrub years of dirt and dust from her skin. With one swipe of the soap, she felt it pull away at everything she had been carrying. The loss of her parents that she had never truly known. The years spent as a forgotten child in Aunt Martha's home. The courageous and terrifying trip to London when she was only a young girl to find work. Samuel.

Oh God, Samuel, she thought, and broke at the image of him as a toddler, an unexpected joy that had been brought into her life.

She kept pushing the soap along her skin, scrubbing harder as she went as if by scrubbing could rid her body of all of it. The work, the neglect, the unexpected. But she would not wash away Samuel. Samuel she clung to, held him against her breast and savored the knowledge that Nathan would bring him back.

Nora set the soap aside and reached for a vial of the oil. Working her hair loose from its braid, she wet the strands before coating them in the scented oil. She indulged and spent precious minutes just massaging her scalp. It felt divine and ridiculous, and she hoped that no one would ever find out that she had been so hedonistic.

Rinsing her hair thoroughly, she wrung the excess water from the thick strands and stood, the now cool water sloshing in the tub about her legs. She paused as the ripples lapped at her knees, and for the first time in a very long time, perhaps ever, Nora looked at her naked body. She was too thin, she could admit that. Her knees stuck out as if her legs each had its own nose. A bulbous one at that. Her ribs were visible beneath her small breasts, and her arms were just elbows and skin. She wondered what Nathan would think should he ever see her like this. He would probably not find much to be intrigued about, and this made her sad. The feeling made her pause, the water continuing to run off her skin. She had never expected to feel sadness over something so trivial. And it was not as if Nathan Black were ever going to see her in such a state.

As gooseflesh sprouted on her skin, she stepped from the tub and picked up one of the lush towels she had admired earlier. Wrapping herself in it, she used another to carefully dry her hair. Once she was done, she stood with one towel wrapped around her, the other hanging from her hand.

What was she supposed to do?

It was not as if she could peek into the hallway and summon the duchess and countess looking like this. And to think her, Eleanora Quinton, would be summoning anyone? So she did what anyone would have done to summon her.

She walked to the corner and tugged on the braided bell pull.

The door to the hall opened almost immediately, and a whirlwind of maids rushed into the room. Nora had not been prepared for such an instantaneous response, and she backed up involuntarily, clutching the towel to her chest.

"Lavender is a lovely color for any young woman," Jane said as she swept into the room behind the Countess of Stryden.

"With her hair? Surely not, Jane. She needs to be put in green," Sarah returned.

It was several moments before Nora realized they were speaking of her.

"I beg your pardon," she said, and it was as if she had screamed it as everyone in the room stopped.

The maids hovered over the tub, their hands filled with unused soaps and vials and towels. Sarah stood at the other side of the chamber, her hand on the frame of the dressing room door. Jane had stopped in the middle of it all, one arm outstretched as if to make a grand address.

"What about red?" Nora asked, not certain where the notion had come from nor the courage to say it out loud.

Jane lowered her outstretched arm. Sarah pursed her lips, one slender finger tapping on the door frame.

"Red would be divine with that chestnut hair you were mentioning," Jane said in Sarah's general direction.

Sarah straightened away from the door, brushing one hand against her forehead as if an invisible piece of her golden blonde hair had come loose from its chignon.

"I believe I have something that may work," she said, disappearing into the dressing room, a maid close on her heels.

"My lady—" Nora heard the maid say before both women disappeared.

Nora turned her attention back to Jane and found the older woman smiling at her.

"This was not what you expected when you awoke this morning, was it, Miss Quinton?"

Nora shook her head. "No, it is—"

She stopped mid-sentence, jumping slightly as a maid touched her arm. There were two of them, and they were pushing her in the direction of a dressing table in the opposite corner of the room from where she stood. They pushed her onto the stool before the dressing table and began to work on her hair, running the locks through a dry towel.

Sarah suddenly emerged from the dressing room with a chattering maid behind her.

"Are you certain, my lady, that that particularly gown would be completely appropriate—"

Sarah stopped in front of her, her hands behind her back.

"How is this?" she said, her hands springing from behind her back, a gown strung between her outstretched hands.

Nora looked at Jane.

Jane looked at Nora.

"Well, at least no one will believe I am a maid," Nora said.

CHAPTER 10

*N*athan stood as his father entered the drawing room. He had not altered his position from the moment someone had been sent to find the Duke of Lofton, and the sudden movement made him realize how tense he was.

"A kidnapping?" Richard said by way of introduction.

"Appears so," Alec said, rising from the sofa to pull the bell cord for Reynolds.

Reynolds appeared as Richard removed his hat and gloves.

"A fresh tea cart," Alec said to the butler, who nodded and left just as quickly as he had come.

"Have you briefed Jane?" Richard asked then.

Nathan shook his head.

"We were waiting for you. And the ladies are...well..."

He looked to Alec for assistance.

"I believe the ladies are orchestrating a type of rouse as we speak," Alec finished.

"Ladies?"

Now Alec turned away, walking to the front of the room to stare out the window at the passing traffic.

Richard turned and looked at his other son. Nathan only nodded.

"I see. How is the lady countess?" Richard said, taking a seat on the sofa Alec had just vacated.

"Lovely as always," Alec muttered.

"And what sort of rouse are the ladies concocting?" Richard asked.

Nathan resumed his seat.

"One of camouflage. I believe they are preparing Miss Quinton to appear as a lady and not a servant."

"Miss Quinton is with you then?" Richard raised an eyebrow.

"Of course," Nathan responded automatically, not enjoying his father's questioning expression. "Miss Quinton is obviously in danger. I was not going to leave her unprotected."

"A wise decision," Richard said. "And I am certain Jane was delighted to partake in any endeavor that involved couture."

"It was Sarah's idea actually," Alec muttered from the window.

Richard raised the other eyebrow. "Ah, Lady Stryden then. Interesting." He looked back at Nathan. "And when can we expect the other half of our party to join us?"

"Promptly, Your Grace," came Jane's voice from the doorway.

Nathan stood automatically, turning to face the door. And then he froze.

Alec's laughter filtered into his muddled mind. "Well, this certainly makes me feel better about my own situation," he mumbled.

But Nathan was truly not hearing anything.

Nora stood outlined in the doorway from the corridor. While Sarah and Jane had entered the room to join Richard and Nathan in the sitting area, Nora stayed where she was as Nathan outwardly perused her appearance. Her hair was luscious and glowing, swept up in a mass of braids that he was sure would not come as easily undone as her simple maid's style had. Her face was clean of any rice powder and glowed with a warmth he had not seen before. The brown of her eyes was magnified by the red hues of her hair.

And her gown.

Her gown was...magnificent. Whatever the fabric, it was a deep crimson with long sleeves that puffed at the shoulders, making her look regal and capable. The high waist of the gown suddenly gave her a bosom that Nathan admired very much. Some sort of gold ribbon framed the plunging neckline, and his eyes traveled the length of it up to her shoulders and back to her face.

But his eyes darted down once more to her hands.

She wore no gloves.

He wanted to reach out and take her hands into his own. To feel her skin against his.

He wanted to care for her more now than ever. In everyday attire, she looked like a woman most suitable to be his wife, but with this thought came another. He could not care for her. His gaze drifted quickly to Jane and back, memories of a time long ago stinging with an intensity that would not fade.

Nathan stepped aside and gestured for Nora to sit, unable to say anything at that moment.

Richard stepped forward, blocking her entrance, and the movement broke Nathan from whatever trance had enveloped him when Nora had come into the room.

"Miss Quinton, I believe," Richard said, as he bowed to

Nora, "It is a pleasure to finally make your acquaintance. People have much to say about you. I am very sorry to hear about your son, but I assure you that we will do everything necessary to resolve the matter quickly."

"What he is trying to say is do not fret," Jane said from where she had taken a seat on the sofa behind him.

"Precisely," Richard affirmed, stepping aside so Nora could take the place next to Jane on the sofa.

With a fresh tea cart arriving promptly, the discussion quickly turned to the matter at hand, and Nathan forced himself to focus and not stare at Nora transformed.

"So what is it we know about the situation?" Richard began.

"Nothing. Or next to nothing," Nathan said. "There were three big men and one smaller one, which I suspect was a woman with red hair. Samuel was taken from behind Gregenden House by the stables. There was no carriage waiting, but that does not mean there was not one farther down the alley. I found this." Nathan drew the four of clubs from his pocket and held it up. "I am assuming Samuel dropped it, as right before he was taken, I was teaching him how to play poker."

Jane made a tsking noise in his general direction but otherwise did not comment.

"The four of clubs. Like the gaming hell?" Sarah asked.

Alec and Nathan both looked at her.

"The gaming hell?" Alec nearly screeched. "What do you know about a gaming hell called The Four of Clubs?"

"I know more than you would think, my lord," she returned, assuming a seat in the chair opposite the sofa. "The gaming hell down by the wharf. By Madame Hort's."

Nathan nodded. "I know where you mean."

Alec asked, "Do you think Samuel dropped it on purpose?"

"He is smart enough to," Nathan answered automatically, and he caught Nora hiding a smile behind her hand.

"Why would they take him to The Four of Clubs?" Sarah asked.

"Why would they take him?" Alec countered.

Sarah looked at him, annoyed.

"They took him because of Nora."

Everyone looked at Nathan.

"What did I do?" Nora asked as if offended.

Nathan had the nerve to smile. "I think you did something that you do not know you did."

Nora raised a single eyebrow and made Alec muffle a laugh.

"When I went into the alley where Samuel was taken, I was given a message from a street boy. He told me to stay out of it. If it had anything to do with me and my business, he would not have told me that. There was also the night of the ball when Nora and I were shot at."

"Someone shot at you?" Sarah asked.

"Someone shot at us," Nora said.

"Someone shot at you," Nathan corrected her.

Alec shook his head. "How can you be sure?"

"I cannot. But I have been thinking. No one knows me," Nathan said. "That is a profile I have been careful to create. However, everyone knows Nora. So why would someone take a shot at a nobody when there was a somebody standing right next to him?"

"Everyone does not know me," Nora huffed, making Nathan look at her in surprise.

Could he actually be getting to the infallible Miss Quinton?

"Yes, everyone does," Sarah argued.

Nora looked over at her. "Everyone?"

"Quite possibly everyone." Sarah adjusted her skirts.

"Everyone knows who Lady Gregenden's housekeeper is. The infallible Miss Quinton."

"They do not say that." Nora actually wrinkled her nose, and it was Nathan's turn to hide a smile.

"Oh, they do," Jane concurred.

"We have established that everyone knows Nora, but what does it mean?" Richard interjected.

Nora was silent.

"It means that she is the likely target for all of this," Jane offered.

"But why now?" This from Alec who had returned to his spot by the window.

Sarah leaned forward in her seat. "I think it would be best to find out what Nora knows first. Or at least, what she thinks she knows."

Nora shook her head quickly. "Nothing. At least not something worth kidnapping my son over."

"It is probably something that you do not realize is important. Something that they are afraid you know is important," Nathan added.

Nora remained silent, but he could tell that she was thinking. There was something in her memory. It would only be a matter of time before she would find it. He was sure of it.

* * *

"WHY WOULD SOMEONE WANT SAMUEL?" Richard, the Duke of Lofton, asked the fireplace.

Nora sat on the sofa keeping her hands loose in her lap, the tension and fear of being in this strange, elegant place not quite so gripping. The unfamiliarity of fine fabrics and lace made her uncomfortable, but she resolutely did not fidget.

The Duke of Lofton was indeed speaking to the fireplace, or more directly, to the empty grate. Jane sat on the sofa beside her, sipping from a new cup of tea as if nothing were amiss. The Countess of Stryden, too, enjoyed a cup of tea without so much as a fidget. Nora found it difficult to simply remain seated.

Did these people speak of kidnapping and threats so often that it became normal drawing room conversation? And among mixed company even. She pulled on the sleeves of the gown as if to ease her mental discomfort with a physical action, her resolve to not fidget dying under her tenacious anxiety.

Nathan stood somewhere behind her now, but she resolutely kept her face forward in case she was caught glancing at him too much. But the look on his face when she had entered the room in the new gown, her hair swept up in an intricate braided style for the first time in her life, that expression she would never forget. The look of sheer desire in his eyes, a desire that should have frightened her, but somehow pulled her toward him, as if his desire were an attractant itself.

Alec asked, "Did Samuel have any enemies?"

Sarah, who had demonstrably taken a position on the opposite side of the room as her husband, replied, "How do nine-year-olds acquire enemies?"

Nathan answered, "I think he has got a point. Samuel is smarter than most nine-year-olds. Maybe he saw something he was not supposed to and knew it."

Nora nodded. "Samuel is often used as an errand boy at the house. I do not always know where he goes, so it is quite possible he did encounter something. However, I am not certain he would know how truly important the thing would be."

Jane handed her a cup of tea suddenly. "You need this,

darling," she said, "And what about you? You are always in a position to see things certain members of the peerage would rather have left unseen. What have you seen lately?"

Nora accepted the teacup and shook her head. "Nothing lately. It has been rather quiet."

Richard turned around. "Maybe it was not something lately. Revenge does not always come quickly."

He sat in one of the chairs framing the sofa and took a cup from Jane as well.

Nora stared at the tea in her cup, thinking. "How far should I go back?"

Nathan sat on the arm of the sofa just then, startling her just enough to make her look up. His gaze remained sharp, but the desire she had seen before was somehow banked. His attention focused purely on the matter at hand.

"How far back is there to go?" he asked.

"Thirteen years. I have been working in London for thirteen years."

Richard grunted. "Fabulous. How about just the highlights then?"

Nora nodded. "All right. Let us get started then." She paused, sorting through all the dirty secrets in her mind. "Last November I came upon Lord Trenton and his valet when they were guests at the House." She paused again.

Richard interrupted, "How is that important?"

"She came upon them, Richard," Jane said.

Richard sat back. "Oh. Well I guess that explains some things."

Nora continued, "There was the Earl of Glouton and Mrs. Fairby last August." She thought some more. "And Mr. Havenbaum and one of my maids." She suddenly looked up. "Maybe that is it. Maybe it is Mr. Havenbaum."

"Why would it be him?" Nathan asked.

"Because I whacked him over the head with a bottle of champagne. He could not be happy about that." Nora switched her attention to Richard because she could not say the next part while looking at Nathan. "My maid did not want Mr. Havenbaum's attentions."

The shockwave from Nathan suddenly straightening hit her. Richard nodded, and Jane cleared her throat.

"Did he see you, Nora?" Alec asked.

She thought and frowned. "No, I do not think he did. I came from behind him, and he was out before he knew anything was amiss."

Nathan relaxed slightly. "I do not think that is it then."

"What about innocent looking things, Nora?" Sarah came closer to the cluster. "Something that did not look odd at all. Or maybe just odd but not scandalous."

Nora thought, as the tea grew cold in her cup. "I overheard a conversation that Lord Archer was having with the Duke of Chesterfield that seemed odd."

The room buzzed with silence, and Nora looked up to make sure she was not suddenly alone.

"What did you hear, Nora?" Alec asked, drawing softly closer.

"It was at Lord Gregenden's birthday gala last month. The two men were in an alcove alone together. It seemed odd because the two hate each other, so I went over to take a listen."

Richard interrupted again, "Why do they hate each other?"

"The duke won the hand of the lady that Archer wanted," Jane supplied.

Richard nodded and motioned for Nora to continue.

"They were discussing yachts, racing yachts." Nora paused, thinking back. "Archer said he had the fastest, but then His Grace countered saying it might be fastest but did it run shallow."

"Yachts to break through the blockade," Sarah whispered.

Nathan leaned forward, took the teacup from Nora and, setting the cup aside, gripped her hands. "Did they know you were listening, Nora?"

Nora shook her head but stopped. "They might have."

Nathan gripped her hands tighter.

"They were still speaking when Niles Turning came to tell me we were running low on lemonade. He might have said my name." She looked over at Richard. "They might have heard him."

"So Chesterfield is spying for Napoleon as well," Alec said, mostly to himself.

Nora's fingers tingled from lack of blood as Nathan's grip tightened. She had to shake their hands to get him to notice. He loosened his fingers. Slightly.

"How do you know Chesterfield is...um, a spy?" Nora asked, feeling ridiculously left out of the conversation that was beginning to pulse around her.

"We have known of Lord Archer's activities for the better part of a year. If he were discussing yachts with a man he disliked in secret in a public place, we must assume his intentions were less than honorable," the duke said, standing to return to his spot by the fireplace.

"That seems a rather large assumption," she offered, but Alec quickly shook his head.

"I do not think so. Not with the resulting circumstances. The assassination of the wrong Lord Archer, someone attempting to shoot either you or Nathan and then Samuel missing. It must be connected."

"What do we do now?" Nathan asked his father.

Richard did not answer right away. Alec came up against

the back of the sofa, his wife beside him, and Nora wondered if either of them noticed their proximity to one another.

"The Four of Clubs," Richard said finally.

"The Four of Clubs?" Sarah asked.

"Yes. That is our only clue, and we must assume that Samuel is going to react to this more cleverly than a typical child would." He went over to the table and picked up the card where Nathan had discarded it. "We are going to assume he dropped this on purpose. Now, who is going to go?"

"I will," Sarah volunteered.

"You bloody well will not," Alec responded.

Nora expected the conversation to end at that, but Sarah was not one to be so dismissed it seemed.

"You are not in charge of what I do and do not do, Lord Stryden, and it would be best—"

"It would be best if you did not constantly try to—"

"I do nothing constantly but—"

"Children!"

This last bit came from Jane at a pitch and volume Nora did not know her capable of. It made Nora sit up straighter, setting down her tea cup lest she spill it.

"I think I had better go," Nathan said, looking down at his clothes.

Richard nodded in agreement. "You do appear more fit for the part," Richard said.

Nora looked at Nathan. He wore a typical greatcoat, worn but not shoddy, and working boots. A clean collar and cravat were noticeable beneath the top of the greatcoat. Nothing he wore looked particularly remarkable, but when Nora turned her attention back to the Duke of Lofton, the difference became clear. Nathan was a working man, whereas the duke was a member of the peerage. Nathan would blend in with greater ability at a gaming hell, whereas everyone would remark on the presence of the Duke of Lofton.

"Very well," Alec said. "We must prepare to leave immediately. I will have a carriage summoned."

Alec left the room with a still fuming Sarah trailing after him. Nora imagined the conversation that was likely occurring between the pair just then. Nathan stood, and so did Nora.

"Jane, a moment, please?" Richard said, and Jane set down her tea as she stood.

"Of course," she said, turning to Nora. "Excuse us, dear."

Richard and Jane left the room, leaving Nora quite alone with Mr. Nathan Black.

* * *

NORA DID NOT KNOW what to do with her hands. Or her tea. Or her breath.

Everything felt suddenly awkward when moments before she had been feeling nothing but physical tension as her mind wandered over and over again to her son.

"Did you truly hit some bloke over the head with a bottle of champagne?" Nathan asked, sitting beside her on the sofa.

She turned and, at the quizzical look on his face, felt the sudden awkwardness melt from her. She may have had her hair done by a lady's maid, and she may be wearing a countess's gown, but she was still Nora, and this was still Nathan. Everything seemed a little bit more all right with Nathan.

She nodded. "I did. A big bottle at that." She shrugged. "I just thought it lucky that I decided to come above stairs by way of the east wing that night, or I never would have come upon them in the green drawing room."

She paused as the memory of that night surfaced. She had not really been thinking so much as reacting. The noises that had been coming from the green drawing room in the east wing of Gregenden House had sounded frighteningly familiar. Familiar in a way Nora never cared to remember or have reason to hear again. The sounds of a struggle and muffled pleas for help in a soft, feminine contralto with just the slightest of Irish accents. It took but a moment for Nora to realize what was happening in the room, for her to turn her course, enter the drawing room, and smash the bottle of drink over the grunting man's head. She had not even known who the man was at the time. She had only seen the young maid's face as she lay pinned on the sofa in the room, her skirts thrown up and the pale skin of her thighs exposed above the top of her stockings a beacon in the dim light of the room. And then there was the girl's face. Drawn with fright, her eyes were mere pools of despair. And so, Nora had reacted more than anything, a primal urge within her for justice swinging her arm up and landing the champagne bottle directly on the man's head. He had collapsed with a grunt, and it took both of them to free the poor girl trapped beneath his body. One such occasion in her life had been enough, but having a second chance to escape a room with one's skirts solidly held to one's legs was more than enough for Nora.

She watched Nathan, and she knew he wanted to ask her something. She saw the way his jaw tightened, and a muscle in his eyelid jumped as he tried to decide whether or not he would ask it. Nora admired him more then than ever before for his consideration and subsequent restraint. She waited another breath before she saved him from his own propriety.

"Yes," she heard herself say, but her mind did not believe she was actually speaking of the one thing she swore never to speak of again. "Yes, that is what happened to me. Only there was no one with a bottle of champagne to save me in time."

Her words were simple, but it had taken all of her

courage to say them. Not once in nearly ten years had she so much as whispered a hint to someone about how Samuel had come to be in this world, and now she had admitted the whole truth in one sentence to a man she had known for only a week. But somehow its declaration did not carry the thrust she had expected. She had expected a retaliation, recriminations about having asked for it by behaving in a certain way or dressing improperly.

But Nathan only sat watching her, and for the briefest of moments, she saw it again, the look of dark sadness that crossed his features fleetingly, the one she could not name nor dare ask him about. Nathan Black had his own demons, and there was something about Nora that brought them to the surface. And just like Nathan, she was too polite to ask of them.

He raised a hand, and she was not sure what he was going to do with it, but there was something about the gesture that made her speak.

"Please, Nathan," she said, "I cannot take anyone else being nice to me today. It is taking all that I have to keep my composure. If you so much as tell me it will be all right, I may start crying on you like a silly girl."

Nathan's hand hung in the air between them as Nora watched his expression. The look of sadness that had crossed his features was replaced by his usual casual mien, his mouth not quite smiling, yet not frowning, and his eyes interested but not engaged, the perfect mask of ease. The look made her feel ridiculously better about everything, and she clamped down on her emotions, holding together her calm with everything she had. Until Nathan spoke.

"But it is going to be all right," he said, and then he did smile, and Nora could do nothing except smile in return.

"You are rather annoying, Mr. Black. You are aware of that, are you not?" Nora said then.

Nathan adjusted the lapels of his greatcoat as if assuming an elegant pose. "It is a necessary trait of any great spy, Miss Quinton," he said, and Nora continued to smile.

Silence descended on them, and Nora did not mind it in the least. There was something about Nathan that made her feel comfortable not speaking, just letting herself be with him. It was an unusual feeling, and one to which Nora feared she was becoming accustomed.

"Nathan, are you certain you should be doing this? Going to the Four of Clubs? It sounds like an awful place. Is there not someone else that can be sent?"

Nathan moved a little closer to her, taking one of her hands in his. She did not retreat at his touch as his hands moved with more curiosity than comfort.

"Do you know when truly terrible things happen, and they send someone to help?" he asked.

Nora nodded.

"Well, they are the War Office, and I am the someone," he said, looking up from his exploration of her hand.

Nora had known all along that he was a spy, but it had all seemed too surreal. As if it were the truth but not really. But as Nathan held her hand in his, the reality came crowding in, and she realized just how dangerous this man must be. She had noted his height, surely over six feet, and the wide span of his shoulders when she had first seen him enter the ballroom at Gregenden House, but his eyes told a story that had put her at ease. And although her body may have been scared of Nathan Black, she had never truly been afraid of him.

"Is it really as simple as all that?" she asked, returning the pressure of his hand with her own, locking their fingers together.

Nathan looked down briefly as if to see what it was she had done with their fingers, but he looked up quickly.

"Sometimes it is. Other times, it can get rather complicated."

"But you shall find Samuel?"

She did not know why she asked the question. It seemed ridiculous to question him when he would at any moment head into danger to follow the only clue they had as to her son's whereabouts.

"Yes, Nora, we will find him," he said, squeezing her hand one more time before standing.

Nora looked down at her hand now resting on the fine crimson fabric of her borrowed gown. It looked lost and alone suddenly without his hand holding it. Nathan moved away from the sofa in the direction of the door. She heard his footfalls grow fainter as the distance between them grew greater.

She stood. "Nathan. Wait."

Nathan turned around on his way to the door, surprise showing on his face. He bent his head as she came right up to him. Her heart thundered in her chest, feeling as if it may break directly through her skin at any moment. Her breathing was shallow and sporadic. Her hands grabbed fistfuls of her skirt to keep from shaking.

"Be careful. Please," she said and kissed him.

She did not know if she felt resistance from Nathan or merely surprise, but when his arms came around her, pulling her against his body, she decided she felt neither.

Her hands came up, bracing herself against his solid chest. She felt his heart pounding beneath her fingertips, a beat strong and erratic to match her own. He deepened the kiss then. Her head fell back along his arm as he slid one hand up to cup her cheek. She wanted to cry at the sheer gentleness of his gesture, how precious he must find her to treat her with such care. But just as quickly, he eased her away, his hands dropping to his sides as he leaned his forehead against hers. Their heaving breaths mingled, and Nora worried she may faint. After everything the day had brought, she found it ironic that it would be Nathan's kiss to bring her down.

"I will be careful, Nora," he whispered, cupping her cheek once more in the barest of touches.

And then he turned and left, leaving Nora all alone in her borrowed gown.

CHAPTER 11

*a*lec watched his brother from his seat opposite him in the carriage. He noticed the tension in the other man's face, the way his jaw kept clenching almost imperceptibly, the tightness of his shoulders. His brother watched out the window as the scenes of London moved past, one row of townhouses after another. One sidewalk full of people blurred into the next. Finally, his brother looked at him and noticed his careful gaze.

"What?" Nathan asked.

"Bastard," Alec said.

Nathan raised an eyebrow. "And to what do I owe that term of endearment?"

Alec shrugged. "What are you doing with the infallible Miss Eleanora Quinton?" Alec asked.

He may have just laughed at his brother's obvious predicament, but he was growing to care for the infallible housekeeper, and he would not see her reputation sullied.

"Oh," was all Nathan said before returning his gaze to the window.

Alec waited patiently. If there were something truly bothering Nathan, he would get around to speaking of it eventually. Alec would not press him.

Finally, Nathan shook his head. "I do not know," he whispered.

"Do you want to talk about it?" Alec asked, wondering why his brother would suddenly become reticent when they had discussed any number of weightier topics in the past. Perhaps the matter of Eleanora Quinton ran deeper than Alec believed.

"I do not know what there is to talk about," Nathan said.

Alec frowned. "There most certainly is something to talk about," he said and then shut his mouth, having regretted the sentence as soon as he had spoken it. He did not know what it was that plagued his brother, and proclaiming that he knew there was something amiss just made him appear foolish.

Nathan's head swung around though. "Of course there is. But I do not know what it is."

Alec did not speak. He had never seen Nathan like this. Nathan had a casual affair maybe once a year. He had always talked about them. He did not brag, but they were not a secret. And now he did not know what to say? The matter of Eleanora Quinton truly did run deeper than he had believed.

Nathan turned back to the window while Alec worried.

"I just want to take care of her," Nathan finally said, his voice so soft the rattling of the carriage almost drowned it out.

The carriage hit a particularly deep rut, and Alec was concentrating so hard on Nathan's statement, he was almost thrown off the bench.

"What do you mean by take care of her? You mean, because someone is trying to kill her, and they have kidnapped her son?"

Alec hoped that is what Nathan meant, but a little trickle

of dread had started at the base of his neck and began to work its way into a pounding at his temples. "You have only known the woman a mere week at most."

Nathan continued to stare out the window. "I know, but there is something..." His voice trailed off, but Alec's worry grew despite the silence.

"Something?" he finally prompted.

Nathan nodded at the window. "There is something about her that makes me think of family," Nathan said.

The worry was now a pounding along his brow. The matter of Eleanora Quinton ran deep indeed.

"What are you going to do?" Alec asked.

Nathan looked at him. "I do not know. I can barely take care of myself. How am I to take care of her and Samuel?"

Alec let the carriage roll over a few more ruts before responding. "Father would help," he said.

Nathan did not respond, but he did not need to. Neither of Richard's sons would ask their father for help. Richard would give it without a thought, but the sons were too proud to ask.

So that left the sons bouncing around in a carriage in silence on their way to a gaming hell by the wharf at three o'clock on a Tuesday afternoon.

"How is Sarah?" Nathan abruptly asked.

Alec looked down at his hands, fumbling with his thumbs.

"I am sorry," Nathan said.

Alec nodded. "Me, too."

* * *

THE FOUR of Clubs looked like something a cat had retched out of its stomach.

Mold oozed from around the stones that constructed its base as they were constantly blasted with salt watery air. The door was large, wooden, cracked and tilting to one side. The windows that were on the front were blacked out with dark material. A man, limping on a wooden stick, missing one leg and with a coat torn around the hem, knocked on the door and waited. The door opened a crack, and the man with one leg spoke. The door opened wide enough to let him shuffle in.

Nathan and Alec leaned away from the window of the carriage.

"This might be a problem," Alec said, watching the door close on the one-legged man.

"Whoever is doing this knows who I am," Nathan said.

Alec nodded. "If you try to go inside, and they are in there, they will recognize you, surely."

Nathan looked at Alec, and he could tell that Alec was thinking the same thing as him. "I believe this is the one time that our similarity will bite us in the ass," Nathan said.

Alec looked down at himself and then studied Nathan. "Maybe not."

"How do you figure?" Nathan asked.

"They are expecting you to look like that." Alec pointed at Nathan's greatcoat and muddy boots. "They are not expecting you to look like this." He then pointed to his own fine attire.

Nathan nodded. "Strip," he said and began to unbutton his greatcoat.

Minutes later Nathan felt the bile rise in his throat when something resembling a human being opened the door of the Four of Clubs.

"Wata ye want?" it asked.

Assuming it was English, Nathan responded. "Afternoon. I have come to rid myself of a lot of money." Actually, between him and Alec, they had managed five pounds. But It did not have to know that.

It nodded and held open the door.

Nathan drew a last breath of fresh air and plunged into the crowded gaming hell.

* * *

ALEC THOUGHT he could climb that.

Nathan's greatcoat billowed around him in the breeze behind the Four of Clubs, and Alec suddenly wanted his hat back. His ears were cold.

The open window was on the second floor. He could climb not so rotted looking crates, use the drainpipe for leverage to the hole in the crumbling rock of the building. and then just one last heave into the window. He could do it.

So he did.

The hole in the crumbling rock was slightly smaller than it looked from the ground. He struggled to wedge his boot in it. The drainpipe creaked ominously, and Alec tried to remember a prayer. Then his boot caught, and Alec heaved in the direction of the open window. He flew, less than gracefully, over the ledge and into the worst stench he had ever experienced. Beer, smoke, and way too many bodily fluids mixed together. He stuck his head back out the window, gasping.

And then he heard a voice. A small voice. A voice that said, rather politely, that it had to use the chamberpot.

Alec brought his head back in and looked around. The hallway was dark, and the floor was sticky as Alec shifted his boots. There were three doors to the right and a stairway to the left. Which door was the lucky one?

He tried a step on the sticky boards, and when no creaking erupted, he took another one. Pausing in front of the first door, he listened. A woman was breathily asking someone to do something to her harder, so Alec moved quietly to the next door. This door was silent. Alec moved to the last one. He heard some shuffling. There was a pause. More shuffling. Alec waited.

Finally a voice came. "Aren't ye done yet?"

The response was too muffled for Alec to hear it, but he did not need to. He grabbed the knob and found it loose. He swung open the door, beaming whoever was standing behind it. The man was thrown into the wall and lost his balance. On his way down, he tried to draw the pistol stuck in his trousers. Alec searched for something to knock the man out with.

"Here." A heavy wine bottle was stuck in his hand.

Alec brought it up and swung it before the man could dislodge the pistol.

The man grunted and passed out.

Alec looked down at his side. "Thank you," he said to the boy.

The boy backed up. "You are not Nathan."

Alec saw the wariness but turned to shut the door first. "No, I am not. I am Nathan's brother, Alec." He set the bolt this time, hoping it would hold. The screws were starting to work their way out of the boards of the door though, so he doubted it would.

The young boy who Alec presumed was Samuel did not speak. Alec glanced over him, attempting not to frighten him. The boy looked to be in solid shape. A bit dirty, but he did not appear to be hurt.

"Your mother is safe with our father, the Duke of Lofton." Alec kept talking with his voice low, as if soothing a wild animal.

"You are wearing Nathan's coat," Samuel said.

"Yes, I am. And he is wearing mine." Alec smiled slowly, trying not to frighten.

"What are you two doing?" Samuel asked, scrutiny written on his face.

"Honestly?"

Samuel nodded.

"I do not really know," Alec said.

* * *

NATHAN HELD the mug of ale but was not brave enough to drink it.

He studied the people around him. Mostly what the gutters had spit back out with the rare gentlemen between them. The gentlemen were not ones that Nathan had ever seen. He wondered as to their reasons for being in such a dive. Then he remembered what he was wearing and wondered even more.

"Ye lookin' to 'ave some fun, sir?"

A skinny woman with little hair and less teeth bumped into him, sending ale out of the mug and onto the floor.

"No, thank you," Nathan said, creeping away.

He looked around the room again, seeing if there were three big blokes and one nasty little one with red hair grouped together anywhere. A haze of smoke clouded most of the occupants' heads, but Nathan kept looking anyway.

"Ye be searching a long time, sir, and still not find what quenches ye thirst."

Nathan looked over at the barkeep. "How is that?" he asked.

"What ye seek isn't here. This hole is merely a stopover on a much longer journey." He paused, filled a mug, and slid it down the length of the bar. "The final stop being Dover, o' course."

Nathan waited, leery to take the bait. Dover seemed too obvious, and the War Office had it crawling with agents now.

"But upstairs might slack ye thirst for now."

Nathan still did not move.

The man looked left and right before planting his grimy hands on the sticky bar and leaning in. "For God's sake, Nathan, get your ass upstairs, get the boy, and then get to Dover. Must I make myself more clear?"

Nathan almost dropped his mug.

"Wally?"

"Shh!" the man shot spittle from his grisly beard. "Gibbs, man, it's Gibbs here."

Nathan nodded, set down his mug, and walked away from the bar.

A tiny, red-haired man slouched in the corner, watched, and drank from a mug of ale.

* * *

"HE TRULY IS RATHER good at this sort of thing," Lady Stryden said, probably to reassure Nora, but she did not feel like being reassured.

Nora felt like being rather depressed. First Samuel was taken, and then Nathan went off after him to some dive by the river. She was not open to reassurance.

The Countess of Stryden had returned to the drawing room, rescuing Nora from her own torturous thoughts when the men had left for the gaming hell. The duke and duchess of Lofton had still not returned, and Nora could only imagine what two seasoned spies were discussing in private. Her mind was capable of conjuring up many things at the moment, and she was certain she could formulate an incredible story.

"Alec is not bad either, come to think of it," Sarah murmured, drawing Nora's attention.

Nora looked up at her. "Oh?"

"I am not talking about him," Sarah said firmly, moving briskly to refill her teacup. She held the pot up to Nora questioningly.

"Oh, no thank you. Any more and I may burst."

Sarah smiled and set the pot down.

"May I ask you a question, Sarah?" Nora asked.

Sarah sipped her tea and eyed her warily. "I suppose."

"Why do you dislike your husband so?"

Sarah set her cup back into the saucer. "I do not dislike him. I loathe him," she said.

Nora nodded. "Then why do you watch him so closely when you think no one is looking?"

Sarah choked on her tea, and Nora worried she had overstepped her boundaries. The borrowed gown was giving her a confidence she did not know, and it was going to get her into trouble. But there was something about the Earl and Countess of Stryden that upset Nora. And she wanted the matter resolved.

"I beg your pardon?" Sarah said, wiping her mouth with a napkin from the tea cart.

"You watch him," Nora said. "Like you are afraid he is suddenly going to leave. And you want to make sure you catch him, so you can stop him."

"Alec is not going to leave," Sarah said.

Nora smiled. "I never said he was."

Sarah set her cup on the table between them and leaned back to look at the ceiling.

Nora waited, listening to the fire in the hearth, studying the shelves of fine intricate China figurines that surrounded the drawing room, hearing the tick of the clock.

Finally, Sarah spoke. "He is going to leave, and I do not know when."

"How do you know?" Nora asked.

Sarah brought her head back down and looked at Nora. "He deserves better than an orphan for a wife."

"I beg your pardon?"

"I am an orphan. A whore's accident." Sarah swallowed with difficulty. "The offspring of whores do not marry earls."

"Why not?" Nora asked. She, of course, knew exactly what Sarah meant, but she wanted to hear Sarah say it.

"They just do not," she said, standing up to pace.

Nora watched her make a few passes before speaking again. "Why do you think that?"

Sarah did not stop to answer. "I just know it. It is what everyone tells you every day while you survive on porridge and Bible verses."

Nora did not know what to make of that statement, but for some odd reason, she thought she could relate. Nora said, "And you think everyone else is right?"

Sarah did stop now and faced Nora. "Everyone is right on this."

"I do not think so." Nora stood as well, walking over to Sarah. "I think you need to tell him."

"Tell him?" Sarah backed warily away.

"You need to tell your husband that you love him."

Sarah turned her back and walked to the other end of the room. "I beg your pardon, Miss Quinton, but I do not believe it is your place to give me advice regarding my relationship with my husband."

Nora swallowed, feeling a slight touch of misgiving creep up her spine.

"Oh, but someone must give you advice, darling, before you are both dead and unable to tell each other how you really feel."

Nora and Sarah looked at the door. Jane, on the arm of the Duke of Lofton, stood in the doorway. Nora looked back at Sarah in time to see the other woman's face go instantly red.

"I do not believe I understand what you are speaking of," she said, hurrying to sit in a chair, clearly so she could face the empty fireplace instead of the rest of the occupants in the room.

This time, the Duke of Lofton spoke. "We all know you two love each other. Why you cannot get along is anyone's guess, but it would help smooth the waters between our little group if you two would just get over it already. Love happens. You can deal with it. We all do."

Nora was surprised by the boldness of his words, but why she had expected anything different from a duke she did not know. The matter was quite simple. Sarah was in love with her husband but for some reason was unable to express it, which led to the situation the two were currently in. A kind of truce that was not all that pleasant for the people around them.

But Sarah continued to evade. "I believe the relationship between Alec Black, the Earl of Stryden, and myself is one of the strictest professionalism—"

"Oh, please, darling, you are fooling no one. But if this is the line you are going to carry, I shall not be bothered with it," Jane said, leaving Richard at the door as she swept into the room, taking a seat on the sofa before the vacant fireplace. "We have much more important matters to discuss at this moment." Jane busied herself with the tea things that littered the small table in the middle of the seating arrangement before looking at Nora. "Such as, what on Earth are you going to do when this is all over, Miss Quinton?"

Nora swallowed, no answer coming to her mind.

* * *

NATHAN AVOIDED TWO MORE PROSTITUTES, a man who mistook him for a prostitute, and two pickpockets. He found the stairs in the back, covered by a worn, red velvet curtain on gold hoops. He pushed the curtain aside and tried the first step. The board sagged dangerously but did not snap in two. Taking that as a good sign, Nathan deftly climbed the stairs, avoiding ominous stains and obvious holes in the wood.

The second floor smelled worse than the first. Nathan covered his mouth with his hand and willed his stomach to settle. A breeze twisted sneakily around his face, and he looked into the dimness to find its source. An open window was just to the left. Nathan dove for it, sticking his head into the darkening evening sky, and sucked in gulps of breath.

He really wanted a bath.

Alec was going to have to burn his clothes.

The door behind him opened, and Nathan spun around. A guttersnipe staggered out and right into Nathan. Nathan pushed him off before toppling through the window. He looked out the window to the ground. A large pile of garbage was just below the window. He wouldn't have been hurt had he actually fallen out and landed there. But rotting wooden crates sat just to the left that would have hurt very much. Nathan turned back.

A woman had appeared in the open doorway.

"Are ye next then?"

Nathan's stomach heaved again. "No, ma'am, I am not." He bowed to her and went to move away.

"Who are ye callin' 'ma'am,' ye snobby cad!" She moved out of the doorway, swinging her large, unrestrained bosom at him.

Nathan feinted to his right. Then someone grabbed him, and a door suddenly shut in his face. Nathan spun around, and Samuel was grinning at him.

"What?" Nathan asked.

"You look silly dressed like that." Samuel pointed at his garb.

"I suppose I do," he said, then stepped forward and scooped the boy up, pressing him tightly against him.

He felt Samuel stiffen slightly before relaxing. The boy did not embrace Nathan in return, but he did not push him away.

So Nathan held on.

Eventually, Alec cleared his throat. "Did that seem too easy to anyone else?"

"They wanted it that way," Samuel said, his voice muffled against Nathan's shoulder.

Nathan reluctantly set him down.

"I was just a tool to get all of your attention," he said, straightening his shirt carefully.

"I was told to stay out of it," Nathan said.

"I know you were. That was a trick."

Nathan frowned. "Fabulous."

"Perhaps we should get out of here first. Discuss later." Alec went to the door and popped his head into the hallway.

Nathan studied Samuel. "Are you all right?"

Samuel nodded. "Are you?"

Nathan nodded.

"Let's go," Alec said.

Nathan steered Samuel out first.

"Does anyone know how we get out of here?" Samuel asked.

"The back door?" Alec offered.

"Where is the back door?" Samuel asked.

Alec stopped, and Samuel walked into him.

Nathan looked up. Two beasts loomed at the other end of the hall. Nathan had to look up to see their faces, which were half covered by greasy beards filled with food particles. Their fists were clenched, their fat hands looking like small roasts at the end of logs.

Nathan stepped in front of Samuel.

"Which one of ye called me woman 'ma'am'?" one of the beasts spoke.

"He did." Alec pointed at Nathan without hesitation.

Nathan was still dressed as a gentleman, which did not work in his favor at all. One of the beasts stepped forward.

Nathan spun and grabbed Samuel. "Pardon me, mate," he said and tossed Samuel out the window.

CHAPTER 12

*S*amuel had never been thrown out of a window.

And he definitely had never been thrown into a pile of garbage.

His fingers squished into what had probably been a meat pie and maybe some neeps and tatties. He pulled his hand away and slid down the pile of muck.

His shoes hit the cobblestone, sending sharp staccatos ricocheting down the alley. He turned around and looked up at the window. He could not see anything. And worse, he could not hear anything.

Samuel began to worry.

It was full dark now, and he shivered in his thin shirt and short pants. He backed up against the building opposite The Four of Clubs. He still could not see into the window, and there was no sound to tell him what was happening. He squatted against the building, trying to absorb some heat from the bricks, and waited.

Samuel froze there, squatting by the gaming hell and waiting.

And Alec and Nathan still had not come out of The Four of Clubs.

He had to think. Panic was not going to help. He had to move, or he would be a block of ice in no time. So he stood, running his hands down his legs to work some initial circulation back into them. He walked around the back of the building, side to side.

There was no back door. A single basement window was caked solidly with grime. There were no first floor windows at the rear or back half of the sides of the building. There was only the second floor window from which he had been thrown.

He could go for help. Except he did not know where he was. He could hail a hack. But he doubted a hack would stop for a nine-year-old boy who looked like he had just rolled in the garbage because he had just rolled in the garbage.

He must go in the front door. He had to find Nathan and his brother. They were here for him, so it was up to him to find them.

Samuel squeezed between the buildings and watched the front door of The Four of Clubs from the alley. Two gentlemen in fine overcoats were going inside. Samuel waited, watching the end of the street, waiting for just the right person to walk by.

Ten minutes later, that person did. He was enormous and rolled more than walked down the street. As he passed the alley, Samuel slipped out behind him, hoping the man did not smell him. Then Samuel crossed his fingers, hoping the man was going to The Four of Clubs. His luck held, and the man pounded a jiggly fist on the door. It creaked open, words were exchanged, and the man moved inside. Samuel was right behind him and then darted to the side once he was in the smoke filled front hall of the hell.

The haze of smoke hung just above his head, making the way clear for him to move through the crowd. He was almost through when someone grabbed his arm. Samuel whirled with his fist up. It was a boy smaller than he, so he dropped his fist immediately.

The boy snarled, showing stained teeth. "This 'ere's me turf. Ye best be stayin' out o' it."

Samuel tipped his head. "I beg your pardon."

The boy snarled again and sauntered off, hitching up his baggy pants. Samuel watched him go, feeling sad for the boy. He turned back and continued to the far wall. He found the stairs and ran up them, but the hallway was empty when he reached it. New dark puddles were on the floor, looking suspiciously like blood. Samuel hoped it was not Nathan's blood.

He went back down the stairs and ran along the length of the wall. There was a small door beside the bar, but people were moving in and out, carrying trays of food. He watched and studied their movement. When there was a break, he dashed through the door.

And found the kitchens smelled worse than the garbage.

There were two large counters around which a skinny man cut slabs of meat. There were others milling around with empty trays. Everyone was talking at each other. Samuel was not sure if anyone was listening.

There was a blackened doorway to the right, and Samuel edged toward it. It was just a pantry stocked with smelly cheese. Samuel eased back behind some bags of grain, watching the people grumbling about one thing or another. And that was why he did not see the stairs before he fell down them.

But the landing was soft because he landed on Nathan, who grunted with the impact.

Samuel stood up quickly, apologizing. "I am so sorry, Nathan. Are you all right?"

But Nathan did not look all right. He had his eyes shut as black patches were forming all over his face. Blood was dried in a pool by his nose and mouth.

Samuel got on his knees. "Nathan, can you hear me? Nathan, are you all right? Nathan, are you alive?"

Someone else answered with a moan. Samuel looked over to see the Earl of Stryden in pretty much the same shape. He moved over to him.

"Mister... My l—" Samuel stopped, realizing he did not know the gentleman's proper name. "Alec, are you all right?"

There was no response this time.

Samuel was scared. A sudden burst of noise from above had him cowering back toward Nathan. He watched the man's chest rise and fall, became mesmerized by its movement. Nathan's eyes never opened. Samuel lay down next to him, curling into his warmth.

And then Samuel did something he had never done.

He cried.

* * *

"THEY SHOULD HAVE BEEN BACK by now."

Richard was talking to the empty fireplace again in the drawing room of Stryden Place. He could not remember what he had eaten for supper or what had been supper. He only recalled that his sons had left five hours before and should have returned three hours ago.

"They should have been back by now," he repeated going to sit in one of the chairs by the sofa only to get up and pace a few moments later.

Jane sat on the sofa, one arm around Sarah and the other

around Nora. Both women looked like they could break at the softest of breezes.

Richard walked to the window.

They should have been back by now. This was the only thought moving through his mind at that moment.

He went out into the hall to the front door. He stood on the front stoop listening to the sounds of the night. The air was cold, and he could see his breath. There was scant traffic on the street at this hour. Members of the ton would already be at the evening's festivities they had planned to attend and would not yet be returning home. No one had yet to return to Stryden Place.

He went back to the drawing room, shutting the door harder than he had to, and rang for Reynolds. The butler appeared before the last peal died.

"Your Grace?"

"Have my horse fetched," Richard said. He turned to the women. "I am going for help, and then I am going after them. No one is to leave this house, is that understood?"

The direction was only aimed at one lady, and that one lady knew it. Jane nodded in acknowledgement.

"Good," he said and strode out of the library to get his coat and hat.

The streets were nearly silent as he rode across town into the heart of Bloomsbury. The man he sought was of such a reputation as to be useful in going to such a gaming hell as the Four of Clubs. Upon reaching Amesbury Boarding House where the man in question rented a suite of bachelor's quarters, Richard tied up his horse and made his way inside the building.

Mr. Matthew Thatcher answered his knock in bare feet and no collar. Seeing as how it was ten o'clock on a Tuesday night, Richard did not scold him for the impropriety. He was also generous enough to give him a little leeway when it came to polite society as Mr. Thatcher was newly arrived from America. Some things had to be forgiven.

"Sorry to bother you, Thatcher, but I have a problem," he said by way of greeting, pausing far enough inside the door to allow Matthew to close it for propriety's sake. Thatcher often had the look of a supremely bored hound about his face, and tonight was no exception.

"Do I have time to get my boots on?" he asked.

Richard nodded. "It is rather a complicated tale. I think it best if we got on our way, and I shall explain then."

"Whatever suits you," Thatcher said, already grabbing up coat and hat to follow Richard back into the night.

Richard explained the situation to Matthew Thatcher along the way, giving only enough detail to complete the job at hand. Thatcher only sometimes worked for the War Office, and Richard was reluctant to provide too much information should Thatcher inadvertently become a liability.

The Four of Clubs looked as awful as Richard thought it would look. He was suddenly even more glad than every with his choice to fetch Matthew Thatcher. Thatcher was a private investigator of sorts by trade, and Richard knew he could trust him.

"Any plan, Your Grace?" Thatcher asked.

"Walk in, guns blazing. Is that not how you Americans do it?" Richard asked in reply.

"Yeah, that is usually how it goes. Should I have brought a gun?"

"Probably."

"Well, perhaps next time."

Thatcher slid down from his horse. He dropped the reins in the street and looked back at Richard. "Stay," he said and walked away toward The Four of Clubs.

Richard did not know if Thatcher meant that last command for him or the horse. Regardless, he dismounted, hailing a passing hack as he did so. He tied his horse to the back of the carriage and waited. He stomped his feet in the cold and blew on his hand. Thatcher's horse repeated the gesture behind him. Richard raised an eyebrow at the animal.

Thatcher had been gone for nearly seven minutes. Richard had watched two questionable pairs of gentleman exit the gaming hell and three pairs enter. The establishment seemed to be doing a fair amount of business that evening. Richard waited, hoping his sons would be the next pair of questionable gentlemen to come through the door.

And then they were.

Richard went forward, approaching Nathan first as he carried a bundle in his arms. He was not surprised to find that it was Samuel, huddled into Alec's fine coat. He carried the boy to the hack and set him inside.

"I will take you home now," Richard said, before getting out of the carriage. He faintly heard Samuel repeat the word "home."

Nathan and Alec crawled into the hack but not before Richard noted their various cuts and bruises. What they had encountered inside the gaming hell was surely not at all what they had expected.

Richard turned to shake Thatcher's hand.

"I owe you now, Matthew."

"Put it on my tab," Thatcher said, then mounted his horse and disappeared into the blackness.

Richard got into the hack with his boys.

* * *

NORA HAD ENDURED eighteen hours of mind numbing, fist clenching, body ripping labor to bring Samuel into the world.

That pain came nowhere near to what she was feeling now.

And if that pain did not end soon, she was going to die from it.

No one spoke. Sarah was near to ripping apart the needlepoint cushion on the sofa. Jane had her head thrown back on the chair, her eyes closed. Nora stared out the window, but the darkness only cast her own reflection back until a hackney blotted it out as it pulled up to the curb in front of the house.

Nora ran from the drawing room. She pulled up her skirts far beyond propriety and ran. She was out the front door and down the stoop just as Nathan was coming out of the hack, her son in his arms. She only took a moment to notice the terrible condition he was in before she threw herself at both of them, wrapping them with the force of the pain she had been experiencing only moments earlier. Nathan awkwardly put one arm around her, holding onto Samuel with the other, and squeezed them all until breath became something to fight for.

"Do not ever scare me like that again," Nora said.

Nathan squeezed harder.

Alec had seen Nora fly down the stairs. Had seen the length of stocking exposed from the height to which she had hiked her skirts to get that momentum. Had seen the emotion that she now used to embrace the two people who meant so much to her. He felt worse than ever, and it was not because of the damage to his body.

He stepped down from the carriage and started to the door. And Sarah crashed into him. He reeled, catching his balance at the last moment. Sarah crushed him, and he had never felt anything so wonderful. But then she pushed away and started yelling at him.

"You scared me, Alec Black, and I will not stand for it."

185

She pulled back her fist and swung at him. She was crying though, and her tears blinded her aim. Alec thanked God himself because he had been on the receiving end of one of Sarah's blows more than once. Now he grabbed the wobbling fist and drew his wife back against him, letting her head fall to his shoulder as she cried.

CHAPTER 13

"*D*id you really throw my son out a second story window into a pile of garbage?"

Nathan dropped the soap as he jumped in the bathtub. He swung his head around as his hands scrambled to cover the essential parts.

"Nora! For God's sake, woman." He slipped as far down into the tub as he could get.

"Do not get modest on me now, Nathan Black," she said, taking a step farther into the room but remaining at a proper distance. "I asked you a question. Samuel tells me you threw him out of a window. Into garbage," she said the last bit with far more emphasis.

Richard and Jane had insisted that Nora and Samuel stay at their residence in Mayfair and even though it had been nearly midnight, they had made the journey across the park with an utterly exhausted Samuel and an equally as emotional Nora. Nathan had not bothered to mention that he felt like the pavement itself, trod on by millions without so much as a care. Upon arriving at the Lofton home, Jane had immediately ordered a bath for Samuel, and for Nathan,

although this was an afterthought, and had promptly led
Nora and Samuel away. Richard had demanded a debriefing
in the library, which Nathan reluctantly gave, his mind
wandering to the bath he knew was waiting above stairs.

And Nora and Samuel.

He wondered if the boy was all right. He had been quiet
for the entire ride back to Stryden Place, saying little more
since reuniting with his mother. Nathan was fairly certain
the boy had not been abused in any way, nor had he been
threatened. But Nathan still understood that kidnapping was
a trauma within itself. It would probably take a bit of time
for the boy to come fully around.

But why that led to Nora entering his chambers without
so much as a by your leave, he could not fathom.

"Yes, I did throw him out of a window, and I do believe
there was a pile of garbage beneath said window. Is that all,
madam?"

Nora frowned.

"Do not dismiss me so easily, Nathan. Samuel is calling
the entire night quite an adventure, but I do not see how a
kidnapping can be deemed an adventure. What else did you
do to my son that he is not telling me?"

Now Nathan did smile, even though it was clear that
Nora was concerned.

"He is calling it an adventure? I feel it necessary to warn
you that he may be excellent spy material."

Nora frowned harder. "Do not tease me, Nathan. Was
Samuel all right when you found him?"

Nathan tried pressing his legs tighter together as water
sloshed around him in the tub.

"He seemed quite all right. And Alec found him initially.
Alec said he seemed quite aware for a nine-year-old, but that
he seemed fine despite what was happening to him."

Nora's face began to relax, and her fisted hands, which

had been resting at her hips, slowly slid down her body. "Very well," she said almost in a murmur, and she began to turn as if to go, but something stopped her. "If Samuel was fine, whatever happened to you?"

Nathan wanted to see just how far down in the tub he could get. "There was an altercation," he said.

Nora raised a questioning eyebrow. "Altercation?'

Nathan nodded.

"What was the cause of such an altercation?"

"I showed respect to the wrong woman."

"Interesting," was all Nora said before she pointed a finger at him. "Are you almost done there?"

Nathan looked down at his increasingly uncomfortable essentials.

"Perhaps," he said.

"Very well. I shall return momentarily."

He almost came up out of the tub. "I beg your pardon?" he said.

The very last thing he needed that evening was to have Eleanora Quinton in his rooms in the middle of the night. The whole situation smacked of impropriety and that only led him to want it more.

"You will need someone to apply witch hazel to those bruises. You do not expect to do so yourself, do you? You are not in any condition to be administering aid to your person."

That may have been true, but Nathan could think of many other persons who would be better suited at that moment. Such as Napoleon himself.

"I suppose so," Nathan finally said.

"Good. Get out of that tub and dry off. I shall return," she said as she left the chamber, closing the door softly behind her with a subtle, authoritative click.

* * *

SHE COULD DO THIS. She could. Really.

But she had not been shaking before like she was now. Before when she had brazenly entered Nathan's chambers in Lofton's home to demand an explanation as to why her son smelled of garbage. And it was only then that she realized she had received no explanation beyond admittance to the truth and a declaration of having had quite an adventure. Much the same line Samuel had delivered. Nora frowned, wondering if the two were in cahoots.

But now, she shook, honestly and truly. How was she going to be able to put the witch hazel cream on his face without poking him in the eye or something?

And really, what had propelled her to offer such assistance in the first place? It was a natural reaction she knew, to take action when action was needed. And Nathan obviously needed assistance. But why had she been the one to offer? She was the guest in a duke's home, and it was nearly the middle of the night if not creeping into the early morning, and she was traipsing about like a trollop instead of heeding the rules of polite society. She should never have gone into Nathan's room, but Samuel's gleeful proclamation of being tossed in the garbage had riled her motherly instincts enough to hang propriety and its rules. She had marched into Nathan's room, heedless of the fact that he was likely bathing and indeed, was, and demanded to know something. But offering to apply witch hazel to his bruises was a step too far even for her. Or especially for her.

Nora was getting flustered.

She checked on Samuel, sleeping like the dead in the middle of the gigantic bed that took up almost half of their bedchamber. Their bedchamber was conveniently located just down the hall from Nathan's, and Nora wondered not for the first time if Jane had done that on purpose. Jane had offered them separate bedchambers at first, but Nora would not sleep in a different room from her son that night. Not when she had just gotten him back. And now he slept. Red satin covers were pulled up to his chin with one arm thrown over his head, the other flung out at his side.

Nora paced the bedroom, stalling. The tub of witch hazel a maid had left on the night stand for Samuel's bruises went from one hand to the other. How long did it take for one to get dried off and decent? Had she waited long enough? Had she waited too long?

She stepped forward, grabbed the knob, and tripped through the door into the hallway.

The house was silent. Eerily so. But Nora kept her back straight and carefully shut the door on her sleeping son. She moved carefully down the carpeted hall, her slippered feet silent. The skirts of her borrowed gown barely swished in the stillness. She reached Nathan's door and knocked lightly, not wanting to wake the house. He responded with an equally modest *Enter*, and Nora went inside Nathan's rooms in the middle of the night in a house in which she did not live.

Nathan stood by the fire, a slightly worn silk dressing gown flickering in the light. He turned when she came in, and she had to swallow. He looked terrible, but somehow he still made her stomach turn over.

Pulling her shoulders back, she marched over to him.

"Sit." She pointed to the wingback in front of the fire.

He raised an eyebrow at her. "Is that going to hurt?"

She giggled and covered her mouth with her hand.

Nathan reached up and drew her hand away.

"Don't. I like to see you laugh."

Nora blushed and had to look at her feet. At this rate, she was never going to finish what she had started. She was going to melt into a puddle at his feet.

Nathan released her hand, sat down, and waited. She

unscrewed the lid of the jar and set it aside. Dipping her fingers into the cream, she studied it scrupulously, so she would not have to look at him. This was ridiculous. She set the jar aside too, and with two fingers covered in cream, she attacked his face.

The worst of the bruising was along his jaw and one of his eyes. The swelling had not gotten too bad. It was puffy and tender, but he could still see out of it. She carefully smeared the cream over it, willing her fingers not to shake.

She stood back and surveyed her work. "There. I think that will help."

"Good," Nathan said. And then he grabbed her.

She was in his lap with his lips bruising hers before she realized what he had done. But thinking about what he had done was nowhere near as enjoyable as thinking about what he was doing.

She was on fire.

That was the only thing she could think. His lips seared hers, his hands pulled her closer, tearing at the fabric that stood between her and him. Then his lips nudged hers open, and his tongue dipped into her mouth. She heard someone moan and thought it was very likely her. She did not want to be the only one moaning.

She lifted her hands and speared them through his hair, running her nails along the skin at his neck and along his shoulders. And then he did moan, and she would have smiled, but her mouth was busy.

She became aware of a hand on her leg, underneath her skirt, working on the tie of her stocking. She broke her mouth away.

"It's double knotted," she said, and reached over, batting his hand away. She tugged on just the right strand, and the bow came loose, her stocking sliding down her leg.

"Thank you," he said, plunging his hand down the length

of the stocking and drawing it and her slipper away.

"You are quite welcome." And then she pulled his mouth back to hers.

But there was no way she was going to let him touch bare skin when she could not. She ran a hand up the part in his robe, feeling the crispness of the hair that sprinkled his chest, shocked at the sensation, at the fact that this was happening. She kept going, running her fingers under the silk and pushing it away from his shoulder.

And it was when she touched his bare skin that she realized what was happening, realized it and did not believe it.

The bodice of her gown suddenly felt looser but not quite loose enough. She sat up.

"There is a catch," she said, dragging her mouth once again from Nathan's.

She reached over her head and slipped the hook from the eye at the neckline of the gown.

Nathan tore the bodice away and plundered. His mouth blazed kisses along her exposed shoulder, slipping the strap of her shift away from her collarbone, so he could devour that, too. Nora's head fell back as she was no longer able to hold it up. He placed kisses along the lacy edge of the shift but never strayed any lower. And his hands remained on the bunched fabric of her bodice, never touching her where she longed to be touched.

Finally it got to be too much, and she snapped her head up.

"Nathan, please."

She grabbed his hand and placed it directly on her breast and reeled when Nathan's face turned white as the blood drained from it. And then his hand squeezed, and all thought fled.

She tore at his robe now, dragging both arms out from it and letting it slip down to his waist. She ran her hands down the smooth, tight skin of his back as Nathan's lips finally dared to go lower. Her shift was hanging off of her shoulders now, so she lifted her arms out of the straps and let the material fall away.

Nathan sat up, moving his hands away from her. "Nora, I do not want to—"

"I know, Nathan." She touched the part of his face that was not bruised. "I know, but I want you to. I want to know how good it feels before I remember how bad it felt. Please, Nathan."

He swallowed, and Nora watched the movement, pleading with her eyes.

And then Nathan nodded. He lifted her, and Nora grabbed at his shoulders to hang on. She felt his robe dislodge and fall away, a slight little thrill passing through her at the thought that he was completely and totally naked. Nathan laid her on the rug before the fire, pulling down some cushions from the sofa and pushing them under her head.

"All right?" he asked.

Nora could see the tension in Nathan's face, and she smiled, as warmly and as brightly as she ever had. Nathan slowly smiled back at her. She opened her arms, and he came into them.

He did not crush her. He kept his weight a delicious presence somewhere above her. He pulled at the remainder of her clothing, taking more care not to frighten her, which made her tingle even more. And then he was kissing her again, but with tenderness, and not the jarring emotion of just moments before. His hands were everywhere, sweeping down her sides and back up. And then his mouth was dipping lower, to her collarbone, lower, finally, to the underside of her breast. She bucked beneath him, surprised that her hips moved without her knowing they would or could.

She felt Nathan's smile against her tender flesh just before he drew her nipple into his mouth. She clawed at his back, pressing him closer.

But he was moving again before she could savor what he had done. He was above her, sweeping the hair from the sides of her face.

"Nora, I want to be sure. I want you to be sure. You really want to do this."

There was pain in his eyes, pain of uncertainty, pain of longing, and Nora brought her hands up to his face, mimicking his touch.

"Yes, I am sure. I want to do this with you."

The thought would have startled her had she known she had been thinking it all along, but there in that moment, it just seemed right. It just seemed like destiny that she was lying there in Nathan's arms.

Nathan groaned and kissed her, before going back to first one breast and then the other. Nora squirmed beneath him, and Nathan chuckled. The sound fluttered over her stomach, making her giggle.

Nora brought her legs up, running the heel of her foot along his calf, felt the muscles ripple in response.

Nathan was doing something to her neck, that spot just behind her ear. And then he was in front of her again, framing her face with his hands.

"Are you still all right?"

Nora nodded because she could not speak.

"All right. Um, I am going to—"

Nora nodded, cutting him off. Her stomach had stopped fluttering, and the first icy fingers of fear were starting to creep out. She grabbed Nathan's face and kissed him, kissed him with all she had in her. He broke off the contact, moving his lips to her ear.

"It's all right," he whispered. "It's all right."

And then she felt another part of him, pushing at her. She remembered something else pushing at her.

"Nathan," she whimpered. "Hurry."

Nathan kissed her and pushed all the way into her.

She was on the floor. It was hard against her back. The side of her face that he had struck was numb. He ripped at her pants. She fought him as instinct rebounded. Her fingers bled from scratching at him. Her head pounded. He struck her again. Her hands fell away, her strength to hold them up gone. He was pushing at her. She pleaded with him to stop. He laughed at her. The sound ricocheted in her head. Sensation was blissfully fading. He tore her from the inside.

"Nathan," she gasped, surfacing sharply.

"That's it, Nora. Open your eyes. Look at me."

Nathan was above her, brushing away the tears that she did not know stained her cheeks.

"It's me, Nora. Nathan. You are safe. I am not hurting you."

"Oh, Nathan."

Nathan was no longer inside of her. She felt that almost instantly. There was a quilt covering her, wrapped tightly around her body, and Nathan had his robe on again. She felt cold.

"Oh, Nathan, I am sorry. I am so, so sorry," she whimpered as if she were a lost little girl.

Nathan bent his head, shushing her, and softly kissing her lips. "This is not your fault," he said.

Nora struggled with the quilt and pulled her arms out, wrapping them around Nathan and drawing him closer. She held on as Nathan lay on his back, pulling her against his side.

He held her until the tears finally stopped. And although he had not said a word, she could feel the tension in him. She could feel his reluctance to let her suffer the hurt in her memories. She felt his helplessness in the way his arms remained stiff around her. She recalled the dark look that sometimes crossed his features, his own pain, and she wanted him to know that this was not his fault. That this was something she would need to conquer.

"I was nineteen," she finally said, "Head of the upstairs maids." She cleared her throat. "I was putting out the new set of towels for each of the guests in the east wing. I did not know he was in the dressing room."

She listened for a moment to Nathan's heartbeat below her ear before going on.

"He locked the door and put the key in his pocket. He was smiling, a cruel, mean smile. He struck me once across the face, and I fell. I never got back up."

Her voice got stuck as her throat closed. Nathan's arms tightened around her, but the stiffness remained.

"He pushed up my skirts and ripped my pants. I scratched at his face until I drew blood, but he just struck me again. I do not remember much after that. There was just a lot of pain." She swallowed. "And then Michael, the stableman, was shaking me awake. The floor was covered in blood. My blood. And my first thought was I had to get it cleaned up quickly."

Her voice disappeared then, so she just stopped talking.

The fire crackled in the hearth beyond them. She watched the flames shorten and grow. She rubbed her cheek against Nathan's chest, liking the scrape of skin against skin. But still, his embrace was tight with a pain she could not name.

"Who was he, Nora?" Nathan asked after a while.

"No, Nathan." She shook her head against him. "I will not tell you more. This is a burden you needn't carry."

"Who was it, Nora?" he asked again, an edge she had never heard in his voice before.

She leaned up on her elbow to look him in the face. The

darkness was there, and she suddenly grew tired of not knowing what caused his pain.

"No, Nathan. It does not matter who he was. He's a horrible human being, and that is punishment enough. I do not care what he did to me, because I got Samuel. And now —" Her voice was disappearing on her again, but she pushed it out. "And now I have you."

Nathan nodded. "Yes, you have me."

She leaned down and gently touched his lips with hers. "Then I have everything I need. Except—"

Nathan's expression remained dark even as she went on.

"What is this about?" she said, drawing her hand down the side of his face. "Sometimes there is such sadness in you, and I do not know why."

Nathan made a move as if to get up, and Nora stopped him, her hand firmly on his chest.

"I told you my pain. Now you must tell me yours," she said, refusing to let him slip away from her. "It is only fair."

Nathan's head relaxed against the floor as his eyes drifted to the ceiling. When she thought he would simply ignore her for the rest of the night, he finally spoke.

"Jane," he said, and Nora waited, knowing there must be more. "Jane's first husband was..." his voice trailed off, but Nora knew enough to finish the sentence for him.

"Jane's first husband abused her," she said.

Nathan brought his gaze back to hers, the darkness suddenly receding from his gaze.

"You know?" he asked, and Nora nodded.

"She told me once. It was one of the times she told me stories of you as a little boy, and how grateful she always was that Richard came into her life. She loves you and Alec very much, Nathan."

Nathan's face was a mask of confusion, but Nora did not understand what was so troubling to him.

"Jane told you about...him?"

The last word came out as if Nathan were afraid to speak it.

Nora nodded. "Of course, she did. It is something in the past, Nathan. The past can no longer hurt us unless we let it."

Nathan sat up. The motion was so abrupt Nora would have lost her balance had Nathan not grabbed her by the shoulders.

"Jane...talks to you about these things?"

Nora nodded. "She once told me that the only way she got through her first marriage was seeing you and Alec. She called you her boys. She said no matter how difficult it was, she would keep moving forward because you simply delighted her."

Nathan did not speak. He merely sat, staring at her as if she had suddenly grown another head. So she continued.

"Jane could not have children, Nathan. That was likely one of the reasons her husband was so abusive. Jane could not fulfill her duties as a wife, but the man was already stuck in the bargain so to speak. He was an earl, I think. To have no heir for the title is quite upsetting, I know, but not so upsetting that one's wife deserves to be beaten."

Nathan still did not speak, and Nora grew worried.

"Did you know how much you meant to Jane? How much you still do?"

Nathan finally blinked, finally spoke, but his words did not make sense.

"I thought I could not help," he said.

Nora frowned.

"What do you mean?"

"I saw Jane after...her husband would beat her. She was always so sad, and her skin was mottled with bruises. I would see it, and I would hate it, and I would hate it even more that I could not help her."

Nora finally understood and smiled, raising a gentle hand to his own bruised face.

"You did help, Nathan. You helped by bringing joy into her life."

Nathan's face relaxed, although he did not quite smile or even return to the jovial Nathan she was growing used to seeing. But it was better than the perplexed and disbelieving Nathan of moments before.

"And you helped me, and you helped Samuel. More than you can imagine."

Nathan pulled her against his chest, his arms wrapping so tightly about her, the breath rushed from her lungs.

"I need you, Nathan," she whispered as she could not get the breath to speak louder.

"I need you, too, Nora," he said, and the most incredible feeling of warmth flooded through her.

Eventually, she pushed back.

"Then you need me well rested and ready for whatever is going to happen next, because although I have my Samuel back, I have a feeling this is not over."

Nathan shook his head. "I am afraid you would be right."

He stood and helped her up. She kissed him one more time and drew away to gather her discarded clothing. Nathan helped her put her shift back on. He found her slippers and her stockings. Together, they buttoned the gown enough for her to be decent during the short dash back to her own bedchamber.

"Good night, Mr. Black," she said with her hand on the knob, looking over her shoulder as the firelight danced across Nathan's soft smile.

"Good night, Miss Quinton," he returned, and then she let herself out of the bedchamber, slipping into the darkness beyond.

* * *

THREE BLOCKS over and across the park in the Earl of Stryden's townhouse, Sarah reassured herself that she was just going to check on him. That was a normal, everyday occurrence. It was a humanitarian act, really. From one person to another, a show of concern was typical. Even from an orphan to an earl.

Oh, right.

Sarah adjusted the tie on her dressing gown for the fifth time and knocked resolutely on the door. When Alec said, "Enter," she jumped. Breathe. She had to breathe. And she had to open the door and go in.

He was sitting on the sofa staring at an empty fireplace. The room was cold, and she rubbed her arms. She took only two steps inside, staying behind Alec's line of vision. She had suddenly lost her nerve.

"What is it, Sarah?" Alec asked, without looking back at her.

He, too, wore a dressing gown, but his feet were bare. She shivered in cold for him.

"Sarah?"

"I was just seeing if you were all right," she whispered, knowing he could not possibly have heard her.

"What?" Alec asked, finally turning around. And then he stood, a look of concern on his face as he came toward her. "Sarah, what is wrong?"

She knew she was shaking, and she knew she could probably tell him it was the cold. But she did not want to tell him it was the cold.

"I am cold," she whispered though, unable to say more.

"Is that all?" he asked, studying her face.

"Yes," she lied. "How are you feeling?"

"Fine," he answered too quickly for her.

"Are you sure?" She saw where the bruises had darkened to a dull purple on his cheeks and jaw.

"Yes." He walked away to pour a glass of liquor that he did not drink from. He walked back to the sofa and sat, still holding the glass, still not drinking.

"Good night, Sarah," he said.

He was dismissing her. And her hand was on the door-knob before she realized she was not going to be dismissed. She strode over to the couch, sat next to him, and stole the glass of liquor. She drank it in one gulp that burned the entire way down. She did not cough. She would not cough. And she kept her eyes shut so he would not see the tears the burning had brought on. He had seen too many tears from her tonight.

"Christ, Sarah, that was a lot of whiskey. I am not made of money, you know." He took the empty glass away from her.

When she was sure the tears had stopped and the burning was only a glow in her stomach, she looked at him. He was looking back at her. So she just leaned forward and kissed him.

He did not respond, so she tilted her head and kissed harder, bringing her hand up to pull at the back of his neck. He still did not respond, so she bit him.

"Ow!" Alec pushed her away, and she almost fell off the sofa.

Tears stung her eyes again, so she stood and walked to the door before he could see them.

She did not make it.

He grabbed her and spun her around, kissing her harder than she had been kissing him, bruising her lips. She dug her fingers into his back until she was sure he felt it and sure that it hurt. He pulled on her hair, arching her neck, so he could bite kisses along the length of it. He bit harder on her collarbone, and she retaliated by biting his ear.

He pulled away, bent to stick his shoulder into her stomach, and then lifted her up. He carried her from the library to the stairs.

"What are you doing?" she screeched.

He did not answer. He went up the stairs as if he were not carrying another human being over his shoulder at all. At the top, they turned right and not left. He was taking her to her room. Her stomach clenched, and a burning began low, flaming up through her.

Alec kicked open her door and threw her on the bed. She bounced so hard she almost fell off. She grabbed at the quilt and struggled to sit up. Her robe came loose, and her nightgown was tangled high around her thighs. Alec shut the door, and the sound of the lock clicking into place split the silence.

She backed up against the pillows, slipping on the satin of the shams. He came towards her, slowly, as if he had all the time in the world. Her eyes would not move from his face. And then he was kneeling on the bed bedside her. He reached out a single finger and brushed it along the length of exposed thigh.

"Beautiful," he said, just before he attacked her.

Before she realized, Sarah grabbed handfuls of the quilt and dug her heels into the bed. Her hips came up off the mattress, driving her into Alec.

"Shh, not so fast," Alec said.

Not so fast?

Her robe was long gone, and her nightgown was barely still on. Her hair had come loose from its braid and was splayed across the pillows. Alec kissed the tender skin behind her knee and kept going up the inside of her thigh. That was when she had bolted off the mattress. But that had not stopped him, and he was still making his way farther up, closer to the spot that ached for him. But as much as she wanted him there, she did not want him there. The sooner he reached it, the sooner he would be done with her and leave.

But finally, he did reach it. She grabbed his head, not sure if she was pushing him closer or pulling him away. He sucked and nibbled and drove her crazy. The ache was building, growing, changing. She did not know what was happening.

She said his name, but maybe she did not. She was not sure if she could speak.

The ache was building to something, something she was sure was almost there, but then he stopped. She opened her eyes, forgetting when she had shut them, and he was there above her. He traced the outline of her lips before lowering his mouth to hers. His hand disappeared. Suddenly it was between her legs, cupping her, stroking her, and her hips moved against it. He slipped a single finger into her, then another, still stroking. Now she did say his name, but it was against his mouth and did not really sound like anything at all.

She grabbed the wrist of the hand that was torturing her just as she exploded. She pushed herself more urgently against that hand as her body shook with the force of the blast. The spasms went on forever, flowing from one end of her body to the other.

When she finally opened her eyes, Alec was smiling down at her. She smiled back with energy she did not know she had. She reached a hand toward him, but he slid off the bed before she could reach him.

She sat up, suddenly frightened, and that was when she realized he was still wearing his robe. He straightened it as he walked toward the door.

"Alec?" she said, her voice soft and shaky.

Alec stopped after he turned the lock.

"Good bye, Sarah," he said.

And left.

CHAPTER 14

*N*athan was fairly certain the only thing that made him get out of bed the next morning was the thought of seeing Nora at breakfast.

It was hard to imagine that he had only known her for little more than a week, but he also knew there was something greater than themselves working between them. There was the sense that, whatever it was they were feeling, it was meant to have happened. Meant to have existed. And there was nothing they could do to get in its way.

And what she had told him last night, about Jane, about how Jane had always thought of him and Alec during those years of her first marriage, it seemed somehow right that Nora would ease his feelings of guilt. He was not certain what it meant, or even if it were enough to lift the guilt he had been carrying for years. The guilt of not being able to help Jane when she needed help most. But if he had truly brought her joy at that time in her life, then that was something.

But Nathan still felt awful that morning, and there were many valid reasons for this.

The first of which was the floor. Whoever said making love on a rug before a fire was romantic deserved to be shot. Nathan was intimately aware of every muscle from the top of his head to the heels of his feet. He just hoped that Nora felt better. He would feel like a complete idiot if their first attempts at lovemaking had left her with a sore back from the floor.

The second reason he felt awful was that Nora had spent the night in a bed without him and would probably continue to do so for some time. Last night had made it obvious that Nora's scars ran deeper than he had imagined. When she had retreated to that dark place in her head, his insides had frozen. It was not a sensation he was familiar with, but he had recognized it immediately. He suddenly could not feel his extremities, and he was not sure he could control them. He had rolled off of her, grabbed the quilt from the sofa, and stuffed it around her before grabbing his own robe. But she was still there, in the past, when he had finally come back to her. And he had not known what to do. He had not known how to help her.

The feeling paralyzed him, and even now, thinking of it in the light of day, his stomach still churned. Why was it that he always felt inadequate around women he cared for?

But Nora had helped herself. His name was the first thing she had said, coming to on the floor beneath him. She had latched onto him, used him as a buoy to save her from scary, turbulent waters. And if he were her buoy, he would stay her buoy for as long as she needed. Had she not told him that she needed him? That would have to be enough.

He looked at the door to the hallway as he pulled on his other boot. He had not heard the occupants of the chamber down the hall get up this morning, but it was still fairly early. So he stood and left the sitting room.

And was surprised to find Nora stumbling out of the

door down the hall. She caught herself against the opposite wall and stood a moment, blinking dazedly.

Nathan watched from his own open door, both confused and delighted. Miss Quinton was not infallible this morning.

"Nora."

She jumped and turned toward him, her hand coming up to her mouth to stifle whatever noise had been about to emerge. Her hair was pinned up in a bun but looser than she normally wore. And the gown from the day before had been replaced with an emerald one. This gown was a touch more demure, but it still sent Nathan's heart racing with the way it sent sparks through her hair and turned her eyes into pools of pulsating color.

And she was smiling.

"Good morning, Nathan," she whispered and pointed at the door. "Samuel's still sleeping."

She tiptoed toward him, and a hot thrill spiraled through him.

Her arms slipped around him, and her head fell back, her eyes shut.

He kissed her before whatever mood had overcome her disappeared. He let his hands stray down to her buttocks and pulled her closer. A moan came from deep in her throat, and she wiggled even closer. Nathan was hard in an instant and wrenched Nora away from him. He pulled in deep breaths holding onto Nora's shoulders to keep upright.

And then Nora giggled.

He glowered at her. "This is not funny."

She turned serious instantly. "I know, Nathan."

She brought her hands up to take his in her grip. She was not wearing gloves, and the skin on the backs of her hands was raw under his callused fingertips. He felt a little of the fire die in him. He wanted to take care of her. He wanted it so much.

"Nathan?"

He drew her back to him, cradling her softly. She laid her head on his chest, tucking it carefully under his chin. They stood just like that as the grandfather clock ticked somberly somewhere behind them.

"I slept," she said after a few ticks. "I slept a lot."

Nathan felt a grin, and--

The front door flew open, banging against the wall, and someone screamed hysterically, "Nora!"

The sound shot up the stairs from the front foyer and smashed into them, making both of them jump.

"Nora!"

Nathan pushed her toward the stairs, following two steps behind her.

Downstairs in the foyer, Sarah was frantically tearing at her hat and gloves. Her hands shook so badly neither of them would come off. Her hair was in complete disarray from all the tugging. Tears were pouring out of her eyes as her cheeks blotched with red.

Nora ran to her and dragged her into her arms.

Sarah was mumbling, and Nathan could not understand a word. But Nora held onto the woman, rubbing her back and making cooing noises to her as if to soothe her.

Richard and Jane appeared on the stairs above him, both still in their dressing gowns, just as Samuel slipped under Nathan's arm, rumpled from sleep. Nathan pulled him closer as they watched Sarah hysterically crying in Nora's embrace.

Sarah reared back once and shouted at Nora, "He left! He left! Do you understand that? He left!"

And she dissolved. She collapsed right there, and Nathan sprinted to catch her, knowing in his gut that he was going to kill his little brother even as confusion as to what had happened still lingered. He scooped her up and carried her into the library.

"Send for tea, Richard," Jane said behind him.

Richard grumbled, "She is going to need something a bit stronger than tea, I think."

Nora sat on the sofa, cradling Sarah's head in her lap, stroking her messy hair away from her face. Sarah had stopped sobbing, the tears now sliding soundlessly down her cheeks and into her hair. Nora kept silent. Nathan kept silent. Samuel kept silent.

And Richard poured Sarah a tumbler of whiskey while Jane fussed with a teacart, from where, Nathan could not say.

He stood behind the sofa with Samuel under his arm feeling as uncomfortable as a nun in Madame Hort's House of Leisure.

He was definitely going to kill Alec.

And he was going to enjoy it.

"He just left," Sarah mumbled now, the words soft and without context, confusing.

"He left? Did he leave willingly?" Nora asked just as quietly.

Sarah shook her head in her lap. "He left me. And I cannot find him," she said before her eyes closed and her breathing evened out.

Finally, Sarah slept.

* * *

NORA EASED out from under her head, replacing her lap with pillows. Jane covered her with a quilt, and they left the library, the tea growing cold on the cart and the whiskey untouched in its glass.

"Where the bloody hell did he go, and why would he go there, the bastard!" Richard roared as soon they reached the morning room.

Nora sat heavily on one of the chairs, which brought

Nathan quickly up behind her, clearly worried. His hand was tense on her shoulder. She smoothed it with one of her own.

"Nathan's the bastard, dear," Jane said, also taking a seat.

A maid scampered in, setting dishes on the sideboard. Nora smiled in reflex. The maid shyly smiled back and scampered out faster than she had scampered in. Nora wondered for a moment how she really felt, sitting there as maids bustled about her.

"She was afraid he was going to leave," Nora said into the sudden silence, "and he did."

"But where would he go?" Jane asked.

Samuel, who was once again under Nathan's arm as if he had become permanently fixed there, said, "Maybe he went to Dover."

"Why would he go to Dover?" Richard asked.

"Because they told him to," Samuel replied.

Nathan nodded, his grip on Nora's shoulder tightening so that she almost winced. "Wally's been placed as the barkeep at The Four of Clubs. He told me to go to Dover."

Richard frowned. Deeply. "What's in Dover besides half the War Office?"

Nathan shrugged.

Nora pried his hand loose and wove her fingers through his, her shoulder throbbing with relief.

"And why would someone who is shooting at Nora and kidnapping her son be telling us to go to Dover?" Jane asked.

"Are they all connected?" Nathan countered.

"I think so," Richard said.

A different maid came in carrying more dishes to the sideboard, and Nora smiled again. This maid blanched and almost dropped the dishes before running out.

Nora turned back to the conversation. "But how are they connected?"

Nathan sat down, bringing a startled Samuel onto his lap.

Nora watched Samuel's face register shock and squelch panic. And then he started to settle into Nathan's lap, and Nora wanted to smile.

"Let's start at the beginning," Nathan said. "I shoot the wrong man."

Richard shook his head. "It started before that. It started with the conversation Nora overheard."

Nora felt the bile rise in her throat as she stared at her son. "It may have started before that."

Everyone looked at her, and Nathan's fingers clenched in her grip.

"What haven't you told us?" Richard's voice had gotten smoother, fatally smoother.

Nora swallowed. She could do this. She looked at her son. She had to do this.

Nora looked at Nathan and said, "The Duke of Chesterfield."

* * *

Nathan had been shot once. It had hurt. Tremendously. But the white hot fire that was the pain of being shot was not anything he could compare to the feeling he got just then.

He was scorched in half by a blazing fire iron.

And only Nora's strong grip on his fingers kept the halves from falling to the floor.

"The Duke of Chesterfield?" Richard asked.

"The Duke of Chesterfield," Jane said, her mouth hanging slightly open.

Samuel burrowed deeper into Nathan, and Nathan pulled him closer. Samuel's heart beat rapidly against Nathan's chest, and he felt the two burnt halves of himself meld back together.

Now he was ready to the kill the man who had raped the woman Nathan feared he was starting to love.

"You have reason for revenge," Nathan said.

Nora nodded.

"Reason enough to tattle. To spy, even," Jane said.

Nora nodded.

Richard sat down. "I think I am missing something," he said.

Nathan turned Samuel to look at him.

"Cover your ears," he said.

Samuel looked at him.

"Just do it," Nathan said.

Samuel responded almost immediately, his look of wonderment casting about the room.

Nathan nodded to Nora.

"Almost ten years ago, the Duke of Chesterfield raped me at Gregenden House," she said, and for the first time in almost ten years, saying it out loud left her feeling...nothing.

Richard looked at her. "He thinks you're the snitch."

Nora nodded. Nathan poked Samuel in the ribs, and Samuel lowered his hands.

"All's good now, son," Nathan said and smiled.

Samuel returned his smile with an equally bright one, and Nora wondered if it was at Nathan's use of the word *son*.

"So out of revenge, you spy on Chesterfield and tell the War Office what you hear," Nathan said. "Chesterfield is at the ball and sees Archer's brother get shot. He then takes a shot at you, hoping to get rid of you."

"But he misses," Jane picked up the story. "And has to steal your son?"

Richard jumped in, "He kidnaps Samuel because his plans have changed. He missed Nora because Nathan got her out of the way. So if he was waiting to shoot Nora till then, then he—"

"He heard us talking about shooting the wrong man," Nathan finished.

"Has to change his plans now because there are more players," Richard continued. "And he wants all of those players in Dover. So why?"

Nora stood up and went over to the sideboard. The first time she tried to pick up a plate it rattled because of her shaking hands, so she had to set it back down to take a breath. The second time she picked it up, it was steady. She put eggs and sausages on the plate and brought them back to the table. She set it in front of her son, who obediently picked up his fork and poked at it. He did not take any bites as he continued to listen to the story about him.

Nora sat back down.

"Why would the Duke of Chesterfield spy for the French?"

Every head in the room swung to the door.

Sarah stood calmly with her hands folded in front of her. Her hair was clumped, half up and half down. Her eyes were red, and she had not bothered to wipe her cheeks so her skin was stripes of shiny and pale skin where the tears had dried on her face.

Nora stood up and filled another plate, pushing Sarah into a chair before setting the plate in front of her.

"What do we know about Chesterfield?" Nora said, sitting back down.

"He actually is wealthy," Jane said, getting up and filling two plates. She returned, setting one plate in front of Richard.

"While Archer spies for the money," Nathan said, starting to poke Samuel to get him to eat something.

"Gambling," Nora murmured, thinking of the well-known reason why Archer would need money.

Sarah took a bite and chewed. Nora waited for her to

swallow. It came eventually. Nora felt the sudden urge to brush Sarah's hair.

And then she forgot that.

And could not really think of anything else.

"She has red hair," she said.

"What?" Richard asked, spearing a kipper and looking up.

"She has red hair," she repeated louder, turning to Jane.

Jane's fork stopped mid-air. "She does have red hair."

"Who has red hair?" Samuel asked, swallowing his eggs.

"The Duchess of Chesterfield," Sarah said, looking brighter than she had all morning.

"What do we know about the Duchess of Chesterfield?" Nora asked Jane.

Jane lowered her fork and thought. "Almost nothing. She is some Scottish girl. I do not even recall her family name," Jane finished with a shake of her head.

"Jacobite Scottish?" Richard raised an eyebrow.

"Jacobite? You think someone would still hold a grudge over that?" Sarah asked.

"Why not?" Nathan shrugged and stole a sausage off of Samuel's plate.

"How are we going to find out more about the Duchess of Chesterfield?" Richard pushed his plate away.

"We cannot pay a social visit." Jane smirked. "She probably knows who I am now."

Richard nodded in agreement.

"We could follow her," Nora said.

"She's going to be at Temple Church today at noon," Samuel said into his eggs.

Nora and everyone else looked at the boy.

"What?" Samuel said when he finally looked up and saw everyone was looking at him.

"Temple Church? On Fleet Street?" Richard asked.

Samuel answered, "By the river. She's meeting someone there about a man named Franklin."

Nora went to ask how her son could possibly know this, but she was interrupted.

"Which one of us is going to be there as well?" Sarah asked, reaching for the teapot on the table.

"I am," Nora and Nathan said together.

They looked at each other.

Nora thought she should feel like sticking her tongue out, but she felt oddly tingly instead.

"You will both go," Richard said, standing up. "And I am going to figure out what the hell we are going to do after that."

Sarah picked up her head. "What about Alec?"

Nora paused, half sitting, half standing. Samuel was hanging onto Nathan's neck so he did not fall on the floor, as Nathan was about to stand up as well. Jane sipped her tea.

"I'll find him," Richard said and stomped from the room.

* * *

NATHAN TORE his mouth from Nora's and moved to the opposite seat.

"No," he barked, when she went to move next to him or onto him as it appeared. "We are on assignment, and if you keep doing what you're doing, I won't be able to pay attention to what I'm supposed to be paying attention to."

The hack dipped into a rut, and Nora bounced against his knees, frowning.

"All right," she said and looked out the window.

Nathan felt his stomach tighten at her casual manner.

"Well, maybe you can sit next to me," he heard himself say, "but no touching."

She jumped to the other seat, smiling.

This was not the Nora he was familiar with, but considering the circumstances, he rather liked her.

"What's gotten into you?" he asked.

And she smiled even more broadly. "I slept."

"You slept? That's it?"

"That's...part of it."

Her hand was reaching for him, and he batted it away.

"No touching."

"Nathan, I have not slept like I slept last night in years. Years, Nathan. That is a long time. And I spend one night, half of one night really, with you, and I sleep like it is my only purpose in the world. Excuse me for being excited." She turned sharply away to look out the window.

The hack bounced again, sending her against him.

"I'm sorry, Nora. I didn't realize—"

"No, you didn't realize. I have spent every night for the past nine years in a chair. A chair, Nathan. Dozing if I'm lucky. Staring at a stove if I'm not. And last night, I slept in a bed. Full out slept. Slept so hard I woke up confused, and the only thing that made sense was you. You were the first thing I remembered. And that makes me very happy."

The last sentence ended on a choked sob, and Nathan felt his stomach roll over. Nora started to cry. She put her face in her hands and bent over, as if hiding from him. Why were all the females in his life suddenly so weepy? She had gone through an entire kidnapping ordeal without so much as a whimper, and now she was crying? He was afraid he would have to touch her.

Nathan hauled her upright and onto his lap. Her head fell to his chest as she kept crying. It was not a loud cry, just a slow, soft release of anger, frustration, and grief. The wetness penetrated to his chest, and he held her tighter as the hack bounced along.

"It makes me very happy as well," Nathan whispered.

Nora shook one more time and fell silent.

Nathan waited, feeling his heart beating against his ribs, wondering if Nora felt it.

"Nathan?"

"Yes?"

"Don't...leave...me. Ever."

"I won't. Ever."

And with a sigh he felt down to his toes, Nora sat up in his lap.

"I feel better now," she said. "I think I may just have needed to get that out."

Nathan smiled at her. The hack took one more roll and stopped.

Nathan leaned forward, gripping Nora, and looked out the window.

Temple Church was partly visible through the other traffic on the street. People of questionable hygienic standards strolled the sidewalks. Women shouted their wares for sale. Men spit on the ground at their feet. Nathan reluctantly let Nora slide off his lap onto the bench. Nora kept one hand in his.

Hacks passed by, the rare carriage filtered in between. A woman hocked the sad looking flowers in her arms.

And then a hack rolled up in front of the church, and a short person jumped out and ran into the Chancel.

Nora reached for the door and was out before Nathan could get off the bench to follow her. They crossed the street carefully and went through the door moments after their short prey.

The organ loomed up far in the distant gloom. Rows of pillars lined up like slightly intoxicated soldiers, leaning outward. There were no people scattered throughout the pews. The Duchess of Chesterfield was nowhere to be seen.

Nora walked brazenly to the front and spun a circle. Nathan ran after her.

"You don't spy by walking out into the open. You get shot by doing that," he whispered harshly to her.

"There's no one here, Nathan." Nora pursed her lips at him.

The happy Nora of the hack was apparently gone for the time being, and the infallible Miss Quinton had returned.

"Well, where did she go?" Nathan whispered.

He swung his head in all directions, but there was literally nothing that should not be in a church. Candles, pews, marble, stained glass windows. It was a church without a single parishioner.

Until one stepped out from behind a pillar and looked right at him.

The muscles in Nathan's midsection unraveled.

Nora turned behind him, and he knew the moment when she saw the big figure in the distant gloom staring at them. She went absolutely rigid.

It was a man, a large one, and Nathan felt all his bruises start to throb in response. He also took a minuscule step in front of Nora. The man watched them. His trousers and boots were muddy and looked too big for him, where as his coat was just a touch too snug and too fine. Like it had just been removed from the original, smaller owner.

Nathan took another step in front of Nora.

The man watched them as he made his way to the back of the Chancel, slipping something into an inner pocket of the fine coat.

The man stopped.

Nora moved in front of Nathan, and he reached to get her out of the way.

"You must be the happy couple then?"

Nathan and Nora spun in the other direction, staring up

at the altar where the voice had originated. A priest was coming out from behind the pulpit carrying a Bible.

"Happy couple?" Nora asked.

"Aye, the pair who wished to be wed today at noon. I was afraid you were going to be late, but here you are. Prompt as prompt can be." The priest's bushy eyebrows rose and fell with his smile. There was more hair in his eyebrows than on his head.

"Shall we get started then? The special license arrived just as you said it would. You must only fill in the names." He extended a roll of parchment. "Shall we sign it then and see you two married?"

Nora looked around Nathan back at the large man by the door. Nathan looked as well. The man watched them, assessing, and then settled a hip against the farthest pew as if getting ready for the show.

Nora turned back to the priest, Nathan following her movement.

"Yes, we shall," Nora said and grabbed the special license.

* * *

RICHARD HAD no idea where his son was.

His valet was gone. Some of his clothes were gone.

And the servants knew he was gone.

But no one in the house knew where he had gone.

Richard was getting angry.

He stormed up the steps to his house and nearly collided with Jane in the foyer. Which was rather sad, since he liked colliding with Jane normally. But Jane looked worried, so he controlled himself. Mostly.

"What is it now?" he asked.

Jane frowned, and Richard was chastised. "Sarah."

"Sarah?"

"She's gone after him."

"Sarah's gone after him where? We don't know where he is!" Richard slammed his hat and gloves down on the hall table so hard the mirror hanging above it jumped.

Jane put her hands on his face and tilted his head down to look at her.

Her brown eyes were soft and drew him in. He felt his blood cooling almost immediately.

"She left me a note. I didn't see her leave, so I couldn't stop her to ask her where she was going, but I'm sure she will find him. She's smart, Richard. She will find him."

Richard brought his hands up to Jane's and drew them away.

"Is your son all right?"

Richard jumped as if he'd been caught with his hand up Jane's skirt and looked up the stairs where Samuel stood.

"I don't know," Richard answered him truthfully.

Samuel came down the stairs. "I am certain he is. He is a very resourceful man. He knows what he is doing."

Samuel stopped at the bottom of the stairs but would not come any closer to them.

Richard still held Jane's hands in his and suddenly released them. He did not miss the smirk Jane gave him. He just chose to ignore it.

"And how do you come about that conclusion?" he asked the boy.

"He found me, did he not?"

"Yes, but he had Nathan's help. And yours."

Samuel shook his head. "That does not make a difference."

"I'm still afraid he's going to do something extremely stupid."

"He won't," Samuel was quick to say. "He is too afraid of disappointing you."

Richard looked at the boy, how shyly he stood with his

hands behind his back and his shoulder not quite out from behind the newel post. And Richard suddenly had an idea.

"Do you know how to play poker, Samuel?" Richard asked.

Samuel grinned hugely. "Yes, I do, sir."

It was hours later when Jane swept the pot toward her and declared, "Full house, gentlemen."

Samuel frowned and threw his cards into the pile.

"I told you we shouldn't let her play," Richard said from the side of his mouth.

Samuel shrugged. "But you did not tell me to listen to you."

Richard laughed, and Samuel felt his cheeks turn slightly pink. He did not really make people laugh. It was getting to be a nice experience. One he would not mind repeating.

And he liked the Duke of Lofton. He had a voice that made Samuel feel safe. He knew that sounded silly, but that was how he felt. The duchess was still a little scary, but he was starting to not shake when he first saw her. And he liked the little wrinkles around her eyes when she smiled. She must smile a lot to get those wrinkles, he figured.

Jane dealt the new hand, sliding the cards across the table at him. He scooped them up and tried not to react. Nathan had told him to put his emotions in his pocket when he sat down at the card table. So that is what Samuel did. He had two nines, an ace, a four, and a jack. Not too bad to start.

He went to toss in his bet.

"Playing poker, again?"

Samuel jumped, and the chip went flying. The Duke of Lofton caught it deftly and winked. Samuel turned to his mother who had suddenly appeared at the library door and became immediately alarmed.

She looked weird.

Her cheeks were reddish, and her hands were loose at her

sides. Her hair was in a braid across her shoulder when he was sure she had left with it in a bun. The dark circles that were normally under her eyes were only gray smudges that were mostly hidden by her big smile.

Samuel was terrified.

"Mama, what did you do?"

She grinned more, and Samuel almost peed himself.

Nathan appeared in the doorway behind her. "We got married!" he shouted, also grinning stupidly.

Samuel felt himself stand, but then he could not move.

"Really?" he whispered, almost afraid that everything would suddenly change back to what it had been if he questioned it.

"Yes, really," his mother answered him.

And then he ran. He ran across the room and knocked his mother into Nathan with the force of his hug.

"Really really?" he asked, looking up at her.

"Really really."

Samuel jumped back and looked up at Nathan, feeling terrified again. "That means you're my father now?"

Nathan nodded, probably because he was still smiling and could not really speak.

Samuel did not know what to do. How did one greet one's new father? So he went back to what he knew. He straightened his shoulders and stuck out his hand.

Nathan stopped smiling, and Samuel's heart stopped. He had done the wrong thing.

But then Nathan grabbed him. Not his hand. Him. He was airborne with Nathan swinging him around as Nathan laughed. Samuel scrambled to grab ahold of Nathan's shoulders to keep from flying across the room. He felt like throwing up, but he felt more like laughing because Nathan was laughing. So he laughed.

Nathan stopped spinning and pulled him against him.

Samuel had to stop laughing because breathing was suddenly hard with how fiercely Nathan was hugging him. But he did not care if he could not breathe. He had never been so happy in his life.

Finally, Nathan set him down but did not let go of his hand. Samuel stood, looking up at his new father and feeling very, very lucky.

* * *

"I GET to sleep in this big bed all by myself?"

Nora giggled. She had been doing it all night, but it never seemed to get old.

It had been a long night of celebration. Nora had not expected the Duke and Duchess of Lofton to be so delighted with their son's sudden marriage. Nora was not sure how she even felt about it. But the Loftons were quick to order a cake be made for that night's supper. There was a feast and champagne. And then they all played charades and sang songs as Jane played the piano. It was a night unlike anything Nora had lived before.

Before she was married.

Before she had a husband like Nathan Black.

"Yes, you get to sleep in this big bed all by yourself," she answered Samuel.

She tucked the covers tighter around Samuel's chin.

"I might get lost."

Nora giggled again and felt a warmth spread through her limbs. Her son had never joked before. Nathan was so good for them.

"Try really hard not to."

"Okay." Samuel smiled but let it fade. "Mama?"

Nora felt her throat closing. "Yes, dear?"

"I really like Nathan. I am glad you married him."

Nora's throat stopped constricting. "I really like him, too."

"Good night."

"Good night, Samuel." Nora kissed his forehead and slid off the bed. She closed the hallway door softly behind her and turned to look at the door opposite.

Her husband was waiting for her behind it.

A feral smoldering began low in her belly and spread through her, licking at her emotions.

She loved her husband.

She knew that. She did not know how long she had known it. But she knew it now. She just did not know if she was brave enough to tell him. What would happen if she did? When they had faced each other in the church, there had only been survival in mind. Perform the act to fool the enemy, so that big bloke of a fellow at the back of the church did not make the unbruised side of Nathan's face match the other.

But did Nathan really mean it?

When the priest had announced them man and wife and they had finally kissed, she had not noticed if the man was still at the back of the Chancel. She did not notice anything as Nathan had rushed them to the street and hailed a hackney. And once inside the hackney, she had not noticed anything except Nathan, and she suspected that had been Nathan's plot all along. They had not been kissing. Kissing was far too sedate a word for what they had done. True, she had not managed to get any of his clothes off, but then the ride had been too short, and really, she had been a little distracted. They had lost all of her hairpins though, and she had had to resort to a braid for decency.

Surely, Nathan would not have done all of that if she had not mattered at least a little. And the way he had held her last night after...after...well, after she had made a ninny of herself. Surely, he must care.

But standing in the hallway looking at a door was not going to get her any closer to finding out if he cared.

So she opened the door to his bedchamber and strode inside.

To find her husband soundly asleep.

Nora felt the wind rush out of her.

Nathan lay on the bed, and his chest rose and fell in a steady rhythm. His very naked chest.

Nora looked around the room at the discarded clothes. It appeared as though he had been in a hurry to get them off.

And then he had fallen asleep.

She smiled sadly for him as she crept over to the bed. A single candle flickered on the table beside him, and she bent to pick it up before studying his calm face. The bruises were healing nicely, faint green patches along his jaw and one cheek. The light flickered off the smattering of hair on his chest, and Nora wanted to run her fingers over it. Of course, she did not dare. Nathan was likely exhausted and deserved the merits of good sleep. She walked to the other side of the bed, extinguishing the candle before climbing onto the bed.

The mattress dipped only a little, and she settled carefully beside him, wrapping the cloth of her nightgown around her legs. His breathing remained steady as she laid her head on the pillow beside his. She curled as close as she could get to him without actually touching him.

He slept.

And so did she.

CHAPTER 15

*I*t was raining.

Nathan heard it pattering against the window-panes. The grandfather clock in the hall was a distant pulse. He listened to their battling beats and the sound of his own breath going in and out. He finally opened his eyes.

And his breath stopped going in and out.

His wife was lying beside him.

And she was asleep.

Nathan stared at her. Her face was right next to his on the pillow, her breath softly brushing his ear. One hand was curled under her chin. She was so beautiful. Nathan carefully rolled onto his side to get a better look at her, but he did not touch her. He just watched her sleep.

And fell totally and completely in love.

When he had gotten into his bedroom that night, his last thought was that his wife would be joining him. He had merely stripped off his clothes, not caring where they landed, and fell into bed, exhausted and frustrated as hell. He had married Nora, but that did not make her any closer to him, any more comfortable with what it meant to be together.

Frankly, it just made everything worse. And yet he had never been so happy in his whole life.

He could still see her face, the way her mouth tilted up, and how she struggled to keep from smiling hugely when he had been saying his vows. He had been shaking while he had said the words, but he had forced his hands to be still as he held hers. He did not want her to doubt that he meant what he said. And he did not doubt that she meant what she said. She had grabbed the license and signed it before Nathan realized what she was doing. She had shoved it at him with the quill, pointing out exactly where he was to sign. And she had watched him carefully as he did it. He had scrawled his name next to hers and dragged her up to the altar.

He had completely forgotten that they were being watched.

And now she slept soundly beside him. Absolutely at peace, and he hoped, happy.

And then he did have to touch her.

He slid his arms carefully around her, cradling her against him. Her head rested just below his chin, and he breathed in the scent of her. She made a little noise and wiggled closer, her arms pushing to get around him. He obliged, and he felt her settle back into sleep, content. He held her as the rain struck the windows, and the grandfather clock chimed the hour. He held her as his heart pounded against his ribs when he thought about being able to do this every night for the rest of his life.

And then she stiffened, all at once and suddenly.

He felt his happiness dissolve.

"Nathan?"

He stroked her back, hoping to restore the calm, contented mood he had just been in. "Shh, it's all right."

She pulled her arms away and pushed against his chest,

bringing her head up to stare at him in alarm. His faltering happiness turned to icy hot anger.

"I didn't wake you, did I?" she asked.

"No."

She let out a rush of air that ended on a small sigh, and then she smiled softly. "Good."

Nathan felt the anger sloshing back toward happiness, and he was getting very confused.

Then Nora squeezed her arms back around him, tighter this time, and put her head back under his chin. She wiggled once against him, for her pleasure or his, he did not know, and then sighed again before going still in relaxation against him.

Nathan stared at the untouched pillow beside them and tried to figure out what the hell was going on. His wife had clearly just snuggled up to him. His wife, who by all accounts should have been terrified at the thought of getting anywhere near him and a bed at the same time.

But there she was, quite firmly pressed against him and holding on like she expected to do so for some time.

"Nora?"

"Hmm?"

"I didn't wake you, did I?"

It was not what he had meant to ask, but it was what came out of his mouth.

"No. Yes. I don't know. I just suddenly woke up." She wiggled back a little to look up at him. "I was a little scared, you know, waking up. I'm not used to waking up in a bed. I'm still a little confused when I do. But you were there, and I knew I was all right. And I am." She smiled and returned her head to its place under his chin.

Nathan wondered if Nora realized he was completely naked under the sheets and that, in fact, the only thing separating them was her nightgown. He hardened instantly, and he sucked in his breath. He thought about moving his hips away, but then wondered if it might be too late. He closed his eyes and waited.

"Nathan?"

Should he pretend to be asleep again?

Did he have to answer her?

"Yes?"

"Nathan, do you...do you...want me?"

Her unsteady voice made his teeth grind.

But he had to be honest with her.

"Yes, Nora, I do, but I don't want you to think that I will do anything that you don't want. So if you don't want to...do anything, I won't. I promise."

He kept his eyes shut, willing his tormented senses to stop their torrent. But it really was no use, not with Nora plastered against him.

"And what if I do want...to do something?"

Nathan's eyes shot open. "If you do want?"

"Yes."

He eased her away from him, so he could see her eyes. "Do you want?"

"I think so."

She thought so? "Nora, I—"

"I get this weird feeling when I'm around you. Down here." She took his hand and put it low on her stomach almost—

He pulled his hand away. "Nora, I—"

"Would you light a candle, please?"

A candle? She wanted to light a candle now?

He rolled over and got the flint out of the drawer of the table beside the bed and lit one of the candles on the table-top. Its light flickered faintly, barely casting an orange glow beyond the tabletop.

He went to roll back toward Nora, but she was moving.

She had her arms and most of her head under the covers, pulling at something. He lay on his back and waited, suddenly terrified that he knew what she was doing.

Her nightgown came up over her head, and she flung it off the bed.

Nathan could not move. He wanted to reach out and...and...touch. But he did not know where his hands were or if his fingertips would be able to feel anything.

Nora was sitting up, and she pulled the braid of her hair around to untie the ribbon holding it. She shook back her head, and the strands loosened, spraying around her shoulders in straight trickles that barely touched her breasts. The candlelight flickered over her pale skin and the brownish tips of her nipples. Her ribs stuck out a little as she twisted to throw away the ribbon. He sat up then and touched the lines of her ribs, skimming his fingertips over them. She twisted back, and the lines disappeared. She looked up at him, her eyes shadowed as he blocked the candlelight.

"I want to take care of you," he said, his fingers still on the place where her ribs had been visible. The skin under his fingertips moved as she breathed.

"I want you to take care of me," she said in response.

He kissed her, bringing his other hand up to hold her head. She leaned into him, her small breasts crushed against his chest.

And then she pushed him away, hard. He fell back against the pillows, his heart thundering erratically.

She was smiling.

Impishly.

His heart almost came out of his chest, and the room spun. Or maybe it was just his head.

She leaned over him and nipped his lower lip before moving to his jaw, then his neck, and then lower. She pressed her lips in a searing line down his chest, her hands kneading the muscles along the way. He thought she would stop at his stomach, but she kept going lower. And lower. And—

He grabbed her shoulders and hauled her up. She squeaked, and he loosened his grip on her.

"What are you doing?" His voice was scratchy and sounded not at all like himself.

Her eyes grew wide, and her voice came out feebly. "Am I doing something wrong?"

"Not wrong. Just dangerous."

"Dangerous?" She had the nerve to smile at him.

And then she licked her lips.

He growled, actually growled, and flipped them, so Nora was pinned underneath him. He took her mouth, plunging his tongue inside, no longer caring if he was being gentle or not. It appeared his wife was more ready than he had thought. Nora rose up against him, and he used his hands to push her back down, smoothing his hands down her sides and back up, coming painfully close to her breasts only to pull away and make her groan. He liked that sound.

She pulled on his hair, and he tilted back his head, surprised.

"This isn't fair. I started this," she said, gasping for air.

"Fair?" He raised his eyebrows.

He was making love to his wife, and she wanted to discuss fairness?

"Yes, it isn't. I had an agenda here, Mr. Black, and you are seriously deviating from it."

"Is that so?"

"Yes. It is."

She reached down and grabbed his fully erect penis. He sucked in his breath and tried to pull away from her. Her hand slid down the length of him, and his eyes rolled back into his head. His arms gave out, and he fell down, just avoiding crushing Nora. She came up on her elbow over him, her hand still stroking him slowly.

"That's more like it," she said and disappeared out of his vision.

Nora had never done what she was about to do before, but she had seen it done. Accidentally, of course, but she had seen it. That was all that mattered, was it not? And the man had enjoyed it; at least he appeared to enjoy it. And she wanted Nathan to enjoy himself.

So she took him into her mouth.

Nathan neither moved nor made a noise, and she was afraid she was not doing it right. She noticed the fistful of sheets he was attempting to shred and felt much better.

But then Nathan grabbed her again, pulling her up the length of him, which really felt pretty good, so she was not going to complain. He rolled on top of her, taking her mouth again before settling himself between her thighs. She felt a tiny spasm of fear and resolutely pushed it away. There was nothing here to be afraid of. This was her husband, and she loved him. She wrapped her arms around his neck and her legs around his hips.

The pleasant pain began to throb again in that place that she never touched, not even in the bath. It started as a low hum and built to a swirling crescendo. She pushed on Nathan's shoulders to get his mouth off of hers.

"It's happening again," she said, heaving in gulps of air.

"What's happening?" Nathan's eyes had grown wide and frightened.

She shook her head furiously. "Not that. The pain, it's there, and it's getting bigger, and I don't know what it is."

Nathan's face relaxed into a smile. "Oh, that's happening again."

His hand slid down her side, across her stomach, and between her legs. He touched her, and her hips came off the mattress, pushing harder against him, a tiny pulse of air escaping her lips.

"That's supposed to happen, sweetheart," he whispered against her ear and then entered her.

The pain stopped all at once, and she dropped her legs from around his hips. Now she just felt full and not the least bit thrilled at the idea of continuing.

She tapped Nathan's shoulder. "Could I have a moment, please?" she said once Nathan stopped nuzzling her neck.

He nodded and stayed still above her, watching her face.

"What?" she asked.

"I'm giving you a moment."

"Oh."

She took deep, slow breaths, willing her muscles to relax. Nathan kept watching her.

"You know I don't believe I've ever talked this much while making love to a woman," Nathan said, making himself comfortable above her. He framed her face in his hands, skimming his thumb along the outline of her lips and over her cheeks.

Her relaxing muscles suddenly clenched, and Nathan cursed, sucking air in between his teeth.

Nora winced. "I'm sorry, but that felt good. Did I hurt you?"

Nathan smiled tensely. "Yes, but it felt good."

Except he no longer touched her face.

Nora adjusted her hips, letting her body become fluid again.

"All right," she said.

Nathan had been staring at the headboard and flinched when she spoke. He looked down at her.

"All right?"

His voice was oddly squeaky.

"Yes. Nathan, are you going to be all right if we do this?"

"I'm afraid probably not."

And then he began to move. Not a lot. Just a little. Just enough to make her muscles compress again, but softer this time, as if her body were stroking him. The pain started once more, low and pulsating...blooming. Nathan was sweating above her with his jaw taut. She brought his mouth down to hers, easing away the strain. The feeling grew towards something, but what it was she did not know. She lifted her legs around his rocking hips, and the pain stabbed at her. She moaned against Nathan's mouth, urging him to move faster, to move her toward whatever it was that was crashing around inside of her just out of her reach.

And then it was there, and she ripped her mouth away from Nathan's to scream, but nothing came out. She dug her nails into his back and hung onto him as he pounded into her. He stiffened and collapsed on top of her.

She stared at the ceiling as the delicious spasms continued to rock her body. She held onto Nathan as her heartbeat slowed with his.

She watched the candle send shadows dancing across the ceiling, and she said to those shadows, "I love you."

* * *

I LOVE YOU.

Nathan had been almost asleep, but he had heard her just fine.

She loved him?

They had known each other for little more than a week, and she loved him?

But then why would he doubt it since he had just recently come to the same conclusion? Did people really fall in love in little more than a week? His father always said he fell in love with Jane in just a look, so perhaps a week was too long to fall in love. Maybe he was really lazy when it came to love.

Since his bones had most certainly just turned to water, he did not mind feeling lazy. But he was crushing Nora, so he reluctantly pulled himself off of her, which was more a chore than he thought as she clung to him, her grip unbelievably strong for a woman who had just been thoroughly loved. Maybe he had been lazy, but then Nora was a lot stronger than he ever gave her credit for. He really needed to change that.

He settled Nora against his side, her head falling into the hollow of his shoulder, one arm slung over his stomach. He thought he should reach down and find the sheet, but the strength necessary for such a move was not to be found, so he just lay where he was, enjoying the feeling of holding his wife.

And wondering if he should tell her how he felt as well.

But then there was that whole issue of telling a woman you loved her for the first time before, during, or after one made love to her that was always a little skeptical. Did anyone really believe such a statement in that situation, even if one really meant it? Nathan believed Nora when she said it because Nora did not think in such complicated ways. She was simple and straightforward. She said what she was thinking, and she acted on what she was feeling. Had she not just seduced him? He smiled and tightened his arm around her.

The rain still beat against the windows while the clock still ticked in the hallway, and the candle flicked shadows around the room.

And he wanted to tell his wife that he loved her.

"Nora?"

Her breathing never faltered, and her heartbeat was a steady pulse against his side.

"Nora?"

He tilted his head and found her to be soundly asleep.

He sat up, carefully sliding her head to the pillow, and pulled up the sheets around her. He extinguished the candle and leaned back against the pillows, sitting against the headboard.

He watched his wife sleep and wondered how he was going to take care of her.

* * *

IT WAS NEARLY dawn when Nathan pulled his wife toward him. He woke her slowly with a kiss. She hummed in her throat, and her arms came fiercely around him, startling him with their intensity. They were facing each other, and he slid into her, finding some resistance because she was not ready for him. But he moved against her, letting the friction of their bodies bring her fully awake. He ran his hand down her back to the cleft of her buttocks and relished the shudder that went through her before her eyes flew open to stare at him.

She smiled against his mouth and then pulled away. "Good morning, Mr. Black."

"Good morning, Mrs. Black."

He cupped her buttocks to hold her more snuggly against him and increased his pace. Nora's eyes closed, and she purred.

Nathan felt his control slipping and pivoted to bring her beneath him. He reached down to where they were joined and stroked her sensitive nub. She shattered in his arms, and he followed on the wake of her orgasm, spilling his seed into her. He fell onto his back, bringing her with him so that she draped across his chest, her head falling just below his chin. Her thighs fell on either side of his, and he kept his hands firmly on her buttocks to keep himself in her.

"Nora?" he said before she had a chance to really settle.

"Mmm?"

"I love you."

"I know," she mumbled against his throat.

He sat up. Nora grabbed at his shoulders as if to steady herself. He kept his hands firmly on her hips to keep her from squirming. He did not need distraction right now. Her hair had fallen over one side of her face, and she brushed it back to see him.

When he was sure she was paying attention, he said, "You know?"

She nodded. "You're not a man to seduce a woman such as myself unless he loved her."

"Seduce a woman? Excuse me, but I believe I was the one being seduced."

Nora thought a moment. "Well, perhaps, once. But you clearly started it every other time. And I know you wouldn't have done that if you didn't at least care. A little." She lifted her shoulders in a small shrug.

"I care a good deal more than a little," he said, his tone harsher than he intended.

Nora bit her lower lip, and he felt like a cad. But then he realized she was trying not to smile. He frowned at her. She wrapped her arms tightly around his neck, crushing her breasts against his chest, and he resolutely ignored how damn good it felt. They were having a serious conversation, and she was not going to distract him.

"I care a lot more than a little. I love you, and well, that's that."

He sounded like a first rate idiot, but really, how did one profess one's love to said love when said love was straddling one, naked, in a bed?

"I love you, too. Now is that settled?"

He leaned back a bit to get a really good look at her. "Yes, I suppose it is."

"All right then, we have something else we need to discuss."

He raised his eyebrows. "We do?"

"Yes."

"Right now?"

"I think the sooner we talk about it the better."

He felt a lick of fear work its way up his spine. "What do we need to talk about?" he asked.

"Samuel."

"What about Samuel? I love him, too, in case you're worried—"

She shook her head. "I know that, and it's not about Samuel existing in our lives, it's Samuel as a thing."

"Samuel as a thing?"

Nora nodded. "Samuel is my son. Samuel was a result of..."

Nathan paled. "One time. You were pregnant after one time."

Nora nodded. "Yes, I was. And I might be inexperienced, but I'm fairly certain I know how this works, and I was just wondering if we should perhaps be a little more cautious."

Nathan started to nod but stopped. "Why?"

It was Nora's turn to back up. "Why?"

"Why not? Why can't we have a baby?" Nathan asked.

"You want to have a baby?" Nora asked, her eyes wide.

"I want to have a baby with you," he corrected.

"Oh."

"You don't want to have a baby with me?"

Nora nodded furiously. "I do. I do want to have a baby with you, but," she looked down, pink staining her cheeks, "how are we going to take care of a baby?"

He brought his hand up to lift her chin. He wanted to be looking at her when he said this. "I'll take care of us."

She shook her head again. "You can't, not all by yourself. I'll have to find a post now as it is, but with a baby—"

He covered her lips with his thumb. "My father. I'm going to ask my father for help." He felt his breath catch, but he forced air into his lungs.

Nora's lips parted under his thumb, and her eyes widened even more. "I didn't think you would do that," she finally whispered.

"For you and my family, I would." He forced more air into his lungs. He could not hold his breath waiting for her response since she had suddenly gone still in his lap. If he was going to wait for a reaction, he was going to have to breathe.

"Nora?" he prompted when she had remained still for longer than he had patience for.

"I love you," she whispered.

He nodded quickly, urging her to go on. She did not, so he answered with, "I love you, too."

She shook her head slowly, left and right, and whispered again, "I love you. I love you very much."

Nathan smiled, "And?"

"That's it."

"That's it?"

She nodded slowly, up and down. "You said that was it."

He nodded, mimicking her slow movement. "That is it."

He kissed her, pouring himself into it as she met him with the same force. He fell back against the pillows. Her hair cascaded around them. Nathan grabbed her arms and levered her back up away from him.

"Have you ever had the opportunity to ride a horse?" he asked.

"A horse?" She raised her eyebrow at him. He was getting to like that eyebrow.

"Yes, a horse."

"No, I haven't. Why?"

"I think you should learn." He adjusted her, settling her more tightly against him.

The look of confusion quickly disappeared from her face. "Oh."

"I think we should begin our first lesson right now."

"I think so, too," she agreed.

CHAPTER 16

*N*ora hid the yawn with her hand and walked into the morning room to find a stranger helping himself to the eggs.

"Excuse me," she said pertly, lapsing back into house-keeper mode.

The man turned around.

And smiled.

"Good morning. You must be Nora. Mrs. Black, lately, I hear." He set down his plate and came over to her. "I'm Matthew Thatcher. I pulled your husband out of that gaming hell a few nights back." He extended his hand.

Nora shook it firmly and nodded. "You're from the Colonies."

He laughed softly. "I'm American, you mean."

Nora nodded more quickly. "Oh, yes, of course. American. Feels strange to say that."

"It's even stranger correcting people." He smiled again and went back to his eggs.

Nora helped herself to tea and sat.

"So, Mr. Thatcher, what brings you to England?"

"Oh, you can just call me Thatcher. I needed a change of scenery." He piled even more food on his plate, which had Nora staring. Mr. Thatcher was quite a large man, probably the same size as Nathan, so he probably needed all that food. But that logical reasoning still did not stop Nora from staring. She caught herself, though, before Mr. Thatcher turned around to take a chair at the table.

"A change of scenery? You came all the way to London for a change of scenery?"

"Actually, I went to Dublin first, and then Glasgow, and then York and now I'm here." He raised his eyebrows briefly and settled into his food.

"Have you found London's scenery to be to your liking?"

He looked up at her. "I'm enjoying it right now."

"Watch it, Thatcher. She's mine."

Nora turned around in her chair to see her husband standing in the door with his fists on his hips, a furious expression on his face.

"Oh, please," she said under her breath and rose to fix Nathan a plate.

"What are you doing here, Thatcher?" Nathan asked, walking over to shake the man's hand and slap him rather hard on the back.

Nora set the plate down and pushed Nathan towards it. He would not budge and instead raised a single eyebrow at her. She knew that look and did not like what it meant.

"What?" she asked.

"You eat it," he said and pushed her into the chair with the plate of food before going to help himself at the sideboard.

She picked up her fork before she realized he was ordering her around and stopped to look at him.

He sat in the chair beside her and leaned over to discreetly pat her stomach under the table. She looked down where his hand briefly rested and then swung her gaze back to his. He smiled softly at her. She nodded and started eating.

"Your father asked me to come," Thatcher said from the other side of the table. "I hear your brother's run off, and his wife has followed him."

Nathan grunted as a response.

"Do you work for the War Office as well?" Nora asked.

Thatcher shook his head, laughing. "God, no. Not technically anyway. I am what you would call a private detective, I suppose."

"I see. And what is it you privately detect?"

Thatcher thought a moment. "I'm not sure I should tell a woman."

Nathan raised his head from his food. "You can tell this woman." He pointed at Nora with his fork.

"Tell this woman what?" Jane asked, sailing through the door and heading straight for the food. She backtracked abruptly, and a huge smile bloomed on her face. "Thatcher!"

Thatcher stood. "Ma'am," he drawled before grabbing Jane in a crushing hug.

Nora forgot her fork was halfway to her mouth and stared.

When Thatcher finally let go of her, Jane fanned herself.

"You Americans," she mumbled.

"What's going on here?" Richard demanded.

Nora turned around again to look at the door. Richard was the exact image of his son moments before.

Nathan swallowed his food. "He's making the rounds, Father."

"I see." Richard stomped into the room. "Why don't you make the rounds somewhere else?" he said, coming to stand between Jane and Thatcher.

"But you invited me," Thatcher said.

"Oh, that's right. I did. My fault, then." Richard shrugged and slapped Thatcher on the back.

Nora started to become curious about this back slapping ritual these men types seemed to embrace.

"Mama?"

Nora turned to find Samuel tugging on her sleeve. She looked down at her son and immediately brought up her hand to brush the hair from his forehead.

"Is something wrong?" he asked.

Nora's brow furrowed. "Wrong? Why would anything be wrong?"

"It is nearly eight o'clock, and you did not wake me," he said, his voice gravelly with sleep.

Nora wanted to laugh. She wanted to laugh very loudly so that everyone in London heard her.

"I don't have to wake you anymore, dear. You can wake yourself whenever you'd like."

Nathan leaned over her to put in, "But I'd advise waking early as the food in this house tends to disappear quickly." He nodded very seriously.

Samuel smiled and rubbed his eyes. "Could I have some of the food then?" he asked.

"Absolutely." Nora went to rise, but Nathan stopped her.

"I'll get it," he said, standing up.

Nora helped her yawning son into a chair and felt a yawn coming on herself. She put her hand to her mouth to hide it, but Samuel was too quick.

"Mama, are you all right? You look sleepy."

Nora felt heat rush to her cheeks. "Aren't I always sleepy?"

Samuel shook his head. "No, you always look tired. But now you look sleepy. There is a difference."

"Oh," Nora said, turning her attention back to the table to find everyone staring at her.

Nathan set a plate of food in front of Samuel more loudly than necessary, and everyone snapped back to themselves.

"So, how are you feeling this morning, Samuel?" Thatcher asked.

Samuel looked up from the food. "Fine, thank you, sir." He paused. "You are not English. I did not notice that the other night."

Thatcher smiled. "No, but then you were a tad distracted the other night."

"From where in the Colonies have you come?" Samuel asked.

"I'm from the southern states in America."

"States. That will never last," Richard murmured into his cup of tea.

"Why not?" Thatcher defended.

"You're already on your second form of government, and you're not even out of knee pants," Jane said.

Nora watched the conversation go back and forth and broke in. "What do you mean, second government?"

Thatcher smirked shyly. "Well, the Articles of Confederation didn't work so well, so the people in charge over there got together and created a new government under a little piece of paper called the Constitution."

"They can do that?"

"Sure can. Power of the people and all that."

"Huh." Nora sat and thought a moment. "What happens if people you don't like are in power?"

"We vote them out," Thatcher said.

"We vote? Are you allowed to vote, Mr. Thatcher?"

"Currently, no. I don't own land over there right now, but if I did, sure. I could vote for anything and anybody."

"And people trust each other to make the right decision?"

Thatcher shrugged. "I guess so. It's been working all right so far."

Nathan reached for the teapot. "As fascinating as this talk about the attributes of democracy is, I think we should get down to business."

Nora nodded and looked at Richard. "What is the plan, sir?"

"The plan is for you to stop calling me sir and start calling me Father, and then we'll discuss the plan."

Nora felt a smile tugging at her mouth. "All right...Father."

Richard smiled at her.

"Does that mean I'm supposed to call you Grandfather?" Samuel asked quietly.

Nora felt her heart constrict at the faint sound of hope in her son's voice.

"Of course," Richard said, speaking with such casual assurance Samuel could not doubt his sincerity.

Samuel's shoulders straightened immediately, and Nora's heart constricted more. Nathan laid a hand on hers under the table. She turned her hand over and squeezed his.

"First things first," Richard said, "I need to bestow my wedding gift upon my son."

Nathan's, Nora's, and Samuel's heads all swung around at once.

"Gift?" Nathan asked, his voice suddenly weak.

"Yes, gift. I set it aside a long time ago in case you ever got married. Frankly, I never thought you would, but now that you have, I'm very pleased to hand it over to you."

He pulled a folded piece of parchment out of the inside of his jacket and extended his arm across the table. Nathan did not reach up to grab it, so Nora did, taking the parchment in her fingertips and holding it in front of her husband.

Nathan stared at it, and Nora squeezed his hand harder under the table. He looked at her and finally took the parchment.

He was silent for some moments after he unfolded it, and the anxiety was starting to make Nora insane.

"What is it?" she finally hissed at him.

Samuel leaned into her. "Yes, what is it, Father?"

Nathan did not look up from the parchment. "It's...land."

"Land?" Nora repeated.

"Land?" Samuel repeated her.

"Holdings really. Down in Kent. A baron died about a decade ago with no heirs and somehow the land came into the family. I didn't need it, so I deeded it off into your name." Richard sipped his tea casually. "I hope you don't mind being a farmer after this whole business with Napoleon is over."

Nora felt tears burning in her eyes and looked up to find Nathan's eyes had gone glassy with tears as well. His fingers had lost their grip on hers, or maybe hers had lost their grip on his. She did not know, but then they both stood together and strode around to the other side of the table. Richard was already on his feet when they got there, taking them into his arms as Nora and Nathan embraced him with all the gratitude that was welling up inside them. Samuel appeared and wrapped his own arms around everyone's waist. Nora did not feel silly at all hugging a duke in the middle of his morning room during breakfast.

When they finally separated, Richard had his own tears in his eyes. "I take care of my children," he said and smiled at all of them, looking down at Samuel to give him his own smile.

"Oh."

Jane jumped up from her chair and embraced them as well. Jane was amazingly strong, and Nora felt a sense of comfort she had not felt in years. She had not only married a man with land, but she had married a man with family. And that meant so much more than any amount of land.

Matthew Thatcher cleared his throat somewhere behind them.

Jane turned and shook her hand at him. "All right, all right. What were we talking about?"

"Saving the world from Napoleon," Thatcher said, leaning back in his chair.

Nora and Nathan sat back down, Nathan drawing Samuel onto his knee.

"What do we know about Dover?" Richard asked.

Nathan was already shaking his head. "Nothing. It's crawling with agents who haven't heard so much as a belch of conspiracy."

"Then why would they want us to go there?" Richard responded.

"I don't know. Unless there is something going on there, and the agents haven't figured it out. Something that they were supposed to figure out."

Richard frowned. "I would hope our men and women are more well trained than that."

"Maybe they are trained well; they're just not looking in the right places."

Everyone looked at Nora.

"What places?" Richard asked.

"Below stairs," she said.

Samuel nodded furiously in Nathan's lap. "Lots happens below stairs."

"What sort of agents do you have in Dover?" Nora asked.

"Mostly members of the peerage. We put all the really top agents down there," Richard replied.

"Members of the peerage wouldn't even know there was a below stairs in which to look," Jane said.

"I agree, so what should we do, and more specifically what should I do?" Thatcher asked.

Richard pointed at Thatcher. "Your only task is to find my wayward son and his wife. I'm afraid he's gone off and done something very stupid, and when he realizes he's done something very stupid, I don't want him to be alone with a wife who will likely murder him." He turned to Nora and Nathan. "You two are going to Dover. Samuel, you're coming with me and Jane."

"I am?" Samuel asked, incredulous.

"I need someone who can scamper below stairs unencumbered." Richard was already standing.

Samuel jumped out of Nathan's lap and nearly ran over to his new grandfather. "Where is it that I'll be scampering?"

"Amongst the servants of Lord Archer's townhouse. I want to know where the good man is."

"I would imagine he's gone on to the Earl of Kent's country dance," Nora put in.

Richard nodded. "Except he never showed up. Our man down there said Lord Archer never left Lord Heathenbaum's."

"The Duchess of Chesterfield passed a note to that man in the church yesterday. Would that have something to do with it?" Nathan asked.

Richard shook his head. "Lord Archer disappeared before that. Right after you shot the wrong man, actually."

"Word traveled that quickly?" Jane asked.

Thatcher spoke up this time. "Maybe it wasn't our word that was traveling."

It was his turn to be stared at by the population of the room.

"Maybe something went down on the other side of the spy game."

"You mean from Napoleon?" Richard asked.

"Yes, I mean, you found Archer out for the spy he was after all. Maybe he was making serious mistakes, and the other team eliminated a weak player before it cost them."

"Who would do the eliminating?" Richard asked.

249

"The Duke of Chesterfield was not at Gregenden House the other night," Nora said.

Richard was already nodding. "But would Napoleon risk one of his top spies on such a trivial task?"

"Maybe they didn't eliminate him. Yet," Nathan said.

"What else would they need him for?" Jane asked.

"That's what I intend to find out," Richard said, grabbing Samuel's hand. "Nora and Nathan, you'd best start for Dover. You have at least a four day ride ahead of you. And if Alec's gone in the same direction, he has a two day head start." He turned to Jane. "My love, would you do me the honor of accompanying me on a spying excursion?"

"Oh, it would be my pleasure," Jane replied.

Nora looked at her son. "Samuel, will you be all right while I'm gone?"

"Of course, Mama, do not worry. I'll be fine. And Nathan, I mean, Father, will take care of you." He smiled and kissed her on the cheek before walking out the door with his grandfather.

Nora felt Nathan's hand slip into hers.

"I've never spent the night away from him," she said, feeling the tears gather in her eyes but not feeling the need to let them fall.

Nathan squeezed her hand in reply, and she felt suddenly, infinitely better.

And then Samuel ran back in the room. Nora turned, startled and worried that maybe Samuel was not as fine with this as he had said.

He ran up to Nathan and leaned in close. "I think of you as my father. Not that other man. I'm very lucky to be able to call you Father," he whispered to Nathan. "I just wanted to make sure you knew that."

Nathan stared at him for a long moment while Nora's heart thundered so loudly in her chest that it hurt her ears.

What was Nathan thinking? What was Samuel thinking? Oh God, the silence was killing her.

But then Nathan carefully gathered Samuel close, and when he shut his eyes, tears fell down his cheeks.

* * *

THE CARRIAGE WAS WELL SPRUNG, but the road was horrendous. Nathan bounced into his sleeping wife again and cursed at himself. She was exhausted, which was mostly his fault, and she needed the rest, but he could not hold onto her with the carriage rocking this way and that. The carriage finally settled again, but Nora was awake. Nathan felt her stretching along his side. Which in turn felt really good to him.

He set his booted feet back up on the opposite bench in an attempt to stretch out himself and most of all, relax. Being in such close proximity to his wife and not being able to do anything was killing him.

"Are we still on the road?" Nora asked, somewhere around his shoulder.

"I hope so."

"Mmm." This was said against his neck, and a shiver spiraled through him.

The carriage rocked along the road. Nathan watched the trees pass by outside the window. The forest was dense, and there was really nothing else to look at. He would have liked to just look at his wife, but she was already far too fetching without looking at her, and he knew he would not be responsible for his actions if he did look at her. So instead, he looked at a bunch of dumb trees.

And thought about what Samuel had said. Samuel was lucky to call him Father? Nathan had thought he had been given everything in the world when Nora had said she loved him, but it turned out there was still something missing. Something very important. He had wanted to be as good of a father as his own father had been. It seemed that Samuel had just told him it was so.

"Do you want to be a farmer?" Nora asked after some time, still nuzzling his neck.

"I don't know. I've never thought about it."

Her hand touched his face, and he looked down at her. He sucked in his breath. When they had gotten into the carriage, she had taken off her bonnet and pulled all the pins from her hair. She had promptly curled up against him and fallen asleep. Now her hair was loose around her shoulders, and the gray bruises that had been so prominent under her eyes were gone. Her eyes were warmer, livelier. Hopeful.

"I'm excited," she said.

He smiled down at her. "I can tell."

She sat up, her hair swishing at her shoulders. "You can?"

He nodded. "You look happy. Really happy, not that secretive I-know-something-you-don't kind of happy you were when we first met."

She scrunched her face, which almost made him laugh since she had never done that before.

"I was what kind of happy?"

"You always kind of smiled but never really smiled. Like you had a secret, and it drove me nuts. I wanted to know your secret, but I also wanted you to be really happy. Not just conditionally happy."

She narrowed her eyes. "Why did you want to know my secret?"

"I wanted to know what made you happy, so I could make you really happy."

"You make me happy," she said plainly, and his heart did a little jig in his chest.

"You make me happy," he said.

"So does this mean we can be farmers?"

"Certainly." He pulled her back against him, because he could. Her head fell to his shoulder, and she nuzzled his neck again. He was beginning to realize she liked doing that. And then her hand crept over his stomach and... lower.

"How long before we stop for the night?" she asked.

Nathan felt the temperature of his blood rise. "A few hours. Why?"

She touched him through his breeches, not making a verbal response but making her intentions clear.

He grabbed her wrist. "Here? Now?"

She sat up again and smiled. "Why not?"

She kissed him, forcing his lips apart so his tongue somehow made its way inside her mouth. The damn woman was seducing him again. He reeled and clutched the bench cushion to keep from falling off the seat. Nora ran her hands under his greatcoat, pushing the material from his shoulders. He felt the cool air stab at his skin through his thin shirt, but the heat of her hands quickly replaced the cold, and he was suddenly burning with a fire so hot he thought he might incinerate right there in the carriage.

The buttons of his shirt came undone, and Nora's wicked hands were on his bare flesh. Her lips broke from his to follow the path of her hands down his chest. He knew where she was going and stopped her.

"You had all the fun last time. Now it's my turn."

He threw her on the opposite bench, her skirts flying up around her waist. He came down between her knees, running his hands up the satin stockings on her calves. There was something incredibly sexy about her covered legs just then. He knew she watched him as he undid the double-knotted bows holding the stockings up. And he watched her watch him as he drew the stockings down and off, slowly and one at a time.

He reached for the ribbon drawstring of her pants. He played with it and watched Nora's eyes glaze over. Finally, he untied it and ran his finger along the waistband, pulling at the ribbon and loosening the fabric around her waist. His hands dove below the waistband at her back, cupping her buttocks and drawing her against him. He brought his hands down and around, pulling her pants with them. He heard her suck in her breath when the cool air hit her throbbing flesh, and he felt his own response as his breeches became uncomfortably snug.

He parted her delicate folds with a single fingertip, watched the way she quivered at the slightest touch. He slipped that one fingertip inside of her, just a little ways in, felt her muscles straining against the intrusion. And then he gripped her thighs, replacing his hand with his mouth.

Nora exploded, her body coming undone at the seams and falling, infinitely falling, down a tunnel of light with no end. She thought she was still holding onto the bench, but she did not know anymore. All of her senses were scattered, except where Nathan continued to touch her. There, they hammered and vibrated in a delirious confusion of touch, taste, sight, and smell. So many feelings at once that none could be defined.

Nathan finally backed away, and she whimpered at the loss of his heat. She heard fabric rustling, and Nathan returned to that throbbing place between her legs. Her eyes were closed, and she did not have the strength to open them, but Nathan's voice was softly asking her to look at him, to watch him. Her eyelids responded without effort from her.

Nathan leaned over her. "I want to watch you when I come into you," he said.

Nora thought she nodded, but again, she could not be sure. She felt him pushing at her. There was no resistance, and he came fully inside of her, deep, so very deep, touching the core of her body. She unconsciously slid farther down the bench to see if he would fit any farther inside of her. Nathan groaned and gripped her hips. He began to move, hard and fast. She threw her head back as the sensation erupted from her in a choked scream. She felt the tide rising again, felt her body fighting the coming climax while urging it on. It came, silently, stealthily, and she shattered before she knew what was happening to her. And all of her senses imploded, leaving her in a mindless void.

Nathan lay half on Nora and half on the bench. The carriage rolled along as if nothing at all had occurred inside of it. Nora panted in Nathan's ear, and a stocking tickled his cheek. He pushed himself up, his legs holding him upright even though they felt remarkably like marmalade. Nora's eyes were closed, and her head was twisted in an awkward angle between the bench and the back of the carriage. She could not be comfortable, but she also did not appear to want to move.

Nathan fastened his breeches and found Nora's pants on the floor of the carriage. He carefully put them back on her but did not bother with her stockings. Through the whole laborious process, Nora never stirred. Nathan was beginning to worry, but when he sat on the bench to pull her on his lap, she snuggled against him, rubbing her nose against his neck.

"I love you," he whispered, simply because he felt like saying it.

Nora mumbled against his neck, and he smiled.

The carriage rolled on, and Nathan slept with his wife in his lap.

Sometime later, Nora placed her palm over Nathan's heartbeat, let it beat against her hand as his chest rose and fell in the steady rhythm of sleep. She felt his breath ruffle her hair and watched the trees pass by the window. The carriage hit a rut, and she gripped Nathan tighter to hold on.

And she thought she could be a farmer. How hard could it be to stick things in the earth and watch them grow? Probably ridiculously hard, but she and Nathan could do it. They would do it. Together.

The parchment in the pocket of Nathan's greatcoat crinkled under Nora's cheek. She wondered where the holdings were in Kent. Not that it made a difference to her since she had never been in Kent. But she wondered if there was a stream on the property, if there were great green fields that rolled on and on or if there were massive forests of daunting old trees that cocooned the farm in safety. Mere days ago she would never have imagined a world beyond her little room with the worn chair and the small fireplace. And now there were holdings. Entire fields ready for her to work with, to watch things grow and prosper.

Her hand drifted down to her stomach. Would she walk with her baby through those fields? She knew Samuel would probably walk her through the fields, but she wanted a new, young life to teach and to watch grow. She wanted to see Nathan holding their child, simply holding the life they created. She wanted Samuel to have a little brother or sister to protect and cherish. Nora briefly thought again of a ratty chair and a tiny stove, and a smile suddenly pulled at her lips. The air whooshed out of her as she realized she was ready to smile about it all. Three full days had not passed, and already she was smiling about the dismal life she had been leading until then.

She leaned her head back to look at Nathan. His face was relaxed in sleep, the bruises along his jaw nearly faded away. She slipped off his lap and retrieved her stockings and shoes. How he had gotten her shoes off without her knowing was beyond her. When she was once more fully presentable, she snuggled up to Nathan's side, dropped her head on his shoulder, and let the safety in his nearness lull her to sleep.

* * *

The carriage had stopped moving.

Nathan came awake slowly, his breath never faltering from a steady rhythm, his muscles never tightening from their relaxed sleep state. Nora was pressed against his side. She had one hand on his thigh and her head resting on his shoulder. His arm was pinned beneath her. After hearing nothing except his wife's inhalations and exhalations, Nathan opened a single eye just enough to see out the window. There was nothing there except the dense woods that had been chasing them for the entire journey since London.

He gently slipped his hand into his greatcoat pocket, letting his fingers cradle the loaded pistol there. He eased forward. Nora stirred as he thought she would and sat up. Nathan laid his now free hand over her mouth. Her eyes flew open. He shook his head, and she became deathly still. Later, he would think about how beautiful she looked when she first woke up. There was probably just a problem with the carriage or the road. Nothing was truly wrong.

He laid his hand on the door handle and pushed. The door swung out and smacked lightly against the carriage. Nathan waited. There was no sound. He could not even hear the horses. He put one foot out on the step, not putting his weight on it. He kept the pistol in his pocket, but his hand softly gripped it. There was still no sound. Nathan put weight on the foot on the step and leaned to see around the edge of the door. Nothing was there. Nathan stopped and focused on his heartbeat. It was steady and solid. He measured his breathing. Calm. He stepped out of the carriage, his boot sinking into the soft mud of the road.

And the world went black.

* * *

THE CARRIAGE ROCKED as whoever had been standing on top of it swung something large and scary at Nathan's head. Nora was flung back against the cushions and slid down the bench, the scream stuck in her throat. She watched Nathan fall, heard the mud as it squished around his prone body.

Someone jumped off the carriage and landed in front of the open doorway. Nora sat up, her hair swinging into her face. She pushed it away, and the air flew out of her lungs. The Duchess of Chesterfield's face was inches from her own.

"What are you doing here?" the duchess demanded.

Nora had suddenly forgotten how to speak English. She saw Nathan unconscious in the road and simply could not breathe. Her heart would not even pump. She could not... live.

The duchess grabbed her and shook, hard. "I asked you a question."

The sing-song cadence of the duchess's voice brought Nora back. "I...I...I should ask you the same thing." Nora reached up and shoved. The duchess fell backward, landing on her butt in the mud. The sudden flare of satisfaction had Nora smiling.

And then three very big men stepped out of the trees, and Nora really did not feel like smiling. She shrank back into the carriage.

"That's not 'im," one of them said. They were identical. Same broken noses, same long, lanky, greasy hair. Same tattered clothes. And, much to Nora's dismay, same God awful smell. She moved farther into the carriage out of choice and not fear.

The duchess was attempting to dislodge herself from the mud. "What do you mean it's not him?"

"This ain't the earl," another of the triplets said.

Her butt came unstuck with a resounding smack, and she stood, wobbly, her hat falling into the mud she had just dislodged herself from. Red hair flamed around her small shoulders. The Duchess of Chesterfield looked every bit like the aristocratic bitch she was. It somehow made Nora feel better about the whole situation.

"It must be the earl," the duchess said.

"Well, it ain't."

Nora leaned forward. "You wanted the earl?"

"Speak when spoken to, servant." The duchess sneered. "Perhaps people of your class do not learn manners, but I belong to a higher peerage, and I will teach you." The duchess huffed.

One of the triplets rolled Nathan over. Mud caked one side of his face. Nora pressed her hand to her stomach to keep from vomiting. Her stomach was suddenly not as strong as it used to be.

"This ain't the earl. It's the other one. The bastard."

The duchess bent clean over at the waist and stared at Nathan. Nora watched the other three men back away. She gauged the distance between her and the trees and instantly discarded the partially formed idea. She was not going to abandon her husband even to go for help. The forest looked far too dense for her to get anywhere anyway. She would be lost a hundred meters in and no good to anyone. So she stepped down from the carriage and stood resolutely beside her unconscious husband.

The Duchess of Chesterfield snapped upright. "Where is the Earl of Stryden?"

"That's a very good question," Nora said.

And that's all she said.

"Well?" the duchess asked.

Nora did not say anything.

"So that's how it's going to be." The duchess sneered, making tiny lines form between her eyes.

Nora raised a finger and pointed at them. "You shouldn't

make that face. You're going to get permanent wrinkles between your eyes, and that would look terribly funny."

The duchess raised a fist, but one of the triplets grabbed it.

"His Grace wouldn't want that. He likes them untouched."

Nora was impressed at this one's English. He did not drop a single "h."

"Load them up. We're going back to the manor." The duchess strode off toward the forest, and a triplet stepped in front of Nora, keeping her from seeing where the duchess was going.

"If you please, ma'am." This was the polite one with the good English. Nora nodded and stepped up into the carriage.

Nathan's body was thrown none too gently in behind her. He landed haphazardly across Nora. She struggled to lay him more comfortably with his head in her lap, but the best she could manage was to just keep him from falling onto the floor as the carriage started moving. She brushed the drying mud from his face.

"Oh, Nathan," she whispered and bent over to lay her lips gently over his as the carriage rolled toward their unknown destination.

The pistol in his pocket bumped her knee.

CHAPTER 17

" *H*ow long should we wait before we start to worry?" Jane asked, leaning over Richard to look out the window of the carriage at Lord Franklin Archer's townhouse.

"I really don't know," Richard answered her.

Jane frowned. It was never a good thing when Richard did not know something. They had sent Samuel through the back door of Archer's townhouse nearly an hour earlier. And Richard and Jane had sat in the carriage staring at the house since then. Just staring. There had been no touching, no inappropriate, wanted groping. No anything.

True, they were here on business. But Richard could at least hold her hand.

Which meant something was really, truly bothering him.

Which bothered Jane, really and truly.

She bumped his booted foot with hers.

Richard looked up at her innocently.

She touched his face, kissed him softly, and felt the sigh escape his lips.

He leaned his forehead against hers. "I'm worried about Alec."

"I know," Jane whispered.

Richard exhaled again, letting his frustrations crash into her, and she welcomed their weight.

And then Richard pulled her into his arms. Jane laid her head on his shoulder, letting their mutual worries coalesce. But she was not worried about Alec. Not at all. She was going to throttle him when she saw him. Putting the people who loved him most through this. She was definitely going to throttle him. But for now, she would steadfastly deny she was worried about him and just let herself rest on Richard.

But Richard was tense beneath her touch.

It was only moments later when Richard said, "I think Samuel's coming."

Jane sat up as Richard opened the door, and the small boy jumped inside the carriage.

"Well?" Richard asked by way of greeting.

Samuel shook his head and climbed onto the bench.

"The Duke of Chesterfield took Lord Archer," Samuel said.

Richard raised his eyebrows. "Took him? How? Nora said he was at the ball the other night. How did he get to Lord Heathenbaum's that quickly?"

Samuel shook his head. "Mama said the Duke of Chesterfield was not at the ball. The butler was certain the duke took Archer but didn't know why. Just that Lord Archer had been seen in the gardens of Lord Heathenbaum's estate chasing after some woman when the Duke of Chesterfield approached him. The duke put an arm around the man and forced him to walk in the other direction."

"Put an arm around him?" Jane asked.

"Then who shot at Nora and Nathan after Nathan shot Archer's brother?" Richard asked on top of Jane's question.

Samuel said, "The Duchess of Chesterfield."

"The duchess?" Richard asked, incredulous.

Jane punched him in the ribs. "Women are more than capable of doing the dirty work.

Richard rubbed his violated ribs.

"So the duchess is behind all of this?" Jane asked.

Samuel nodded. "At least the parts here in London. And she is Jacobite Scottish," he added, looking at Richard.

Richard harrumphed.

Samuel continued, "There's more though. And it's worse."

Richard waited.

"Alec?" he finally said.

Samuel nodded again. "Chesterfield wants him. Something to do with taking him back to France, but the butler wasn't sure. They're only just rumors still."

Richard crushed Jane's hand in his grip but did not notice. "How do servants know so much?"

"How do peers miss so much?" Samuel countered.

Richard grinned unexpectedly. "We'll find Alec first."

Jane interrupted. "How do you know they haven't found him already?"

Now Samuel cut in. "They haven't. Or at least they hadn't as of this afternoon."

Richard and Jane looked at him.

"Flo, an upstairs maid, saw the countess yelling at him in Hyde Park at about four o'clock."

"What the hell was he doing in Hyde Park?" Richard asked.

Samuel shrugged his shoulders. Jane patted their joined hands.

"I think we should ask what we're going to do now," Jane said soothingly.

Richard nodded and looked at her. "We are going on a long overdue honeymoon, my love."

Samuel's eyebrows went up as did Jane's.

"Is that so, dear?"

Richard nodded. "It's the perfect cover for travel. And it appears we are going to be traveling quite a bit in our future."

"What about me?" Samuel asked.

Richard looked at him, put his elbows on his knees, and leaned forward. "I don't want you involved in this anymore. I don't want anything happening to you," Richard added after Samuel had looked hurt after the first statement. The second made him blush.

"Great Aunt Lydia," Jane whispered.

Great Aunt Lydia, indeed.

Great Aunt Lydia had a passion for big dogs and bigger guns. And she lived alone on a huge estate in York, far away from any danger. It sounded perfect.

"Have you ever been to the country, Samuel?" Richard asked.

Samuel shook his head negatively.

"Now is as good a time as any," Jane said.

"Where will you be honeymooning?" Samuel asked.

Richard looked at Jane. "The first stop is Chesterfield Manor."

Jane's eyes widened again. "So blatant, Richard. I'm surprised."

"I'm done playing games."

* * *

THIS MATTRESS WAS VERY, very uncomfortable.

Nathan opened both of his eyes at once.

The mattress was a stone floor.

And it was near pitch black around him. Water trickled somewhere in the void. A rat scurried and squeaked.

Nora.

Nathan sat up too quickly, and the world spun. He grabbed for something to hold him up, and his hand collided with cold, slimy metal. He held onto it as his senses balanced the world around him.

"Easy there, Mr. Black."

Nathan turned his head in the direction of the nasally voice. The gloom was stifling; his eyes strained to dilate and take in more light. Finally, a fuzzy image of iron bars and a face came into focus.

"Who's there?" he asked, but his voice was scratchy and faint. He cleared his throat and repeated it, louder.

"Your good friend," the voice said. "Franklin Archer."

Nathan's eyes stopped trying to dilate. Archer remained a fuzzy shape in the distance.

"What have you done with Nora?"

Archer laughed. "What have I done with her? I haven't done anything. It's hard to do much in this dungeon."

Nathan looked around him again. Heard the water trickling and the rats scurrying.

"Dungeon? I'm in a dungeon?"

Who used dungeons anymore?

"We are in a dungeon, Mr. Black," Archer corrected him.

Nathan looked back at Archer. There were two sets of iron bars. The one Nathan was gripping and the other shadowing the shape that was Archer.

"What's going on, Archer?"

"Now, before I answer your question, I need to ask myself one of my own. Should I answer the questions of the bloke who tried to kill me?" Archer said.

Nathan thought it telling that Archer cared more for his attempted assassination than for the fact that Nathan had killed his brother. Nathan's head was pounding, and he did not need this right now. He wanted to know where his damn wife was and who he was going to have to kill to get to her.

Archer tsked in the dark. "I am thinking I shouldn't."

"I am thinking you should."

"Why?" Archer asked.

Nathan felt his pocket for his pistol. Obviously, it was not there.

"The enemy of my enemy is my enemy. Or the enemy of my enemy is my friend."

Archer shuffled in the distance. "Good point."

Nathan nodded, and the world tilted again. He had been unconscious way too much in the past few days.

"He probably has your wife upstairs somewhere. He figures females will talk," Archer said.

"Who is 'he'?" Nathan's blood boiled, and he started listing in his head all the ways he was going to torture him.

Archer's shape had grown longer, and Nathan figured he had stood up.

"Chesterfield. He likes to play mind games with females. He's a few cards short of a full deck." Archer's head turned right and left as if he was checking to see if anyone was listening. "I should have seen it right off, but well, there was Liza."

Nathan's heart stopped abruptly in his chest. It simply froze and hung suspended by the tissue that surrounded it. The Duke of Chesterfield had Nora. The Duke of Chesterfield. The man who had raped her. Nathan stood up, a roar of frustration and anger surging from his throat as he swung a fist at the blackness. It collided with a solid wall of brick, and Nathan welcomed the pain. He just wished he had swung harder.

"Easy there, mate, easy there," Archer cooed from the darkness.

Nathan concentrated on breathing. He had to be alive in order to kill Chesterfield, which meant he had to breathe. He also had to concentrate on something else before the frustration swamped him into a blubbering mess that was not going to be any help at all to Nora.

So he turned around and sank against the wall, determined to have a conversation with the man he was supposed to have shot a week ago.

"Liza?" Nathan asked, forcing his mind to focus.

"The Duchess of Chesterfield. God, what a woman. I should have known better. A woman like her." Archer was shaking his head.

"You betrayed your country for a woman?" Nathan thought of Nora again, which caused the anger to surge briefly, but he squashed it down and rethought the validity of his question. "Never mind," he said.

"Oh yes, what a woman. But now it doesn't really matter, does it? I'm titled and all."

Nathan knew he had been whacked pretty hard, and his mind was wandering to another subject quite a bit, but he also knew this conversation should be going more smoothly for him.

"What does your title have to do with this?"

Archer did not say anything for a while, as if he were studying Nathan. Nathan felt the urge to smooth his hair, which was ridiculous. Maybe he should punch the wall again.

"You really don't know anything at all, do you?"

Nathan's eyeballs were going to fall out of his head. He leaned his head back against a cold, hard surface. The cold seeped into his head, and he thought it would make it feel better, but laying one's head against a brick wall was never very comfortable for long.

"No, I don't know anything," Nathan mumbled.

Archer rustled in the dark, and his voice came back at Nathan, somehow closer. "What would I get in return for what I know?"

Nathan rolled his head in Archer's direction. "I won't kill you."

Archer laughed. "That's not a very good return considering you're in a dungeon."

"Fine, tell me what you know, and then I will kill you."

Archer laughed again. "Did you not hear what I just said? You can't kill me."

"Not right now. But when Chesterfield comes around, I can keep you from getting killed, or I can let you be killed."

Archer stopped laughing. "What are you talking about?"

"I'm talking about eight months of letters to, what was the name, Liza, or should I call her Lady Lover?"

Nathan let out the breath he had been holding when he heard the outstandingly loud gulp. Nobody in the War Office had actually known who Lady Lover had been, and he had taken a very large gamble in assuming that Lady Lover was indeed this Liza Archer for whom he had committed treason.

"What do you want to know?" Archer asked.

Nathan would have smiled if it had not hurt so much, and if he had not been grinding his teeth quite so hard.

"Everything."

"He's kidnapping titled men. Figures he'll pawn them off for the highest price."

Nathan held up a hand. "Wait. Who is kidnapping titled men and why?"

"Chesterfield. He has desperate orders from above. Kidnap titled men and auction them off. Ransom them if he has to. Napoleon needs liquid assets."

"And he thinks selling noblemen is a good idea?"

"I said desperate. Not good." Archer was speaking quickly. Too quickly.

"What else?" Nathan prompted.

Archer's shape shrugged its shoulders.

Nathan forced himself not to hurt his hands by gripping the iron bars too tightly.

"What else, Archer? Or I am going to call your mate, Chesterfield, down here and tell him all about the milky white skin of Lady Lover's—"

"All right, all right." Archer's head was swinging madly in the gloom, looking for eavesdroppers.

"Archer."

Archer's head stopped pivoting on his neck. "Well, Chesterfield was supposed to snatch the good ones, you know, the spy ones."

"The spies?" Nathan stood up, using the bars as leverage. "What spies?"

"English spies that are noblemen."

Nathan felt the blood rush out of his head, and it was not because he was standing up.

"My father and brother."

Archer's shape shook its head. "No, just your brother. The powers that be specifically want your brother. I don't know why. They just want him. Want him brought to France."

"Napoleon wants my brother brought to France? Why?"

Archer made another one of those really loud gulps.

"Why, Archer?" Nathan pressed and was pleased to hear Archer crack.

"Bait. They're going to use your brother as bait."

Nathan's hands did clench around the iron bars then, and he was amazed the iron simply did not shatter in his grip.

"Napoleon thinks my father and I will follow."

"And then they'll capture you and more will come. Rescue mission, you know." Archer was pacing, one hand trailing back and forth across the bars.

"No. The War Office won't send more after my father and me."

Archer laughed. "I know that. You know that. But again, desperate, not good."

"This isn't even a desperate plan. It's just stupid."

"Fabulous. You can tell good old Nappie when you see him."

The sound of clinking metal stopped their conversation. Keys were being inserted in a door somewhere.

Archer swallowed harshly again. "Uh, oh. They're coming for you." He looked through the bars at Nathan. "I'd play dead again, if I were you." He laughed at his own joke.

Nathan straightened his greatcoat so he looked presentable when they came instead. After all, he did not want to kill a duke without looking at least presentable.

A door opened, and light flooded the small passageway between the cells. Nathan squinted in the intense light. Someone with a heavy trod started down steps, stone steps from the sound of the clinking metal. Another trod interrupted the pattern of the first. This one lighter, more elegant.

Nathan looked away from the light to let his eyes adjust naturally. When he looked back, two men were standing in front of him. One that smelled bad and another that would never be caught smelling in his life.

"Your grace," Nathan nodded at the non-smelling one.

Nathan thought he would feel rage, unstoppable, uncontrollable rage upon seeing the man who had raped the woman he loved. But he did not feel anything like that at all. What he felt was simple. Basic. And, now, he was completely in control of it.

He was going to kill the Duke of Chesterfield. That was it. There was no counter argument; there was no rebuttal. Nathan was going to kill this man.

"Mr. Black, I'm glad to see you are awake. I am having quite a difficult time with your wife, and I was hoping you may be of some use." His voice oozed refinement.

Nathan's teeth were grinding. "What have you done with her?"

"Unfortunately," Chesterfield paused, as if holding onto his words would make Nathan angrier. It did make him angrier, but it also made him deadlier, "nothing. Your wife is a very stubborn woman, Mr. Black. Very stubborn." He let the words linger in the air, casting them back to a long ago place that both of them were sure to be thinking about. "I find stubbornness in women to be an appealing trait. Most of the time I enjoy it." He paused again for the same effect. Then he leaned closer to Nathan's face behind the bars. "I like it when they struggle."

"What do you want?" Nathan forced his teeth apart. The sooner this conversation was over, the sooner he could kill this asshole.

"Answers. I want answers." Chesterfield backed away. "And your wife doesn't seem keen on giving them."

"Answers to what?"

"I want to know where your brother is, Mr. Black. And I will know where your brother is." Chesterfield turned as if to move back the way he had come. "Now, please come along like a good prisoner." The white of his teeth flashed briefly in the surreal light before he disappeared into it.

The smelly man opened the cell and gripped Nathan's elbow.

"Like he said. Be good," the man snarled.

Nathan nodded his head in acknowledgement and allowed himself to be led out of the cell.

"Remember, Mr. Black," Archer shouted behind them, laughing. "Remember."

Nathan did not recognize her because she was wearing a dress. He would have made some pithy comment, but the Duchess of Chesterfield was holding a pistol, which was probably loaded, against the right temple of Nora's head. Another pistol remained at her side. He stayed quiet.

"Now. That's much better, wouldn't you say, Mrs. Black?" Chesterfield asked upon entering the room where Nathan's smelly companion had brought him.

Nora shrugged, moving just her shoulders as she sat perfectly straight and undaunted on the sofa. Nathan's stomach was knotted so tightly at the sight of the gun against her head, at Chesterfield smiling pathetically down at her, Nathan wondered how she could possibly shrug at a time like this.

He forced his eyes to move away from the gun, to see if she was hurt. And then he noticed her uniform. Her housekeeper uniform. She was wearing it, along with that damn starched white apron. She had not been wearing it that morning. He knew. She had been wearing another dress, a blue one. He knew because he had almost removed it from her. Had they made her change? But then he noticed the way the bodice fit a tad too snugly, as if there was something stuck underneath it.

They had not made her change.

Nora had put the uniform over the other dress. And that left him wondering why the hell she had done that. And when. And how. He recalled the carpetbag going into the carriage, but when had she had time to put the dress on? How long had he been unconscious?

"Mrs. Black, you should know by now that I prefer verbal responses," Chesterfield said, coming to stand between where Nathan was being held captive by the smelly man and two other equally detestable gentlemen and where Nora was sitting on the sofa being held captive by the gun Her Grace pointed at her head.

Nora drew in an exaggerated breath. "I told you before, Your Grace," she drawled the last two words. "The room shall not improve until you light a match and burn the whole place down. Those draperies are ghastly, and this upholstery looks like the contents of a full chamberpot." And then she smiled sweetly.

At that Nathan knew. He knew his wife was up to something. Nora was strong, solid, and steady. Not flippant and breezy. Nathan kept his mouth shut. Nora was facing the man who had raped her, and she was brushing him off like the bug he was. She did not need Nathan right now. So he stayed quiet.

Watching for the perfect moment to kill the Duke of Chesterfield.

"I'll ignore your sarcasm, Mrs. Black, as I feel we will get much further if we are civil to one another." The duke walked over to the windows of the small sitting room and huffed his chest out to survey the domain.

Nathan thought this must be the Duke's country home, but he could not be sure. It may be Archer's home for all Nathan knew. He should have asked the whelp.

"Mr. Black, as you can see, your wife is trying my patience. Perhaps you would care to answer my questions."

Nathan did not respond verbally, but in his head, he crushed Chesterfield's windpipe.

Chesterfield turned around. "Where is the Earl of Stryden?"

Nathan saw Nora flinch out of the corner of his eye as the duchess pressed the gun harder against her temple.

"I don't know," Nathan said, turning his head casually behind him. There was a desk with no papers on it. Only a small statue of some kind of a bird, a lantern, and a letter opener that flashed in the watery sunlight that spilled through the window. Sunlight? Should it not be full dark by now? Maybe it was morning again. How long had he been unconscious?

"I think you do." The duke turned around, and Nathan looked quickly back at him. "I think you may need a little incentive to tell me is all."

"I don't need incentive to tell you something that I don't know." Nathan's voice was starting to sound like a growl, and he checked it.

The duke let out a ponderous sigh. "Oh, Mr. Black, I was truly hoping that you would be of a more polite nature, seeing as how you were raised by a duke where as your wife..." He looked at Nora. "Well, she does tend to be...lacking."

The duke flicked a piece of invisible lint off of his fine tailored coat. Nathan glanced at the man on his left. He was slightly smaller than the other two and slightly less smelly. Nathan gauged the height of the man's eye before returning his attention to the duke.

Chesterfield had sauntered over to a mirror on the opposite wall, to the right and behind the sofa Nora sat on. He fixed his waxed hair and mustache in the mirror. Neither of which moved at of his prodding. Nathan checked the two men to his right while Chesterfield continued his primping. The two men were spaced out, one by the door, eight feet from Nathan. The other was only about three feet from Nathan. Nathan looked at Nora's face while studying the placement of the duchess's shoes on the floor.

"I hope you haven't forgotten that I had intended to kill your wife quite a long time ago. It was only a sudden order from my superior that stopped me from completing that objective." The duke was still studying his own reflection.

"I hope you have not forgotten that I do intend to kill you," Nathan said, no longer wishing to go along with whatever Chesterfield had planned.

The duke stopped flicking the unmoving ends of his mustache.

The two men closest to Nathan stepped up and grasped his elbows. Apparently, everyone was past playing.

Chesterfield turned around. "I'll ask you one more time, politely, and then I will be forced to use more extreme methods to get an answer to my question." The duke had strolled over to Nora while he had been speaking, and now he ran a single knuckle along her cheek.

Nathan saw her eyes go out of focus, and he reacted, straining against the arms that held him. The Duchess of Chesterfield moved her pistol, aiming it at his chest.

"Where is your brother, Mr. Black?" Chesterfield asked.

Nathan felt his bones grinding together under the steely grips of his captors. He blinked at the pistol held at the level of his heart and stared into Nora's eyes. Chesterfield slid his hand along her cheek and cupped the back of her head. Nathan felt a growl growing in his throat.

And then somewhere, a door crashed open.

Chesterfield dropped his hand and turned to look at the door leading to the hallway. The three goons turned as well. The Duchess did not waver her stance, one pistol steady at Nathan's chest, one against Nora's temple. Nora's eyes had glazed over, and Nathan focused harder on them, willing her to concentrate on him.

"Go see what that was," Chesterfield said to the man at the door. "You, guard the door," he said to the man holding Nathan's right arm. "I advise you not to move, Mr. Black, or my darling wife will put a bullet in your heart. And then what good would you be to this slut?"

Nathan flexed the fingers of his now free hand, let the blood flow into his fingers, and counted the beats of his heart, slow and steady. He checked his breathing. Footsteps echoed down the hallway to the open door.

Chesterfield had turned back to Nora. "Shall we get

started, my dear?" His fingers went to the fastenings of his trousers.

Nathan breathed. In. Out.

The footsteps in the hallway stopped. Chesterfield pushed Nora back on the sofa, perching himself between her legs, one hand bracing him up on the back of the sofa, the other still working on his trousers. Nora had suddenly gone limp, seeming to meekly obey this man who had raped her. The terror in her eyes told Nathan her control had been swamped.

Shouting came through the open doorway. More footsteps. A gun fired.

The man still holding Nathan jumped. Nathan pivoted. He snatched the letter opener off the desk. The Duchess discharged her weapon into the chest of the man still trying to hold onto Nathan. The man at the door charged at Nathan. Chesterfield was yelling at someone, probably him, but Nathan was not stopping to listen. He raised the letter opener and drove it into the charging man's eye. The now dead man on Nathan's left gripped Nathan's elbow as his muscles clenched in the last spasm before death. Nathan went down. The Duchess aimed the other pistol.

Two shots rent the air at once.

* * *

THIS WAS the second dead man to be dropped in Nora's lap. Only this time, it was a tad more literal as the Duke of Chesterfield lay dead on top of her. She still gripped Nathan's pistol, jammed awkwardly in her stomach as the dead man's weight pressed into her. There was a dampness seeping into her dress that was not blood. Apparently, dead people wet themselves upon the moment of actually ceasing to live. Nora waited, knowing someone was going to lift this man off of her, but she feared it would not be Nathan. She had heard that other shot. Had seen the Duchess lower the weapon at Nathan's falling body.

So when the body did move, and Richard's face appeared above her, she did not flinch. She did not gasp.

She said, "Nathan?"

"What the bloody hell are you doing with my gun, woman?"

Nora turned her head against the cushions of the sofa, a hot hope spiraling through her.

Nathan was attempting to dislodge his elbow from his own dead man. He tripped over the carpet when the dead man suddenly let go and half fell into Nora on the sofa. He knelt on the carpet beside her, smiling goofily.

Nora did not know what to say. Too many emotions were hitting her at once. They were safe. Nathan was alive. Chesterfield was dead. She was married to the man she loved, and they had the rest of their lives in front of them. What did one say?

"He peed on me," she said.

Nathan's eyes traveled down the length of her. "Yes, I'm afraid that tends to happen when people die. They lose muscle control."

"Oh."

Neither of them said anything. They just stared at each other, smiling like fools. And Nora was completely all right with that.

But then Richard cleared his throat. "I think we'd best be getting out of here before some nosy neighbor shows up."

Nathan looked around as if he had realized for the first time that his father was there.

"What are you doing here?" he asked, standing up and drawing Nora with him.

"Saving your ass." He nodded at Nora. "Pardon my French."

Nora just kept smiling.

Nathan looked behind him where the very dead Duchess of Chesterfield was lying in a pool of her own blood. "And shooting duchesses?"

"Only ones who are going to shoot my son," Richard answered.

Nathan nodded, took Nora's hand, and walked out of the room.

"So what are you doing here?" Nathan asked, once they were moving swiftly along the corridor, and he could expect his father to give a clear answer.

He kept Nora tucked under his arm, and Nora did not mind at all.

"Samuel is quite the spy, Nora. The butler at Archer's townhouse told us the French want Alec."

Nathan nodded. "Archer said the like."

Richard stopped. "Archer?"

Nathan stopped as well but did not relinquish his grip on Nora. Nora unconsciously snuggled closer.

"He's in the basement. Or dungeon, rather. I'm sure someone will find him eventually."

Richard nodded and continued moving along the corridor, leaving the treasonous spy to his fate.

Now they only needed to get to Alec before the damned French did.

CHAPTER 18

*N*ora tied the bow of her now clean apron at her back. The material snapped with starch. She smiled appreciatively and turned away from the mirror to find Nathan staring at her from across the small inn room.

"You're beautiful," he whispered, as if saying it too loudly would make her vanish.

She walked over to him, slipped her arms around his waist, and laid her head on his chest.

"And you look rather fetching in that livery, Mr. Black." She tilted her head up to look at him.

He was smiling. "You think so?"

Nora purred in her throat and felt Nathan's reaction stirring low against her stomach. She laughed. "You always look rather fetching, but even more so in the Duke of Lofton's colors."

She laid her head back down, and Nathan nuzzled her hair.

"Are you sure about this, Nora? I don't want to put you in any danger."

Nora only smiled. Her son was a great spy now. Having

found out the plan in store for the Earl of Stryden, Nora had been assured that he was safely tucked away in York under the watchful eye of a formidable woman known only as Great Aunt Lydia. And Nora and Nathan were to act as servants for the Duke and Duchess of Lofton as they traveled on their belated honeymoon. Not that Nora would have to do much acting. But Nathan had been against the whole thing. He did not want to put Nora in danger. And of course, Nora had steadfastly refused to let her husband go on this journey alone. The Earl of Stryden was her family now, too. And she was going to do everything she could to find him before it was too late.

And so Nathan was dashing in his livery, the reds and blacks of the Duke of Lofton's colors. And Nora was back in her housekeeper's uniform.

And they were holding onto each other, because they had been separated for far too long.

"Nora?"

"Mmm?"

"Why were you wearing two dresses?"

Nora blinked. Of course Nathan would have seen that she had been wearing two dresses.

"I needed the layers to conceal your pistol. I used the apron pocket to hold it, but the rest of the material kept the bulk of it hidden."

"Oh."

"Nathan?"

"Mmm?"

"I love you."

He did not say anything. His heart beat against her ear, and Nora listened to it as his breathing countered it. The rhythm of his breathing was interrupted as he eased her away from him.

"Nora, why did you marry me?" he asked, once she was looking up at him.

She looked down at her hands where they had come to rest against his chest. "I trusted you," she whispered.

Nathan's finger under her chin raised her eyes to his. "You trusted me?" he said.

She nodded. "I had not trusted anyone in a really long time. And I knew I could trust you. I could lean on you if I had to."

"And that's...all?"

Nora blushed before she could help it and pushed against Nathan's finger so she would not have to look at him.

Nathan laughed. "What is this? My brave wife has suddenly gone shy on me?"

Nora tried to squirm away from him but ended up in his lap on the bed, giggling. Nathan was laughing, too, trying to hold onto his squirmy wife. The poor, cheap inn's mattress sagged under their combined weight.

Nora forced herself to look at him. "No, that might not have been all."

"What else?"

Nora looked down again, gathering her courage before she started, looking him in the eye. "That night in the library, after you had been shot, I...I...I wanted things."

Nathan raised an eyebrow.

"I wanted to know what it would be like to kiss you. And it was the first time in my life that I had ever thought that about any man, and...and...and it was the first time I actually felt like a woman. You made me feel like a woman."

Nathan's smile made her stop. Maybe she had said enough.

"Is that all now?" he asked.

She nodded, not trusting her voice.

"Are you sure?"

She nodded again.

"Nora?"

"You didn't blame me for what...what happened to me."

Nathan stared at her. "Other people blamed you for being raped?"

Nora nodded, knowing her voice would not hold when she felt the tears burning in her eyes.

"Nora." Nathan cupped the side of her face, and Nora nuzzled his palm, the tears disappearing at his touch.

"That first night when you talked to Samuel, I knew. I knew that you did not judge me and...find me lacking." She barely got the last out and felt deflated in Nathan's arms.

"You did not ask Chesterfield to rape you, Nora. No one can blame you for what happened. And if someone does, I'll give you my gun and you can shoot them."

Nora did not know whether to choose tears or laughter. So she kissed him instead, savoring the sweet softness of his lips. But Nathan pulled away too soon.

"All right, if you can confess, so can I."

Nora felt a trickle of fear at the back of her throat. Confess to what?

"That first night? When you were bandaging my arm? I wanted things, too. You were so brave and beautiful in the firelight, and I wanted you. Wanted you in my bed, in my life, just wanted you. I wanted to see your face every day, to feel your strength. I wanted to make you happy. I wanted to have you here to shoot the bad guys when I can't," he teased.

A laugh burst nervously from her lips.

Nathan continued, "Have I made you happy?"

And that was when Nora started to cry. Not just little whimpers, but full out sobs. Nathan's face went white in terror, and she reached up to touch it, as if her soft caress would make him feel better. He reached up and snatched her hand, gripping it hard in his.

"Nora, what is it? What did I do?"

Nora just shook her head because she was crying too hard to speak or even smile. Her lips wobbled around on her face. Finally she just laid her head on his shoulder and nuzzled her nose into his neck like she liked to do. Nathan stroked her back, and the sobs eventually died away.

When she could draw a full breath, she said, "Do you know when I first realized I loved you?"

She heard the tentative smile in Nathan's voice. "No."

"When you stepped out of that carriage holding my son. You were ten different shades of purple, but you didn't seem to notice because you were cradling Samuel like he was the most precious thing in the world."

"He is one of the most precious things in the world," Nathan said, quietly interrupting her.

Nora sat up. "One of them? What else is precious?"

"You," he said, falling back on the bed and rolling her beneath him.

"Nathan," Nora began to admonish him for wrinkling her uniform, but the wicked glint in his eyes had her quickly changing directions. "Do we have enough time?"

Nathan looked up toward the clock on the wall by the door. "I would say we have about, oh," he looked down at his wife, and a smile spread across his face, "all the rest of our lives."

And then he kissed her.

And she let him.

ABOUT THE AUTHOR

Jessie decided to be a writer because the job of Indiana Jones was already filled.

Taking her history degree dangerously, Jessie tells the stories of courageous heroines, the men who dared to love them, and the world that tried to defeat them.

Jessie makes her home in the great state of New Hampshire where she lives with her husband and two very opinionated Basset hounds. For more, visit her website at jessieclever.com.

Printed in Great Britain
by Amazon

Printed in Great Britain
by Amazon